Revelation

To find happiness, ... s...

Prudence Carstairs is spirited and fiercely intelligent. Badly scarred from a childhood accident, she lives her life in the shadows. Her sister, Mercy, is famously beautiful but unhappily married. Living in Victorian society's spotlight has taught her to hide her pain well. Both sisters want—*need*—change. But can they be brave enough to let go of their past in order to remake their future?

Prudence's story:
The Earl Who Sees Her Beauty

And now Mercy's story:
Lady Armstrong's Scandalous Awakening

Available now,
from Marguerite Kaye!

MARGUERITE KAYE

Lady Armstrong's
Scandalous Awakening

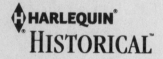

HARLEQUIN®
HISTORICAL™

ISBN-13: 978-1-335-40774-0

Lady Armstrong's Scandalous Awakening

Copyright © 2022 by Marguerite Kaye

Harlequin Enterprises ULC
22 Adelaide St. West, 41st Floor
Toronto, Ontario M5H 4E3, Canada
www.Harlequin.com

Printed in U.S.A.

Marguerite Kaye has written over fifty historical romances featuring feisty heroines and a strong sense of place and time. She is also coauthor with Sarah Ferguson, Duchess of York, of the *Sunday Times* bestseller *Her Heart for a Compass*. They are currently working on their second book together. Marguerite lives in Argyll on the west coast of Scotland. When not writing, she loves to read, cook, garden, drink martinis and sew, though rarely at the same time.

Visit the Author Profile page
at Harlequin.com for more titles.

This book is dedicated to Glasgow,
birthplace of my hero, who, like the city itself,
is warmhearted, a bit of a rough diamond,
but well worth getting to know.

Prologue

Killellan Manor, Sussex, November 1862

Unseasonal sunlight streamed in through the windows of the drawing room, causing several of those gathered there to squint and shield their eyes. It seemed cruelly incongruous since this was, by any definition, a gloomy occasion. Standing at the window, Mercy, the Dowager Lady Armstrong, usually the most observant and thoughtful of hostesses, neglected to signal to the butler to have the heavy scarlet drapes drawn. Instead, she continued to stare out sightlessly at the autumnal gardens, which were bare apart from a few leaves clinging on valiantly to the huge, ancient oak tree.

Like everyone else in the room, Mercy was dressed in heavy mourning. Her gown of plain black silk was unadorned with any of the beads, braid, swags or lace which her late husband had liked to see festoon her toilette. Now that Henry was dead, there was no need to pander to his ostentatious tastes.

The man who had dictated her every move, had tried

to control her every thought, was gone. When it had become apparent that her husband would not survive his brief illness, Mercy had examined her conscience for any trace of emotion. But any affection she'd once had had been eroded by the harsh reality of seventeen years of increasingly arid marriage. Now it was over, and she felt nothing save an overwhelming sense of relief.

'They're ready to begin,' her brother, Clement, said, interrupting her reverie. 'One last formality to endure and then we can be on our way.'

He ushered her towards the waiting guests, his hand hovering protectively a few inches away from her shoulder. Knowing that Clement was desperate to support her in any way possible, Mercy forced herself to lean into his embrace for a second. 'I'm fine,' she whispered.

'I wish I could spare you this,' he muttered as he sat down.

'You have been a rock.' She perched on her own chair, noting wryly that they had been deliberately placed at a distance from those of Harry's brothers. Major Lord George Armstrong, her husband's brother and heir, sat beside his younger twin, Captain Frederick Armstrong, the pair flanked by their respective wives. Harry's identical twin brothers were very like him, with the same hooded eyes and determined chins.

Frederick looked over, catching her eye, his mouth forming a thin, snide smile. Mercy shuddered and reached instinctively for Clement's hand. Clearly surprised by her rare display of physical intimacy, he squeezed her fingers, smiling warmly at her, his smile reflected in his cornflower-blue eyes, his expression one of gentle concern.

At last, the lawyer cleared his throat and began to read. Mercy clasped her hands in her lap and began to count the minutes until she could leave the Armstrong country seat for ever. His opening words declared that this was the last will and testament of the late Lord Harry, known as Henry Atticus Percival Armstrong. The will had been written following their marriage, and Mercy had been unable to provide her husband with a scintilla of hope that there would be any need for it to be altered to accommodate an heir in the course of seventeen years.

As the lawyer droned on about settlements and properties, in which she no longer had any interest, the tears which had failed to fall upon her husband's death now stung her eyes. She blinked them back. She had shed too many tears for the child she had desperately longed for, and for the pain and suffering its absence had brought to her marriage. Harry had been devastated by his lack of a son. She had paid the price for that.

'Provision for my wife, Mercy, Lady Armstrong, née Carstairs, is on the terms already specified in the marriage contract.'

Hearing her own name, Mercy stirred herself. Not long now, she thought, anticipating that the lawyer would move on to the list of bequests for servants and distant relatives. But instead the lawyer cleared his throat and produced a second piece of paper.

'With regard to the provisions made for Lord Armstrong's widow, at this juncture I will read from a codicil written by His late Lordship a week before he tragically passed away.'

Mercy glanced at Clement, but he shook his head, looking irritated. 'No idea,' he whispered.

However, a glance in the direction of her two brothers-in-law gave her a horrible premonition, for both had their gazes fixed firmly on her. Years of practice allowed her to maintain a blank countenance, casting her eyes demurely down, but Mercy was now listening intently.

'"In the eyes of the world, my marriage to Lady Armstrong has been an exemplary one, marred only by the absence of any progeny. The reality, however, has been very different. For the duration of our marriage, I have been a dutiful and faithful husband. No one could fault my assiduous regard for my wife's comfort and well-being. I wish it to be recorded for the sake of posterity, as I lie on my deathbed, that my devotion to the wedding vows I made seventeen years ago was not reciprocated by my wife, as witnessed by her obstinate and determined failure to provide me with an heir. While the law of the land prevents me from altering the provisions already made for her in the contract I so hopefully signed upon our marriage, it is my personal belief that morally she has no such entitlement."'

A sharp intake of breath from all but the two brothers followed this announcement. Clement leapt to his feet. 'This is an outrage! How dare you utter such slander, sir?'

'The words belong to my late brother, and as such cannot be deemed slanderous,' the new Lord Armstrong said. 'The lawyer is merely acting on my brother's last and final wishes in reading them, Mr Carstairs. The codicil is perfectly legal and properly witnessed. It therefore forms part of the last will and testament and as such I wish it to be read aloud.'

'Sit down, Clement.' Sickened, Mercy grasped her brother's wrist, tugging him back to his seat. 'He cannot take my jointure away from me. Let him have his final say. The sooner this is over, the sooner we may quit this place and never return.'

'If you insist, though it goes very much against the grain.' Clement glowered at the lawyer. 'Get on with it.'

'Ahem. As I was saying… "I spared no expense and left no stone unturned…" ah, yes… "investing a great deal of money and my own personal time escorting Lady Armstrong to various treatments, spas and clinics."' Here the lawyer stopped, flushing scarlet. 'My lord, I really do not feel it is appropriate to continue. The content of the final paragraph is most personal in nature.'

'My brother wished it to be read out in its entirety,' Lord Armstrong reiterated. 'I insist you continue.'

The look he threw Mercy was one of undisguised contempt. Clearly he had read the codicil already. She sat up straighter, tucking her hands beneath the folds of her gown, out of sight, curling them into tight fists.

'Very well, my lord, though I must protest in all decency that I do not— However, very well.' The lawyer cleared his throat again and began to read, stumbling over the words in his haste to be done. '"Lady Armstrong remained most stubbornly resistant to all ministrations. At the risk of shocking any of the fairer sex in attendance, I wish it further to be known that I have concluded the fault was not biological but of the mind.

As a husband, I know myself to be without fault, unfailing in my attentions to her, yet no ardour could awaken a womanly response, making it impossible for me to succeed in my most natural quest for a son and heir."'

Mercy uttered an outraged gasp. Harry's utter refusal to discuss any matter of a personal nature had made their marriage a sterile wasteland in every sense. He had never accepted their childlessness, though the attempts to remedy the situation had become a grim endurance test for both of them. To have him accuse her like this from beyond the grave—and to have everyone listen, study her reaction and, worse, know that was exactly what he wanted—was abhorrent. Had he really resented her so much that he must destroy the facade they had so painstakingly presented to the world for so long? Had he truly hated her that much?

Shaking her head vehemently at Clement, Mercy dug her nails into her palms, outrage giving way to a cold anger. 'Carry on,' she said, glaring at the lawyer who, under other circumstances, she would have felt sorry for. 'I am sure we are all agog to hear what else I am accused of.'

The solicitor winced, muttered something which might have been an apology and once more began to read. '"Behind the peerless beauty of the woman who was my wife lies a heart of stone and a body of marble. I hereby declare, in an effort to prevent any other man from suffering as I have done, that she is a disgrace to the gentle sex she purports to represent and not fit to be a wife. Lady Mercy Armstrong is frigid. Engage with her at your peril."'

The lawyer set aside the letter with abject relief.

'And here ends the codicil. I will now return to the remaining bequests, beginning with...'

'Bitch,' hissed Frederick Armstrong.

'Barren bitch,' Major Lord Armstrong added.

A sharp silence filled the room. Shocked to the core, as much by the fury as the vitriol which her dead husband had expressed—his dying words redolent with emotions he had kept from her when he'd been alive—Mercy shakily got to her feet. She allowed her gaze to sweep slowly round the small gathering before coming to rest on Harry's twin brothers. 'Whatever other faults I may have, gentlemen, at least I am not a hypocrite. I do not pretend to have feelings that I don't have.'

'You don't *have* any feelings.' Lord Armstrong got to his feet. 'My brother—'

'Is dead,' Mercy interrupted him. 'And you could hardly wait, George, for him to breathe his last. You were hovering over his sick bed like a vulture.'

'I was there, fervently hoping that my brother would recover. I did not see you in attendance. Why, when he first took ill, instead of nursing him as any wife worthy of the name would, you scurried off to attend a wedding.'

'My sister's wedding, which *he* wouldn't have attended even if he had been in rude health and invited. Which he was not.'

'Since you clearly prefer the company of your family to my own, I suggest you leave.' Lord Armstrong snapped his fingers. 'Immediately.'

'I am more than happy to. I wish you joy in your new position, my lord.'

'And I wish you all that my late brother would for you, his frigid, barren widow. I believe...'

But what Major Lord Armstrong believed would never be known, for at that point Clement leapt out of his chair and landed him a vicious punch under the jaw that lifted him clean off his feet. His lordship staggered backwards and then crumpled with a look of utter astonishment onto the drawing room floor.

'I have been waiting a great many years to do that,' Clement said coolly. 'My only regret is that it wasn't Harry. Shall we go, my dear? I had the foresight to order our carriage.' Giving Mercy no time to respond, Clement took her arm and led her briskly out of the drawing room.

Chapter One

Hampshire, November 1863, one year later

It had been a long day, and Jack Dalmuir had spent far more time than he had intended inspecting the water features which dotted the gardens of Hawthorn Manor. They were oddly charming pieces, a little eccentric and most certainly ingenious, though the engineer in him couldn't help but deconstruct the workings and imagine a few minor improvements.

He was glad he'd made the journey. It had been a constructive use of his free day, and a much-needed change of scenery. With no burning need to return to the city until the morning, he decided on the spur of the moment not to head to the train station, but instead to take dinner and spend the night at the inn where he had hired a horse and gig.

It was already dusk as he began to slow up to make the sharp turn into the inn's yard, his focus on the entrance of the inn, when a woman appeared from nowhere, it seemed to him, and threw herself in front of the carriage. Jack cried out a warning, yanking on the reins to pull his horse out of her path. The horse reared, the woman crumpled onto the road and Jack leapt down from the gig, handing the reins to an ostler who had come running out of the courtyard.

'Careful,' he said urgently to the woman as she struggled to sit up. 'Are you hurt?'

'No, I don't think so. I didn't see you. I was deep in thought. I am so sorry. I gave your horse a fright.'

'And yourself too, I reckon. Here, let me help you up.'

'This is so embarrassing, and entirely my own fault.' The woman took his hand, getting gracefully to her feet, the folds of her long, black cloak falling into place over her grey gown. 'I'm perfectly unhurt, I assure you.'

She smiled shakily at him, and Jack caught his breath, for she was quite the loveliest woman he had ever seen. Not young—he would guess in her early thirties—she had a heart-shaped face with a generous mouth and cornflower-blue eyes, wide-spaced and dark-lashed under perfectly arched brows. Wisps of dark blonde hair streaked with gold had escaped her chignon, and there was a smudge of mud on the sharp plane of one cheek.

'You should rest up for a bit,' he said. 'Are you a guest at the inn?'

'No, I live with my brother at present. He has a house on the other side of the village. I have been out walking and was on my way back. It's not far.'

'Too far for you to walk. If you will allow me to escort you inside, you can have a cup of coffee or, better

still, a medicinal brandy. Please,' Jack added, seeing
her hesitate. 'I feel responsible.'

'You have no need to. I walked right out in front of
your carriage without looking, Mr...'

'Dalmuir. Jack Dalmuir. I have been to Hawthorn
Manor to see the water features—I'm an engineer—
and decided to spend the night here before heading to
London.'

'What did you think of the fountains?'

'I've never seen anything like them. They're quite
remarkable. I would have loved to meet their designer.'

'Prue is away from home at present, but she'll be
very sorry to have missed you. There is nothing she
likes so much as to discuss mechanical intricacies.'

'You are acquainted with Lady Bannatyne?'

'You could say that. She is my sister.' After a moment's hesitation, the woman extended her hand. 'I am
Lady Armstrong. The *Dowager* Lady Armstrong. My
late husband died exactly a year ago today, actually.'

'No wonder you were distracted. Please, accept my
condolences.'

'Thank you, but they are quite unnecessary. I have
completed my mourning duties and owe him nothing
more. Do you know, I think I will take you up on the
offer of a brandy, if you meant it? Though I warn you,
Mr Dalmuir, that unlike my sister I have no interest
whatsoever in mechanical matters.'

They were shown into the best private parlour where
a fire was burning in the grate. A decanter of cognac
with two crystal glasses was set on the table, alongside
a tray of the miniature savoury pastries for which the

innkeeper's wife was locally famed. Mercy removed her cloak and pulled off her gloves, taking a seat by the fireside as Mr Dalmuir spoke to the innkeeper about reserving a room for himself and ordering his dinner.

He was a Scotsman, though not a Highlander, for, while he spoke with a soft burr, his accent was tinged with a harsher, gravelly edge. He looked like an engineer, she thought to herself, exuding health and vitality. Strongly built and solid with tanned, capable hands. His clothes were well-cut but practical—a dark blue coat and trousers, his linen plain and white—and there was a no-nonsense air about him that appealed strongly to her.

He could not be described as handsome in the conventional sense but his face was strong-featured, the short, neatly trimmed beard failing to disguise a determined jaw and high-planed cheekbones separated by a good nose that had nothing hawkish about it. Dark brown hair cut short was swept back from a high brow, but it was his eyes which were his most striking feature—a bright blue that was almost turquoise, thickly lashed like her own, with laughter lines clearly visible at the corners.

He finished his business with the innkeeper and turned round to smile at her, a proper smile that gave her a glimpse of straight white teeth and was reflected in his eyes. It was the type of smile that was impossible not to return.

'Here,' he said, pouring her a generous glass of cognac and handing it to her, before sitting opposite with a glass of his own. 'This will warm the cockles of your heart, as my ma, God rest her, used to say.'

'I doubt anything can do that. I am cold-blooded

by nature, with a heart of stone and a body of marble,' Mercy replied, curling her lip. 'A direct quote from my late husband,' she added by way of explanation. 'However, my heart of stone still beats, Mr Dalmuir, and my body of marble still lives and breathes. Today I have done with allowing my husband to dictate to me from beyond the grave.'

She raised her glass in a toast and downed the cognac in one gulp, sighing with pleasure as the liquid burned a satisfying path down her throat and into her stomach. 'I expect you are thinking you have encountered a madwoman.'

'I can see you're a woman in sore need of another dram,' Mr Dalmuir responded, getting to his feet and topping up her glass. 'By the sounds of it, this is a momentous day.'

'I believe it is.' Mercy took another sip of brandy. 'I am thirty-seven years old. I have been a dutiful and devoted wife for seventeen years. For the last year I have worn widow's weeds. It's about time, don't you think, that I started living my own life?' She took another sip. 'I'll wager you have always lived your own life. You don't strike me as someone beholden to anyone.'

He laughed. 'I've certainly been paying my own way since I stopped being a bairn, but I don't suppose that's what you mean.'

'"Stopped being a bairn"... I am not familiar with that accent. Where in Scotland do you come from, Mr Dalmuir?'

'Glasgow,' he answered, sounding somewhat defensive.

'I was not mocking you. I find your accent charming.'

'Aye, I'm sure you do. It's certainly not what you're used to,' he replied, his tone noticeably hardening.

She had offended him. Mercy's instinct was to retreat, finish her brandy, make her excuses and leave, but it was less than five minutes since she had toasted her freedom, and surely that meant that she was free to explain herself? 'Not charming,' she said. 'That was quite the wrong word. I didn't mean to sound patronising or condescending. I like it, that's all I meant.'

He studied her for a moment, saying nothing, and she realised that it mattered to her—out of all proportion, really—that he believed her, so it was a huge relief when he smiled. 'You wouldn't be the first to underestimate me because of my accent, but fair enough, I'll accept you meant no offence.'

'Thank you.' Mercy took another sip of her drink, surprised to find her glass empty once more. 'May I have another?'

'If you're sure.' He waited for her to nod, then topped up her glass. 'This is good stuff, but it's strong.'

'Good, strong stuff is what I am in need of today.' Mercy settled more comfortably into her chair, putting her glass down.

'Do you want to tell me a bit more about that? I'm a good listener, and I'm not the sort to betray a confidence.'

'I'm not in the habit of talking about myself. Not to Clement, or to Prue, or even Sarah—and, goodness knows, she has tried her level best.'

'I'm sure she has, whoever she is. Another sister?'

'No, Sarah is my friend. If she was my sister, she'd

have been called Chastity or Patience or Charity. Clement is my brother, and Prue is Prudence. My name is—'

'Don't tell me, let me guess. Temperance?'

'I think not,' she said with a small laugh, nodding in the direction of the much-diminished decanter of brandy. 'It's Mercy.'

'Mercy.' Mr Dalmuir nodded. 'It suits you, oddly. You can talk to me, Mercy. If you want to, that is.'

He smiled at her, and his smile Mercy decided, was doing what the brandy could not, warming the cockles of her heart. 'What do you want to know?'

'Ach no, the question is, what do you want to tell me?'

'You are a complete stranger.'

'All the more reason, then, to confide in me. You can tell me your innermost thoughts, get them all off your chest, safe in the knowledge that tomorrow morning I'll be on my way and we'll almost certainly never meet again.'

'Is it so unlikely?'

'I'm an engineer, Lady Armstrong. I earn my living with these hands,' Mr Dalmuir said, holding them up. 'I was brought up in one of the poorest parts of Glasgow—and, trust me, there's some mighty deprived areas in that city—single-handedly by my ma, for my father died when I was a bairn. I'm good at what I do, I've made a success of my life. But, aside from the leg up I was very fortunate to get from the man who put me through school, it's been down to my own hard work. I wasn't born with a silver spoon in my mouth, and there's not a trace of blue blood running in my veins. So, no, I don't think our paths are likely to cross again.'

'Meaning I have been cosseted and indulged since the day I was born—with a *gold* spoon in my mouth—and have not done a stroke of work in my life with these lily-white hands,' Mercy retorted.

Mr Dalmuir looked uncomfortable. 'That's not what I meant.'

Once again, her instinct was to retreat, back down, but once again she reminded herself that she was done with compliantly demure behaviour like that. 'It is exactly what you meant. It is also, I am ashamed to say, true.'

'That's as may be, but that doesn't give me the right to judge you or to patronise you. What I should have said was that we don't mix in the same circles. I'm not your high-society type of man, while you— It's obvious you're what they call quality.'

'My departed but far-from-dear husband would disagree with you,' she retorted mockingly. 'According to him, I am something less than useless as a woman. He took the trouble to say so in a codicil to his will read out after his funeral in front of his family and my brother. I knew he had come to resent me, but he really must have hated me to be driven to such a spiteful act.'

'He did what?'

He did whit?

His outrage was a balm. 'I am not fit to be any man's wife, apparently. His very words, I assure you.'

'Good God! What kind of a monster were you married to?'

'That is a very good question. He was not a monster, but a most respectable member of the nobility, and ours was hailed by both families as a very good match.

I did not pretend to love him, but I believed he had all the necessary qualities to make a good husband and father. He did claim to love me, though I quickly realised that he merely coveted me. I happen to be beautiful, although I can take no credit for that. It was simply the hand that nature dealt me. It mattered to him, though, that his wife's complexion was flawless, her figure incomparable, that she was and remained the toast of society. I was a prize, you see, and he never tired of reminding others that he had won me.'

'You make it sound as if he worshipped you.'

'That is what everyone believed—well, almost everyone—but it couldn't be further from the truth. No matter how I tried, I never could live up to his expectations of me.'

'He must have had impossibly high expectations.'

'Impossible, though neither of us knew it when we married. I have one glaring imperfection, you see.' She braced herself to say it. It was *important* for her to say it. 'I cannot have children.'

The words produced a brief, extremely awkward silence. 'I'm very sorry,' Mr Dalmuir said gently. 'I can't begin to imagine how painful that fact must be to bear.'

Painful! She would not allow herself to cry. 'No,' Mercy said gruffly. 'I don't expect you can. It is not a subject which people discuss, is it? My husband and I never did.' Though she had tried. She winced, recalling Harry's fury, his utter refusal to consider the possibility of failure.

'We continued,' Mercy said, lost in the memory, 'With what I would describe as grim determination to do our duty to the title and hope that our efforts would be rewarded—' She broke off, shuddering. 'At least, I thought that's what we were doing, until the codicil was read out, placing the blame squarely on my shoulders.'

Mr Dalmuir looked satisfyingly disgusted. 'That was a very cruel thing to do.'

'It was vile! You cannot imagine how it felt to hear all that vitriol spewed out in front of everyone, and to realise that he'd been keeping it bottled up for all those years.' Mercy took a shaky breath. 'I couldn't believe it.'

Mr Dalmuir looked stunned. 'No bloody wonder.'

'Yes! No bloody wonder! Exactly! I was furious too, though. I had no idea, you see, that he felt like that. I don't mean he kept up the pretence of having more tender feelings while we were alone, I mean that I thought he had no feelings left for me, save his proprietorial zeal. I expect you are sorry you asked now.'

'I'm not sorry, if it's helping you to talk. It sounds like it's long overdue that you did. You must have been miserable.'

'Miserable.' Mercy nodded, unable to speak for a moment for the lump in her throat. 'I didn't allow myself to think about it when Harry was alive, for it would have been pointless. There was nothing to be done, save to carry on regardless. Though Prue and Clement and Sarah all guessed at how unhappy I must be, I dared not admit it, for to do so would only make them miserable too.'

She picked up the glass but did not drink from it, clasping it tightly in her hand and forcing herself to speak. 'But I was truly miserable,' she confessed, her jaw clenched. 'When I allowed myself to think, to see what everyone else could save him—that we had no hope of a child—I was miserable then, because I knew I couldn't make him happy. The only thing to be done was to pretend to hope, as I thought he did, and to continue to play the role of devoted wife. But it's clear now that he too had given up, that he blamed me and resented me. I had no idea at all how angry he was with me.'

'It was a foul thing to do, to declare all that when he knew you'd no chance of having your say in return. And in front of his family too.'

'Who ensured that it was reported in the press, and doubtless also ensured that those who missed reading about it heard about it—discreetly, and in complete confidence, of course. What relish they will all have taken in re-evaluating the outwardly perfect marriage of the devoted Lord and Lady Armstrong. What delight Harry would have taken in seeing me cast firmly in the role of the villain. Sarah and Clement and Prue all tried to keep the newspapers from me, but I saw enough to be able to imagine the rest. Harry's ploy was masterly, really, when you think about it.'

'You'll excuse my being blunt, but he was a bloody coward.'

'I *hadn't* thought of that, but you're quite right, he was. Do you know what I think, Mr Dalmuir? I think he would have taken me with him if he could have. He didn't love me, he didn't even care for me, but I was his, you see—for better and most definitely for worse. So he didn't want anyone else to have me. That's why he wrote that codicil. I see it now. My goodness, I see it now quite clearly! He wanted to make sure that I remain alone, and his property, for the rest of my life.'

Mercy wriggled deeper into her chair, a slow smile dawning. 'Thank you. It has been a relief to finally unburden myself. As of today, I've completed my mourning. I owe him nothing more. He's dead and I'm alive. I'm free, and I belong to no one.'

'Hear, hear.' Mr Dalmuir raised his glass in a toast and took a small sip. 'The big question now is, what are you planning to do with your new-found freedom?'

'Ah, there's the rub. Another most excellent question. The answer is obvious enough, I suppose. I have hidden away from the world, just as he wanted me to, for the last year. Now I must re-join it. No, more than that. Embrace it.'

'Bravo!'

'Thank you!' Mercy made an attempt at a seated bow and finished the last of her cognac. She rarely drank, but she found it was making her pleasantly numb. 'May I please have some more brandy?'

'You wouldn't prefer some coffee?'

'No, thank you, I'm not it the least light-headed. Only relieved.' She wrinkled her nose. 'That's not the right word, but it will do. I have been keeping everything in for so long, you see. Well, yes, you do see, for it was you who encouraged me to talk. I hope you are not regretting doing so.'

'I'm not, not a whit of it, I promise. So, what's your plan, then?'

'A change of abode, for a start—and I don't mean moving to the Armstrong Dower House. I've been living at my brother's house since the will was read. I've been recuperating. Yes, that's the word, recuperating. But I am ready to make a fresh start now, and I can't stay with Clement for the rest of my life. Apart from anything else, it would not do for me to be a cuckoo in the nest if he ever gets around to marrying.'

'Is that likely?'

'I don't know. I hoped he would marry Sarah, my friend, but he is almost forty and quite set in his ways. He is a classical scholar, and happier imagining himself in ancient Greece than taking part in the modern world, while she is quite the opposite, and very much against marriage into the bargain. There was a spark between them, but it seems to have died. If I could stop them worrying about me, they might rekindle it. So I shall find a house of my own choosing in town. And then, well, I've no idea what I will do when I am there. I shall take my life a step at a time.'

'You never know, you might marry again.'

'Good heavens, haven't you been listening at all, Mr Dalmuir? Why on earth would I do such a thing? As a widow, I have financial and personal independence. If I married, not only would I lose my jointure, I would once again become my husband's property. Besides, you are forgetting the fact that I cannot have children, and that surely is the whole point of a marriage?'

'Not quite the whole point. There's companionship and finding a helpmeet.'

'I am looking forward to living alone, and I have no need of a helpmeet. Poor Harry,' Mercy said sarcastically. 'He went to such trouble to brand me as unmarriageable, and he had no idea that remarrying is the last thing I would ever wish to do.'

'When you put it like that, I can see why.'

'It's different for a man, though. Are you married, Mr Dalmuir?'

'Not yet. I'm waiting to meet the right woman.'

'To fall in love, do you mean?'

He snorted. 'Marriage is far too important to rely on love to see you through the trials and tribulations of life together.'

'Now, there we are in complete agreement. Tell me, for I have done far too much talking, what qualities do you seek in a wife?'

'I am not actively seeking a wife at present, Lady Armstrong.'

'Don't call me that! Call me Mercy. Come, now, you must have thought about it. You strike me as a man with very strong ideas about his life, a man who likes to have everything just so. Or am I wrong?'

He laughed. 'You make me sound like an uptight bore.'

'No, no, not at all. I meant it as a compliment. I wish I— But we are talking about you, Mr Dalmuir—or may I call you Jack?'

'Please do.'

'Jack. You see? That's a good, strong name for an engineer, isn't it? I expect you want a practical wife, don't you? A helpmeet, to use your own word, a woman who can run your house, bear your children and—and do your accounts and charm all your business associates and—and all that sort of thing. Am I right?'

'I want a wife who would share my life, certainly. A strong woman, practical, with the same roots as myself.'

'A woman like your mother, perhaps?'

Jack grinned sheepishly. 'I reckon so. I could do a hell of a lot worse.'

'And children?'

'I'd like a family, yes.'

'You needn't look so uncomfortable, it's a perfectly natural thing to want children. My sister, Prue, and her husband, Dominic, are expecting their first child. Poor Prue. She was afraid to tell me, she tried to hide it from me for fear of upsetting me, but I guessed.'

'And were you upset?'

She shook her head vehemently. 'I'm happy for them. Very happy. Looking at them has made me see that it wouldn't have been right. Not for me. Not with him—whose name I will no longer speak, I have decided. Do you think that's a good decision?'

'An excellent one. I think I'll get you some coffee after all, though. Excuse me a moment.' He got up and left the room, returning with a tray. 'Here,' he said, pouring her a cup. 'Have some of this.'

'If it will make you happy, but I am not in the least affected. My head is perfectly clear. Tomorrow, I am going to cast off my widow's weeds, roll my sleeves up and make all sorts of decisions. Tomorrow, Jack, is the first day of the rest of my life. I am going to start afresh. What do you think of that?'

'It's an excellent plan.'

Mercy beamed. 'Yes, it is. Quite excellent. I am going to prove him wrong about me. Though I am not at all sure,' she added, her face falling, 'how precisely I am going to do that. If I was truly set on proving him wrong, I should wear the willow for the rest of my life just to show the world how he had unfairly maligned me and what a terribly devoted wife I was.'

'Aye, but that would be playing straight into his hands. What you really need to do is let everyone see how miserable he made you by showing how much happier you are without him.'

'You're right! You are absolutely right. That's it in a nutshell. How shall I do that?'

'You said that money isn't one of your worries?'

'No, I have plenty of money. That is one thing that Har—I mean, *he*—couldn't take away from me.'

'Then why not spend some of it? Enjoy yourself, kick over the traces a bit. Do some of the things that you've always wanted to.'

'What sort of things?'

'I don't know. The kind of things that he wouldn't have wanted you to do. He sounds like he was a right stuffed shirt.'

'Oh, indeed he was. Stiff-necked, prudish and so boring! A model of propriety, who liked nothing better than to read the reports of the tedious, exclusive dinner parties and balls where his wife was the most beautiful woman there, and her gown the most expensive.

'What he didn't like,' Mercy said, her lip curling, 'was when the same newspapers speculated about whether his beautiful wife was at last in an interesting condition when she cried off from an engagement with a head cold or a stomach ache. The scandal sheets were almost as obsessed with the contents of my womb as he was. And now I really have shocked you. I apologise, that was vulgar.'

'You're exaggerating, surely?'

Mercy shrugged. 'On the contrary. Even when he died, they printed their condolences to his "beautiful widow, whose grief will be made even more painful by her heart-breaking failure to provide him with an heir". You are looking sceptical, but I assure you it was so.'

'I'd have gone round to whoever was responsible and given him a piece of my mind, if that had been me,' Jack said scornfully. 'If he hated the newspaper coverage so much, why didn't your husband do just that and stop them publishing such intrusive speculation? He must have had some clout—strings he could pull, I mean?'

'"Never question, never explain" is what my parents always taught me. It is not the done thing in polite society to give any credence to what the reporters might say. For a start, it would require one to admit that one had read it.'

'Which your husband clearly did.'

'Yes, but it would have been even more scandalous if he'd admitted he'd read it and tried to have the editor retract it, if that's what you mean. "Lord Armstrong was most upset by the allegations that his wife might be expecting an heir and wishes it to be known that in fact the halibut she ate for dinner was the culprit". Thus letting the world know that our kitchen serves questionable fish and he has still been unable to get his wife with child. Do you see?'

'I see you live in a very different world from mine. The only time my name appears in the papers is when I've signed a big commercial contract. If you really want that husband of yours to be turning in his grave, it seems to me the best way of doing it would be to get yourself splashed all over the front pages of the scandal sheets.'

'Now, there's an idea.'

'I was joking.'

'I doubt they'll be interested in me anyway, now. I am no longer the beautiful wife of a powerful peer, I'm a barren widow with few friends and no influence.' She thought for a moment, then smiled. 'How lovely it will be not to have to *worry* about what people say about me. I am so sick and tired of behaving with *propriety*. I don't want to cause a scandal. What I want is to be a little bit outrageous. I don't suppose you have a notion of how I could make a start on that?'

Jack bit back the obvious reply as Mercy gazed at him, her huge eyes dancing with merriment, and decided that he might as well go along with her. 'Well, if you want to start modestly, you could take up dancing the polka,' he said. 'I don't mean the polite version danced at a ball, but the rough and tumble style of the dance hall.'

'I've never been to a dance hall, and I'm not at all sure I know what you mean by "rough and tumble style". Do you think I'd enjoy that?'

'Why don't we try it now, see what you think?'

'Here?'

'Aye, why not?'

Why not? What the hell was he playing at?

Another of his very good questions, and he had no idea of the answer, but he was committed now. So he set about clearing a space for them in the middle of the room, pushing the table and chairs back into the window embrasure. Of course he wanted to dance with her. Mercy was lovely. In fact, she was bloody gorgeous. But, aside from the fact that she'd downed half a decanter of brandy, she was clearly in an extremely fragile state of mind. She was precisely the kind of woman he'd usually run a mile from, but he felt no inclination to run.

Though she'd been sparse on details about her marriage, she'd clearly had a rough time. But, rather than weep and wail, and sob on someone's shoulder about it, she was staunchly stoic, keeping her suffering even from her nearest and dearest. Now she wanted to get her own back, and he admired her spirit, even if he doubted she had the strength of mind to carry it through.

'Right,' Jack said, putting a screen in front of the fire. 'Are you sure you're ready for this?'

Mercy nodded, looking not at all certain, taking the hand he held out to her and getting to her feet. Her fingers were long and slender, her nails cut to the quick and the skin around the edges frayed with traces of dried blood. He took her into his hold, but she flinched and he immediately let her go. 'What...?'

'Nothing. I am not accustomed to— My dancing with anyone was frowned on, that's all.' She put her hand on his left shoulder. 'Is that correct?'

She seemed to be steeling herself. Carefully, he put his left hand flat and very lightly on her back, then took her other hand in a clasp, and as he began to talk her through the basic moves she relaxed marginally.

She did not wear perfume but smelt of lemon soap and smoke from the fire which she had been seated by. Her mouth pursed with concentration and a tiny frown brought her brows together as she listened to him, nodding slowly, which he found both endearing and arousing. From a distance, she was beautiful. Close to, her skin was flawless, her mouth softly pink, her body intensely feminine.

Flustered by his own reaction, Jack increased the distance between them and began to walk them through the dance. Her crinoline brushed the furniture as they circled, slowly at first, and then picked up the tempo, Mercy unbending a little more, counting under her breath, easily matching her steps to his. It was she who stepped closer into his embrace, tightening her clasp on his hand, making him forget his own reticence as they began to polka properly, faster and with less restraint. Faster and faster they went, swirling in a tight circle in the cramped space, until the leg of a chair caught them both out and they came to a halt, laughing and breathless.

'That was wonderful!' Mercy panted. A few tendrils of hair clung to her cheeks, which were flushed with colour. Smiling, her eyes bright with laughter, she dropped down onto the sofa that Jack had moved into the window embrasure. 'I loved it.'

'You'll love it even more in a dance hall with a proper sprung floor and an orchestra,' Jack said, joining her.

Her face fell. 'One can't dance the polka alone.'

'Not a problem. I'll dance it with you,' he said, taking them both by surprise. 'I've business in London that will keep me there a good few months more,' he continued, for his own good as much as hers. 'I'm responsible for the engines being built for the new pumping stations they're constructing. It doesn't require my presence on site full-time, but it's too important not to be on hand if any issues arise, so my returning to Scotland is out of the question.

'That's why I'm here today, in fact—trying to make good use of my free time now that I've seen all that London has to offer—or at least, all the bits that I want to see. In fact, if you require an escort at any point,' he concluded, quite happy with his reasoning now, 'I'd be happy to oblige you.'

Mercy was less convinced. 'You don't even know me.'

'I know enough to want to know more. Unless *you'd* rather not…'

'I would, very much, like to. But why, Jack?'

He frowned, thinking it over before he answered. 'Because you've had a hard time of it, and I think you could do with a bit of a laugh and a bit of moral support, just until you find your feet.'

'I don't want your motive to be pity.'

'Trust me,' he said with a short laugh, 'It's not pity I feel for you. Look, you'd be doing me a favour. I'd much rather spend my spare time with you than a bunch of architects and engineers. To say you're easy on the eye is just about the biggest understatement I could make, but it's what's going on behind that lovely face of yours that interests me.'

'Why?'

'I don't know, and that's the God's honest truth. We've next to nothing in common, but it seems to me that we've just…' He snapped his fingers. 'Do you see what I mean?'

'We understand one another? Get along?'

'Both of those. Aye, both of those. And we could have some fun together.'

'So are you offering to be my partner in crime, then, Jack Dalmuir?'

'Proving to the world that you're no longer living in that man's shadow is no crime.'

She chuckled. 'No, you're right. It is a—a very necessary campaign, that's what it is. Are you serious about offering to keep me company?'

'It looks like I am. If you want me?' He hadn't meant the words to sound suggestive and he hadn't meant the hand he held out to her to be anything other than the mock signifying of a deal. But, as her gaze met his and as their hands clasped, something other than liking sparked between them. She licked her lower lip and swallowed, and the effect it had on him was immediate and embarrassing. 'Want me to be your escort, I meant,' he said, unable to tear his eyes away from her, though he knew he should, his foolish words making it worse.

'Yes. I mean, I do. I want you.' Her colour was high now. She pulled her hand away just as he let her go and she dropped her gaze.

'Then it's a deal,' Jack said, getting up, sounding discordantly jovial. 'I'll give you my card. You let me know when you're settled in London and, first chance we have, we'll go dancing.'

Mercy got up, her own colour fading. 'I will look forward to that.'

'If you change your mind, you can just forget you ever met me, and no harm done.'

'I won't change my mind.' To his surprise, she took

his hand again, lifting it to her cheek. 'Thank you, Jack. I am very glad I threw myself in front of your horse today. I look forward to seeing you in town.'

Chapter Two

London, January 1864

Clement was astounded when Mercy informed him that she intended to move back to town but, after he recovered from the shock of her announcement—which she made the morning after her unsettling encounter with Jack Dalmuir—her brother was entirely supportive. It was high time that she made a life for herself, he said, unaware that he was echoing her own thoughts.

The hiring of a house and arrangements for the removal of her personal effects from Hampshire to London took up most of her time since. With Christmas at Hawthorn Manor a pleasant interlude, she had very little time to worry about whether or not she was making the right decision. She didn't mention Jack to her brother and sister, and Sarah being out of town on an extended visit to relatives made it easy for her to keep their acquaintance a secret from her friend.

The agreement they had reached was unconventional, to say the least, and Mercy had no wish to explain it, or to account for her having behaved so out of character, especially as it might come to nothing.

She did, however, mention his name in passing to Dominic, who spoke highly of Mr Dalmuir's engineering company, and of the man himself, who was both respected and well-liked in business circles. Reassured, Mercy wrote to inform Jack of her arrival in town. He responded promptly and tonight, with most of the *ton* still in the country for the Christmas period, Mercy would take the first step towards establishing herself as a merry widow.

The term made her laugh softly to herself. Her dead husband would have been appalled at the little mews house she had taken in Chelsea, an area of London popular with artists and artistes, some more reputable than others. His successor would very likely be taking up residence in the Armstrong town house at Cavendish Square for the season, now that the mourning year was over.

Mercy had hosted a ball to mark the reopening of Parliament at that house every year of her marriage. George would now be responsible for keeping up that and every other tradition. Would he send a card to the Dowager? Mercy grimaced. She loathed that epithet, and she loathed George who, if he discovered tonight's planned escapade, would be delighted to have an excuse to cut her dead.

Fortunately, she was no longer obliged to worry about her reputation or about what the press said of her. Tonight, her biggest worry was whether she and Jack really would get along, as she had so inelegantly put it at the time, or whether their rapport had been the result of the brandy she had drunk.

The day after their strange meeting, she had been astounded by her own lack of inhibition. The brandy had contributed, no doubt, as had the significance of the date, but she had not regretted saying a single thing to him. Or doing anything. Especially not doing anything. Holding his hand, having him clasp her close, feeling his breath on her cheek, the warmth of his skin, had been so strange. She had forgotten to steel herself, forgotten to hold herself aloof, forgotten how much she had come to loathe any such contact.

This last year she had gradually become accustomed to brotherly and sisterly embraces, but Jack was a stranger. Was that it? Because he'd wanted nothing from her, save to dance, she had felt… No, safe in his embrace wasn't the word. She hadn't felt at all safe, she had felt… But why try to explain? She had enjoyed it. She was looking forward to enjoying it again. It was really quite simple.

Mercy surveyed her reflection critically in the long mirror in her bedchamber. Her gown was made of gold silk embossed with a pattern of large, blowsy shrimp-pink roses. A wide belt drew attention to her slim waist, but the V-shaped neckline was cut modestly high and the sleeves were long and cut in the pagoda style. The skirt of the gown was pleated, falling flat over her crinoline, but billowing out when she twirled.

She spun around now, enjoying the effect, revealing the ruffles of her pink lace-trimmed petticoats and the merest glimpse of her pale pink stockings. It was Prue who had suggested the lingerie during a shopping trip just before Christmas, directing her firmly away from her usual decorous white with plain lace.

'Trust me,' her sister had said. 'I have discovered there is a very personal pleasure to be taken in wearing such things.' And Prue was right. Mercy's under garments were completely frivolous and wholly unlike anything she had ever worn before.

It was as if she had donned another, secret identity, that of a woman who was a little bit decadent and a little bit daring. Her entire toilette, including her simply dressed hair and complete lack of jewellery, had contributed to creating a very different woman. Not only did it lack the current fashion for swags, ruffles and copious amounts of expensive trimming, but the colour of the fabric was not in the least demure or restrained, and was only just on the right side of gaudy. Mercy loved it.

She checked the clock and saw that Jack was due in ten minutes. Her stomach fluttered, and it took her a moment to work out that what she was feeling was butterflies of excitement and not sick dread. Tonight, she was going dancing. Not to a ball, where every invitation was vetted, but to a public dance hall, where anyone who could pay the entry fee would be welcome. It was not an adventure she'd ever thought of embarking upon of her own initiative, and it was most certainly not one which any lady of her acquaintance would have dreamed of. Her behaviour tonight, like the petticoats she wore, would be perceived as extremely risqué.

Why were the rules that governed society so very arbitrary? She had never thought to ask herself that question before. Was there really such a difference between a sedate polka at a private ball and what Jack called a 'proper polka' at a public dance?

The doorbell clanged. Mercy pinned her little empress hat in place, picked up her short, plain pink cape and gloves, then dimmed the lamp. She was about to find out.

Jack was shown into the little drawing room by Mercy's maid, Lucy. He was examining Prue's wedding photograph, which took place of pride on the mantlepiece, but set it down when Mercy entered the room and strode forward to greet her. 'How are you? Silly question. You look very well indeed.'

'Thank you.' She took his outstretched hand and dropped a little curtsey. 'I have been extremely extravagant and given my entire old wardrobe away to be sold for Prue's safe drinking water charity. My sister not only designs water features as works of art but she and her husband are ardent campaigners for the provision of clean water in London's poorer areas. Esme, the woman who took that wedding photograph, has also taken some extremely moving pictures of the slums to help with the campaign, which her husband is also closely involved in.'

'I'd like to see those some time,' Jack replied, accepting the glass of sherry she had poured. 'I'm in the business of taking filth out of the city via the steam engines we're building for the new pumping stations, and back home in Glasgow I was involved in bringing fresh water into the city from Loch Katrine. But getting the water into the homes that need it is still an issue. I'm guessing that London is as bad as Glasgow, in that respect?'

'I am ashamed to confess that I know very little of the detail. You would need to speak to Prue and Dominic about that.'

'What happened to your sister's face?' Jack asked, indicating the portrait. 'Is it presumptuous of me to say that I admire her for letting her scars be seen like that? It must have taken courage.'

'Prue is the bravest woman I know. Until she met Dominic, she spent most of her life hiding behind a veil. She was adopted by our parents as a baby—that's something Clement and I have always known, and it has never made any difference to how we feel about her. But it was only relatively recently that she discovered her scars were the result of a terrible accident when the roof of the house her real parents rented collapsed, killing both of them. Her family were very respectable working-class people, but their landlord was a criminal, his homes unsafe and poorly maintained.'

Mercy picked up the photograph, studying her sister's face. 'Prue had Esme take some quite startling photographs in close-up of her face to use in her campaign against slum landlords. They shocked a great many people, my dead husband included, but I was so incredibly proud of her.'

'So she's gifted and brave.'

'Far, far more than I, and much more interesting too. Esme took *cartes de visite* photographs of me for years, to *his* specification. They were much admired, which was good for Esme's business, but I hated them. I looked like a porcelain doll in a party dress, and yet

I never had the courage to protest or to ask her to take a photograph that made me look like me. Perhaps because I was afraid that's how I do look,' she concluded, wincing.

'You must know perfectly well that you're bloody gorgeous.'

Mercy laughed wryly. 'Nature and fashion have conspired to make me a beauty in society's eyes.'

'Well, you're your own woman now. Get a new visiting card made to your own specification.'

'If anyone finds out where I've been tonight, there will be no need to for me to do any such thing.'

'All we're doing is going dancing. It's hardly going to make you notorious.'

Several potential scandal sheet headlines ran through her head.

Dancing Dowager kicks over the traces!

Strip the widow? No, it's the polka for now for daring Dowager!

Lady Armstrong apparently sends a Highlander reeling!

Smiling at her own flights of fancy, Mercy pulled on her cape and tied the fastenings in a large bow. 'Let's go.'

Holborn Casino had been converted from public swimming baths some twenty years ago, when the craze for the polka had first taken off, and was still one of the most popular places in London to dance. The front entrance led straight into a huge room lit by several massive chandeliers which had been adapted for gas. Spectators who did not wish to participate occupied the galleries on the upper floor.

On the ground floor the galleried areas were partitioned off to provide refreshment rooms, where the American cocktail called sherry cobbler was served, as well as the more traditional negus, wine, beer, tea and coffee. There was a Turkish divan room for gentlemen who wished to smoke, and plentiful seating for the dancers needing to rest their weary feet. Plush upholstery, deep carpeting throughout, apart from the famous sprung dancing floor, and immense gilded mirrors added to the general impression of luxury and splendour.

Variety acts occasionally performed at the Holborn. Bedouin acrobats and Carlos Alberto, who specialised in balancing upon bottles while spinning plates, had proved popular in the past. But tonight was devoted to dancing. The modest entrance fee of a shilling was designed to introduce 'dancing for the millions', and the clientele was certainly an eclectic mix of shop workers and clerks from the City and the nearby Inns of Court, with a sprinkling of medical students.

A quadrille was underway when Mercy and Jack arrived, the Master of Ceremonies standing at the head of the floor to ensure that no one broke formation, the orchestra being enthusiastically conducted in the gallery directly above. The dancers, Jack was relieved to note, were for the most part respectable, intent upon enjoying the dancing along with their equally respect-

able partners. The swells who sought more accommo-
dating female company presumably did so in the more
louche Argyll Rooms in the Haymarket, which he had
been advised to give a wide berth.

Mercy, standing close, was looking about her anxiously. 'I doubt very much that we will bump into anyone who knows me here.'

Jack knew for a fact that they let reporters into the
casinos for free, and he also knew that it was a bit early
yet for the swells and the men about town to be out on a
spree. Mercy's beauty was such that she would always
be instantly recognisable, but whether she understood
this herself or not he could not guess. 'Does it matter
if you are spotted?'

'No, you're right. It doesn't matter at all. I must remember that.'

'We can leave if you wish.'

'Certainly not. We came here to dance. Thank goodness you warned me not to wear an evening gown. I
would have looked horribly out of place. I must admit,
I had not expected to dance in my hat and wrap.'

'I have to dance in my hat too,' Jack said. 'And I
don't have the advantage of hat pins to keep it in place,
as you do.'

'You will have to keep your head very still or you
will end up like that gentleman.' Mercy indicated a man
whose top hat had slid down over his brow. 'I wonder
that he can see anything at all, save his feet.'

'As long as he can see his feet, and those of others,
that's all that matters.'

She chuckled. 'Very true.'

The music came to an end and the dancers left the

floor chatting and laughing, in search of refreshment. As they swarmed around them, Jack put a protective arm around Mercy, edging them further into the room to a quieter space by one of the tall pillars which supported the galleries.

'It's a great deal busier than I anticipated,' he said. 'The dance floor is going to be very crowded.'

'This is nothing compared to the crush of some of the balls I have attended over the years. The less space there is to dance, the more successful the occasion is deemed to be.'

'Why not invite less people and have the room to enjoy the dance?'

'An eminently sensible solution, and one I several times suggested myself over the years. But if your ballroom is not full to capacity the assumption is that your invitations have been passed over for another, more prestigious occasion. And that,' Mercy said with a sardonic smile, 'would never do.'

'Were your ballrooms always full?'

'Always. The Armstrong family is very well connected. Our invitations were always sought-after, our parties a resounding success, for I am rather boringly fond of planning, and rather tediously good at it. It is one of my few talents.'

'Don't underestimate yourself. You're also an excellent dancer, as you proved at the inn. Talking of which,' Jack said as the Master of Ceremonies suggested that everyone take their places on the floor for the first polka of the evening, 'shall we?'

'Oh, goodness,' Mercy said, looking around her as

the couples rushed to the dance floor 'I feel suddenly nervous. I don't want to make you look like a fool.'

'I won't let you. Trust me.' He held out his hand, and, after a moment's hesitation, she took it, allowing him to lead her onto the floor. 'Ready?'

'I am committed now.' She checked the fastenings of her cape and patted her hat before putting her hand on his shoulder. 'This feels very odd. People are staring at us.'

They were staring at Mercy. 'Because we're strangers here,' Jack said. 'That's all.'

'Of course. I didn't think.'

'They'll forget all about us when the music starts.'

'Are you sure you'll be able to keep your top hat in place?'

'Don't you worry about anything save keeping in step. If it gets too much for you, just say the word and we'll leave.' Jack put his arm around her waist and, though he kept his touch very light, he could feel her trembling. 'Relax,' he said, smiling down at her. 'No one cares if you make a few false steps. The point is to enjoy yourself, remember?'

Mercy nodded, trying to do as he bid her. She hadn't thought this through properly. She hadn't realised that the pair of them would stand out from the crowd quite so much. Nor had she realised she would have to dance on such a packed floor. She had danced on busier dance floors, but the other dancers had always been people she knew. And the point of being in such a crush at a society ball was to be seen, not to dance.

There! That was a thought she ought to cling to—

she was not on display here. No one cared who she was. Everyone was here to dance. And so was she.

The band struck up. Mercy stepped closer into Jack's arms and then, biting her lip with concentration, followed his lead into the polka. She stumbled, but he held her upright and didn't miss a beat. They made a decorous circuit, and Mercy began to gain confidence. Though the floor was packed, Jack had clearly danced in more crowded and considerably more raucous venues. He steered them both expertly through the throng, the flailing feet, the swirling capes and crinolines and the toppling top hats.

'You're dancing beautifully,' he said as they completed their second circuit. 'Stop worrying about your steps and enjoy yourself.'

'I'm trying.'

A very young man and his very fat partner veered perilously close, and Jack pulled Mercy tight, executing a tight spin that left her breathless. 'You see,' he said in her ear, 'you're much better than you think.'

He was so close she could smell his shaving soap, see the line on his neck where he had carefully trimmed his beard, feel the bump of his shoulder against hers and smell the wool of his coat. His clasp was light but secure, and their steps matched perfectly as he whirled her into another spin that made her gown fly out behind her, her feet barely touching the ground.

She forgot the other couples. She gave herself over to the freedom of being in a strange place where no one knew her, with a man she knew next to nothing about, save that he was the first man she had ever met who looked at her and saw past her looks.

She wished that Sarah could see her now. She wasn't creating a scandal being here, but she was behaving just a little bit scandalously, at last breaking the bonds of decorum that had bound her since she'd first made her debut, and she was thoroughly enjoying it. She was enjoying being in Jack's arms. She was enjoying surrendering to the music, the pulse of the dance and the exhilaration of spinning recklessly. And she was enjoying the thrill of her own pulsing awareness of the man holding her, the surprise of her response to his touch, the hope that it gave her that she might not, after all, be the cold, unresponsive, unfeminine woman the world believed her to be.

When the polka ended Mercy had barely enough time to be disappointed before the orchestra struck up again, and off they whirled. It was hot in the room now, the air thick with the scent of musty clothes, sweat, cheap perfume and the acrid tang of unwashed bodies, the floor bouncing beneath the pounding of feet in time to the music. Sweat trickled down her back as she danced, her body so attuned to Jack's that they moved as one, keeping effortless pace with him as he turned them and whirled them around the perimeter of the floor again, then again and again. When it was over, the crowd clapped and cheered, but she remained breathless in his embrace, pressed close, not wanting it to end.

'Is it very late?' Mercy asked as they left the casino. 'I have lost track and have no idea what the time is.'

Jack checked his watch under a gas light near the entrance. 'Not much after ten. Did you enjoy yourself?'

'Need you ask? I didn't want to stop dancing. It was wonderful. Did you enjoy it?'

'Need you ask?' he retorted, smiling at her. 'You took to the polka like a duck to water.'

'I had an expert guide.'

'Alas, my misspent youth. Are you hungry?'

'Ravenous. I have worked up quite an appetite. Have you?'

'Starving. I'd give a great deal for a piece and chips.'

'What on earth is that?'

'Fried potatoes eaten between two slices of bread and butter.' Jack laughed, seeing her horrified expression. 'A Scottish delicacy. I reckon we'll have to settle for a meat pie. There's a pie stall round the corner.'

'What kind of meat pie?' she asked dubiously.

'Well, now, if you ask the pie man I'm sure he'll tell you it's the best British beef. But, if you'd like a piece of friendly advice, I'd say it's best not to ask. Shall we? I'll risk it if you will.'

'I am not so sure.' But she hurried across the street with him all the same. Even this late at night Holborn was very busy with coaches, hackney carriages and the throngs emerging from the casino. At one corner a man was selling oysters from a barrel, and on another the smell of roasting chestnuts from a brazier was attracting a small crowd. A few more steps brought them to the queue for pies.

'Fresh out the oven from the baker's just a few steps away,' the pie man informed them. 'Finest British beef,' he proclaimed, making Mercy suppress a giggle. 'Delicious gravy made with English ale. You won't get better, sir.'

Jack paid for two pies which came wrapped in newspaper. 'You'd best take off your gloves or you'll ruin them.'

Mercy pulled off her gloves, tucked them into the belt of her dress and accepted the newspaper parcel. The aroma of warm pastry and gravy made her mouth water as she opened it up. Cautiously, she took a bite. The pastry melted on her tongue. She took another bite. The meat was succulent, the gravy rich.

'Well?' Jack asked.

'It is absolutely delicious.' Hot gravy dribbled over her fingers and she licked it off. 'Eating out of a newspaper parcel in the street! Do you know, in a way it feels even more shocking than dancing a polka in a public casino.'

'A bit eccentric, maybe, but hardly shocking. What's wrong with having something to eat if you're hungry, regardless of where you are?'

'Nothing at all.' Nothing at all if she was a man, Mercy thought. Or if she was sixty years old, living in obscurity, and had never been known as the beautiful Lady Armstrong or the barren Lady Armstrong. Then there would have been no harm at all in her walking along Holborn in the dark, eating a meat pie in the company of an attractive Scot.

A very attractive Scot, who for all his experience and success seemed quite oblivious to the world of scandalmongering and the risk he ran of becoming embroiled in it simply by being seen in her company. She didn't want to explain it to him, didn't want him to think she was exaggerating her own importance or making something of nothing, which she hoped she was. But it wouldn't be fair not to warn him.

Raucous singing could be heard through the open doorway of a large gin palace on the opposite side of the road. A little dog started to follow them, and Mercy couldn't resist giving him the remains of her pie, thinking that it would satisfy him. She was wrong. The morsel was quickly gobbled up, and the dog lolloped after her, whining until Jack fed him the scraps from his own supper, handing Mercy his handkerchief to use to wipe her hands and dab at her mouth before he did the same.

'Go on, then,' he said, cramming the handkerchief back into his coat pocket, 'put me straight. What am I not getting?'

She was too surprised at his having read her thoughts to pretend to misunderstand him. 'It's not my eating a pie in public that is scandalous, it's the circumstances. And who I am—or, rather, who I was,' she added self-consciously. 'It is so easy to twist things to tell a different story.'

'Like expecting an heir, instead of a case of off fish, do you mean?'

'Did I say that? Yes, that is what I mean. I'm used to it. I am even setting out to court it, you could say. Once it is known that I have taken a house in Chelsea... That single fact, Jack, could be used against me.'

He shrugged. 'So you live in Chelsea. So what? They can't take your house from you. What have you got to lose unless you care about what they say? And I thought that you didn't.'

'Not any more. But if you are seen with me, then... Oh, never mind. I can see you think I'm making something of nothing.'

'What I can see is that you're getting cold. You're shivering. Come on, let's get you home.'

He hurried them both to a rank of waiting hackneys and gave the driver the address, settling down beside her as they set off towards the river. 'I'll be blunt, for it won't take long to get to Chelsea, and I don't want you hanging about outside once we're there. Are you worried that if we're seen together the newspapers will imply that we are lovers?'

'That is a refreshingly blunt way of putting it.'

'Then let me be even more blunt with you. Provided no one maligns my business or my integrity as a businessman, I couldn't give a damn what they write. My beam engines are the best in the world, which is why I won this contract, and that's all that matters to me. So, if some pathetic reporter wants to make up a load of twaddle about us, let him.'

'I am probably being over-cautious. I suppose if they wrote about me being spotted with an attractive, mysterious man, it might put an end to the myth that I have a "heart of stone and a body of marble".'

Jack snorted. 'The envious ramblings of a man who knows he's going to be cold and buried under marble himself very soon. No one who's met you could believe that of you.'

He didn't understand. The cab was slowing to a halt outside her house, and she didn't want to spoil the night. But Jack was the one person she had always been honest with, and who from the first had tried to understand her.

She braced herself as he jumped down and held out

his hand to help her out. 'I'll see you to your door,' he said, telling the driver to wait.

'He thought me frigid,' Mercy confessed under cover of looking for the key in her pocket, for she did not have any servants living in. '"Lady Mercy Armstrong is frigid. Engage with her at your peril". Those were his very words.' And it was a relief to speak them, to spit them out and to hear Jack's muffled curse in response. She found the key and put it into the lock, opening her door.

'You're not frigid, Mercy,' he said, following her in but leaving the door ajar. 'Frozen, maybe, as a result of what he put you through, but definitely not frigid.'

'Put me through?' It took her a moment to understand his meaning. 'He never harmed me. Not in any way that you're thinking.'

'As a husband, he had a right…'

'No.' She forced herself to meet his eyes in the light of the lamp that her maid had left lit on the side table. 'He never forced himself on me, if that is what you are thinking. He never beat me. He gave me nothing at all to complain of in his treatment of me.'

'Save that he was a tyrant who didn't want you to have a mind or a life of your own.'

Mercy smiled faintly. 'Or a devoted husband who could not bear to have his beautiful wife stray far from his side.'

'Is that what these scandal sheets you're so obsessed with said?'

'I am not obsessed, I'm simply inured to it, and it's what everyone thought.'

Jack took her hand. 'I enjoyed myself tonight. I very

much enjoyed your company. What I said to you that day we met stands. I'd be more than happy to keep you company while I'm in London if you want me to. Forget about proving that man wrong, forget about what other people may or may not say of us being together. Why don't we just enjoy ourselves for the sake of it, you and I?'

'I'd like that. Very much.'

He nodded, smiling at her. 'Good. Then that's what we'll do.'

Her gloves were still tucked into her belt, and his were in his pocket. His kiss was the merest brush of his lips on her fingertips, warm lips on her cold fingers. She shivered, but not with cold, and most certainly not with the more familiar stab of disgust. His touch was making her chest feel tight, as if she couldn't breathe.

Though he was no longer kissing her, he was still holding her hand, and she didn't want him to let go. So she curled her fingers into his and stepped a little closer to him, so that their clasped hands were crushed between them. Their breath mingled. Their eyes met, and her heart thumped in her chest as he leaned into her and she lifted her face for his kiss. But his mouth met her cheek, not her lips, lingering long enough for her to feel the bristle of his beard on her skin, and then he stepped away.

'Goodnight, Mercy.'

Confused and strangely disappointed, she tried to collect herself. 'Goodnight, Jack.'

She watched him walk back down the path and mutter an instruction to the driver, giving her a brief wave before he climbed into the cab. Mercy closed and locked the door and lifted her hand to her cheek, as if she could feel his touch. Closing her eyes, she relived the feeling of his mouth, the warmth of his body, so close but not close enough. Relived the scent of him, and the way his lips had made her shiver. Not with fear, not with disgust and not with cold. The opposite of all those things. What she had felt must be what people called desire.

Stunned, Mercy picked up the oil lamp and made her way upstairs. Smiling to herself, she began to undress, putting her clothes tidily away and pulling on her nightgown before sitting down at her dressing table to unpin and brush out her hair. Her year of mourning had given her the excuse to pay off the haughty French dresser that *he* had insisted she employ, and she had made it clear to the young lady's maid she employed to come in during the day that she preferred to dress and undress herself.

She put down the brush and quickly braided her hair before setting the lamp carefully on the bedside table and climbing in under the covers. Her pillows were soft and plentiful. There was a warming pan at her feet, but the sheets were cool, just as she liked them.

Was Jack in bed in his lodgings, already asleep? Or was he lying awake, thinking of her? When his lips had touched her skin, had he felt the same shivering feeling inside as she had? The look in his eyes seemed to reflect what she had been feeling, but she could be completely wrong.

You're not frigid. Jack had spoken with such conviction. *Frozen, maybe, as a result of what he put you through, but definitely not frigid.*

Was that true? Jack knew nothing of her marriage. No one did, not really, not even Sarah. The intimate side of marriage had come as a complete shock to her, and even when the shock had worn off it had never been anything other than a mildly unpleasant duty. For years, when she had hoped the act would result in a child, she had tried to hide her feelings, but as time had passed and with it her hopes her body had betrayed her.

No ardour could awaken a womanly response.

The cruellest words in the codicil, for they were the truest. She had been cold to his touch, and by association to everyone else's.

Not to Jack, though. Tonight, she had wanted Jack to touch her, and if he had kissed her… But here, she was on less certain ground, not least because she'd had no idea how to respond. Part of her had wanted him to kiss her but at the same time she had been afraid of her own response. Or, worse, possible lack of?

No, that was what was so different about Jack. He made her feel, and in that way he was the antithesis of her husband, which must be part of the reason she was drawn to him, though it couldn't be all of it. He was not classically handsome, but there was something in the way his features were put together that appealed to her. When he smiled, it was a real smile. When she talked, he listened. But, more than anything, the reason she felt so differently about him was because he had no hold over her, and no ambition to have any hold over her. He spent time with her because he wanted to, but he wanted nothing more from her than her company. And that, she decided, was what made *her* different too.

The husband who had commandeered her life and

her bed for seventeen years had declared to the world that she was frigid, cold and heartless. She didn't want to believe him. Tonight had given her hope that he might be wrong. But hope, as she had discovered in those long and painful years, however fervently wished for was not always fulfilled.

Chapter Three

The weather turned wintery in the last week, with temperatures even during the day well below freezing. 'Which means that almost all the construction work on the new embankment and the pumping stations has ground to a halt,' Jack said to Mercy as they descended from a hackney cab at the main gates to Regent's Park. 'The same goes for all the other building works that seem to be a permanent feature of this city. A map of London would be out of date before it was printed.'

'That's disappointing if true,' Mercy said, taking his arm. 'I bought a map only yesterday, actually. I thought I'd get to know London better. It's embarrassing how little I know of the city when I have spent most of my adult life here.'

'I hope you're not thinking of wandering the streets alone. It's very easy to go wrong and find yourself in the wrong place at the wrong time.'

'I won't be *daft* about it,' she teased. 'I only want to be able to walk from my little house to Hyde Park, or

St James's Park. Perfectly safe areas, I assure you. I'm supposed to be learning to stand on my own two feet.'

'You might be better advised getting yourself a carriage and a coachman with a bit of savvy.'

'I might, if I decide to remain in London.'

'You've only just arrived. Are you thinking of moving away already?'

'No. I am making a point of not thinking of the future and enjoying the present.'

Her smile knocked the breath out of him. 'A good plan,' Jack said, willing himself not to start down the road of thinking about kissing her, not here in a public park in broad daylight.

She was looking particularly lovely today, with her hair simply dressed, a few wispy tendrils over her ears and none of those elaborate ringlets that were so fashionable and made him think that the women had styled their hair to mimic their gowns. Mercy's coat and skirt were pale blue, matching the winter sky above them— when it appeared through the smog which hung over the city—and almost the same colour as her eyes. Grey braiding trimmed the edges of both garments, stitched into a geometric pattern. A very long lamb's wool scarf in the same grey covered her hair, and was wound several times around her neck. Her fur-lined gloves and walking boots were the same colour.

She traipsed along beside him, her step light, her skirts swishing against his legs, the crinoline beneath bouncing slightly at the back. It made him speculate about the shape of her beneath it, the indent of her waist, the flare of her hips, the curve of her bottom, the length of her legs. He cursed himself under his breath, reining in his over-active imagination. 'Are you warm enough?' he asked.

'Perfectly. I have woollen stockings and a flannel petticoat on under my skirt,' she replied.

God preserve us, Jack thought. Since when had he found the notion of woollen stockings and flannel petticoats arousing? He wondered, as he had several times now, if Mercy had the slightest inkling of the effect she was having on him, but he was pretty certain it wasn't one-sided. That poor excuse of a husband of hers had branded her frigid, which was the kind of thing a man who wanted to cover up his own shortcomings would be bound to say. Did Mercy know that? He was pretty certain she didn't, though he found it difficult to credit.

In the cramped living conditions where he'd grown up, there'd been no privacy. Weans grew up knowing the basic facts of life, and he knew from the gatherings is his ma's kitchen that women talked to each other about such things. Ignorance was not deemed to be bliss. Quite the opposite.

But in Mercy's world? They went to such pains to keep their young women innocent. After seventeen years of marriage, though? It was none of his business. His involvement with Mercy was temporary, he reminded himself, so why not focus on the here and now rather than rake through the ashes of her marriage, especially when she was doing her best to put it behind her?

'The last time we were out together,' Mercy said, interrupting his musings, 'and also the first time we met, I did nearly all the talking. It occurs to me that I know next to nothing about you,' Mercy said. 'Were you raised in Glasgow?'

'I grew up in the Gorbals. It's a poor district of the city, but full of decent, hard-working people on the whole. My father was born there, a docker by trade, but my ma's family were a cut above that—or so they believed themselves. Her father was a trustee of a bank and they had a house in the West End, not far from the Botanic Gardens. My ma went to one of those fancy schools where they teach girls how to speak properly, stitch samplers, paint watercolours and all manner of absolutely useless things.'

'I had a very similar education myself.'

'Aye, all very well for the likes of you and those who have no need to work for a living, but when my ma found herself in a tenement flat, with a husband and a bairn to keep on a limited budget, not one day of the schooling she'd had was of any use.'

'How did they come to meet, if they were from such different backgrounds?'

'She met my father at the ship yard where he was working. Her mother was there to launch the ship, and my father, if you take ma's word for it, was a good-looking charmer who led her astray. Though, from how she tells it, she was happy to be led away from the cosseted life she was living. To cut a long story short, they married much against her parents' wishes, and were duly cast out and told never to darken the door of their West End house again. Which they did not.'

'But that's dreadful!'

Jack shrugged. 'Ma said she never regretted it. Like I said, she wasn't much interested in living the life she was being raised to, spending her days taking tea and setting fancy stitches, married to a man as boring as her father.'

'But after her husband died, surely…?'

'She was too proud and far too independent-minded to put herself back under their roof. Whether they'd have taken us in or not I've no idea, for she never gave them the opportunity.'

'Was that fair to you, do you think?' Mercy asked. 'For her to refuse help?'

Jack prickled. 'We managed fine on our own.'

'But your mother must have had to work very hard to put you through school.'

'Without doubt,' Jack said shortly, for it was a subject that had always pained him. 'She wouldn't ever talk about those early days, though. It was when she went to work as housekeeper for a woman called Constance Maddox that I got a lucky break. Her husband, Grayson, owned a ship yard and it was thanks to him that I got a sound schooling and went on to train as an engineer. I took to it straight away. I've a good head for numbers, and I've the knack of being in the right place at the right time. As a result, I've done well for myself.'

'And your mother? Did she live long enough to see you make a success of your life? She must have been very proud of you.'

'She wasn't one to say so. She died of stomach cancer almost ten years ago,' Jack said. 'She saw me well-established, but I wish she'd had more time to enjoy—' He broke off, looking away, embarrassed. 'I never really got the chance to pay her back for all her sacrifices. She had a hard life.'

Mercy squeezed his arm. 'But she lived it in her own way. I mean, she chose not to return to her parents—you'd be a very different person if she had.'

'I'm not so sure about that. I reckon I've got engine oil in my veins.'

'Like your mother, you would have forged your own path regardless.'

He frowned. 'What's wrong with that?'

'Nothing. I meant it as a compliment. It takes a very strong will *not* to go along with what is expected of you.'

'Is that something you wish you'd done?'

Though she retained her hold on his arm, he sensed her withdrawal. 'The only expectations my parents had of their children was that they should be happy. I married my husband in the expectation that I *would* be happy. I have never had any ambitions, save to be a wife and a mother.'

'Mercy, I'm sorry. I didn't mean to upset you.'

She shook her head, and now she did take her hand away. 'You think me self-pitying, don't you? I'm well-born, wealthy, privileged and, let us not forget, beautiful. I have so much more than most, and yet I still complain.'

'That's not what I meant at all. I thought that maybe your parents had arranged the match with Lord Armstrong. I thought that was how things were done in your circles. I really didn't mean to upset you. As they say in Glasgow, sometimes I just open my mouth and my stomach rumbles.'

To his relief, she gave a small smile. 'If that means

you speak without thinking, I am not at all sure that I believe you. You are a snob, Jack Dalmuir.'

'Me!' he exclaimed, genuinely taken aback.

'You think that a person who has not fought their way up from nothing is inferior to one who has. And, while I think your view has some merits, I don't think it can be applied to everyone in all circumstances. My marriage was not arranged, but it had the seal of approval from both families. The Carstairs are not so well-born as the Armstrongs, but my mother was very well-connected. My parents died not long after I married and never knew, thank goodness, that it did not turn out as I had hoped. We were a very happy family when I was growing up, and that is all I ever wanted for myself. I have no aptitude for science or for scholarship, as Prue and Clement do. The only thing I am good at is being easy on the eye, and for that I can take no credit.'

'You're very good at pointing out my faults which, let me tell you, few dare to do,' Jack said. 'And you're also excellent company. I was too quick to judge you. There's more than enough people out there ready to do that without me adding to their number. I'm on your side, even though I didn't sound as if I was.'

She took his arm again, smiling up at him. 'Thank you, Jack.'

He wanted to kiss her. It was a huge relief to see her smile again. She was such a slight thing, and so brave, he wanted to wrap his arms around her and tell her he'd keep her safe—which was a bloody stupid thing to think, let alone do. Aside from anything else, given that she was determined to stand on her own two feet, it was the last thing she would want.

'It is very busy here,' Mercy said, looking around, 'Where are all these people going?'

'Same place as we are,' Jack said, belatedly noticing the crowds around them. 'It looks like there's not a bairn in school today. I thought we could go skating. The lake is frozen.'

Mercy gave a little skip of excitement. 'Marvellous! But do you know how to skate?'

'I do, actually. There was an estate about ten miles outside Glasgow called Drumpellier that had a great big loch. I was working there for a bit, when I was learning my trade, servicing the steam engines at the coal mines nearby. A bitter winter it was, and the loch was frozen for weeks. One of the other lads kitted me out with a pair of skates, and I had a rare old time of it, every moment I wasn't at the mine. I've not skated since, mind you.'

'I have only skated once. It is a perfectly acceptable pursuit,' Mercy said. 'Prince Albert was a keen skater.'

'Didn't you enjoy it?'

'Too much, apparently. Don't, Jack,' she added hastily, for he had been unable to suppress a growl of anger. 'It wasn't expressly forbidden—I was almost never expressly forbidden from doing anything—only it was easier to comply. You will think me a poor, weak creature...'

'Browbeaten.'

'But I made no attempt to stop him. When he made arrangements contrary to something I wished to do, I always complied. When I wished to spend an afternoon with Sarah, he would always find something else more urgent that needed done. It was—he made it so—I took the path of least resistance. Even with Prue, I am ashamed to say. He hated her, you see, and he was so vile to her when she visited that it was easier not to invite her. When I think of *that*, I am so deeply ashamed.'

The sparkle had gone from her eyes, and her mouth was set. Appalled to see how quickly she could be overset, Jack led them off the main path away from the crowds, where a large tree lent them an element of privacy. 'Mercy, I am sure that your sister understood your dilemma.'

'She did, horribly well. She stopped visiting, even when she was invited, because she knew I would suffer the consequences.'

'And if you'd stood up to him, demanded that your sister be allowed to visit more often, would that have changed things?'

'No. He made it clear that he thought her physically grotesque—"an affront to his sensibilities", was how he put it. I deeply regret having been so weak.'

'I wasn't there, so I can't be certain, but I've seen his type. To be blunt—'

'Are you ever anything else?'

'He was a bully.'

'I told you, he never laid a hand on me.'

'Physically, but that doesn't mean he wasn't a bully all the same,' Jack said grimly. 'I saw enough of it growing up to know what I'm talking about. Men who took pleasure making others miserable, picking on the easy targets, and their wives were the easiest of all. My ma's kitchen sheltered a few of them over the years. Men like that make me sick to my stomach. You're well rid of him.'

'Thank you. I agree.'

'Good. And, what's more, he's dead and you're not, so you're free to suit yourself.'

'What I want to do right now is to ice skate.'

'Then that's exactly what we'll do.'

Mercy, having already fastened her hired skates, stood on the bank watching the activity on the frozen lake while she waited for Jack. The ice thronged with people. Children formed long chains, the leader calling out a warning as he led the way, weaving precariously through the crowds. A dog barked joyfully, sliding after them, and a warden blew his whistle, shaking his fist to absolutely no effect. The novice skaters stuck to the perimeter of the ice, wobbling, falling, staggering to their feet and starting again. Some clung to the hands of more experienced skaters, dragged along, their expressions a mixture of terror and glee.

There were couples skating arm-in-arm, girls skating hand-in-hand and two young men right in the centre of the lake competed to show off the most complicated jumps and spins. A group of young boys played a game of leap frog on the ice on one of the narrower stretches. A little girl, sitting in an old crate, was pulled along by two older girls, a look of sheer astonishment on her face that made Mercy wave and laugh out loud as she passed.

'She's enjoying herself, any road,' Jack said, joining her.

The little girl was already yards away. Her hair, peeking out from the confines of a bright red knitted hat, was jet-black. Her big eyes were dark brown.

Mercy's daughter, if she had been blessed enough to have one, would have been fair-haired and blue-eyed like both her parents. Her father...

'Mercy?' Jack touched her shoulder lightly.

She turned, so caught up in her thoughts that she spoke without thinking. 'He wouldn't have thanked me for a daughter, if I had given him one, save as proof that I was able to bear a child. He'd have had her given into the care of a nursemaid so that he could begin his quest for a son. And he wouldn't have wanted me to love her because then there would be less of me available for him.'

She rarely cried, but salty tears burned her eyes as she spoke. 'My little girl would have grown up thinking I didn't love her. He wanted an heir. I wanted a family. I've never quite put it that way,' Mercy added, startled. 'Even if I had had a child, he wouldn't have allowed me to...'

'You don't know that,' Jack said urgently. 'A lioness will defend her cubs. Women fight for their bairns when they won't fight for themselves. I've seen it, Mercy. You shouldn't judge yourself so harshly. You're stronger than you think.'

'Thank you.'

'I wish you believed me.'

Moved, she reached up to touch his cheek and he caught her hand, kissing her palm through her glove. Her breath caught, the mood between them altering immediately. Their eyes met, and she was sure this time that he felt as she did. A pull that was almost physical, urging her to step closer, to lift her lips for his kiss. A skater whizzing by too close to the edge skidded, sending up a spray of ice and water, bringing them both to their senses. They broke apart, sharing a sheepish smile.

'Are you ready to join in the fun?' Jack asked.

Mercy nodded, stepping quickly onto the ice. Too quickly. She wobbled, and would have fallen if a man in a black coat and top hat had not grabbed her arm and righted her. 'Thank you, sir, I'm very grateful.'

'A pleasure,' he said, relinquishing her immediately as Jack joined her. 'Good day, ma'am.' He tipped his hat and winked.

'Who was that?' Jack asked as they set out side by side.

'I have no idea.' Mercy glanced over her shoulder. 'He's still staring at me.'

'Can't take his eyes off you, and who can blame him?' Jack stopped to look back. 'There,' he said, as the mysterious stranger finally and reluctantly turned away. 'A good, hard Glasgow stare always works a treat! Nice to know I've not lost my touch. Come on now, forget about him, and let's see if you can skate as well as you can polka. Although the chances of injury are equal with both!'

Enticing smells were coming from a stall set up adjacent to the hut to where they returned their skates. 'Hot chocolate, hot coffee, hot toddy,' the stall holder informed them. 'Which will it be? Tin mugs, or stoneware if you care to pay a bit extra in the way of a deposit, sir?'

Mercy opted for hot chocolate while Jack had coffee. They found an empty bench set away from the lake and sat in silence, enjoying the respite and their steaming hot drinks.

'I will need to invest in a skating costume, if I am going to do this again,' Mercy said when she had finished her beaker. 'It is only thanks to you that I didn't fall when my skates caught in my petticoats, and I hate to think what would have happened if the blades had encountered my crinoline.'

'It seems a bit of a waste to go spending money on a whole new outfit when the ice might only last a few days.'

'I enjoyed it so much, though. It was even better than dancing. Like flying.'

'Have you a fancy for flying? I've never been up in a balloon, and I have to confess I'm not at all sure I want to rectify that.'

'What, are you *feart*, Jack Dalmuir?'

He laughed. 'Your accent's coming along well. We'll have you talking like a native before long.'

'You don't talk like a native.'

'I can if I want, mind, but it's bad for business.' He grimaced. 'People think you're an eejit if you don't *talk proper*.'

'I'm not sure what an eejit is, but I am sure you're not one.'

'It means an idiot, and no, I'm not.' He finished the last of his coffee and set the beaker down on the frozen grass beside hers.

'Do you have a house in Glasgow? Do you still call that city home, or do you travel about too much to have a permanent residence?'

'I've a town house in the West End of the city. It's

very nice but it's too big for me, to be honest, and I don't spend a lot of time there, as my work takes me all over the country these days.'

'Do you think you will wish to settle down when you are married?'

'Settle down.' He winced. 'Just the sound of it makes me shudder. I've no inclination to do any such thing for a while yet.'

'But you plan to have a wife and children at some point. You told me so.'

He shrugged. 'At some point, certainly, but not yet.'

'Don't you get lonely, though?'

'I'm too busy to be lonely, and at the moment I have the perfect company in you.'

'I wasn't fishing for compliments.'

'No, but you *were* fishing.'

Which was her cue to cease doing so and politely change the subject. 'What age are you?'

'Thirty-five.'

'So, two years younger than me, but I am practically middle-aged.'

'Away! What rubbish! Next thing, you'll be telling me you're going to move to Twickenham and install cages full of lovebirds in your parlour to keep you company.'

Mercy giggled. 'I hate lovebirds. I have never understood why people talk to them.'

'Maybe because they know fine and well that they can't answer back. My ma had a budgie—actually she had a whole series of budgies, all called Joey—as did most of our neighbours in the tenement. Like you, I never could understand the liking for them, though they're a lot more practical than a dog when you live three storeys up.'

'Do you have any pets in your Glasgow town house?'

'Two cats to keep the mice at bay, but if they have names I don't know them.'

'And you live alone, save presumably for servants?'

'A couple who live in the mews flat which goes with the house. What is this, Mercy, the Spanish Inquisition or some belated attempt to see if I'm suitable company to keep?'

'Oh no, especially not when what I want is to keep unsuitable company. I simply wanted to know more about you.'

He studied her for a moment, frowning slightly. 'I've had my share of flings, if that's what you're leading up to. Nothing lasting. I've never been in love, but I won't pretend I don't enjoy the company of women—provided, of course, they don't get in the way of my business.'

'Which is your one true love.'

'It is. Seriously though, Mercy, I never make promises I've no intention of keeping. I have never in my life misled any woman with regard to my intentions. Are you worried that I'm some sort of Lothario?'

She blushed furiously. 'You have picked the wrong widow, if you are. I'm frigid, remember?'

He took her hand in a firm clasp. 'You have to stop letting yourself believe the vicious rantings of a dying man, do you hear me?'

'It is not as easy as it should be.'

'I don't know if it helps or hinders, but I spend a good bit of my time with you wanting to kiss you.'

'Jack! Do you?'

'You haven't even noticed?'

'I did wonder the other night, when you kissed my cheek...'

'I wasn't at all sure it was what you wanted, and I'd never force myself on you.'

'I know you wouldn't. That isn't what frightens me. I wanted you to, but I didn't know—' She broke off, mortified and acutely aware of her own shocking ignorance. 'I don't know,' she confessed in a whisper, 'whether I would like it.'

He swore softly under his breath. Then he touched her cheek with his gloved hand, watching her carefully. She leaned into him. She could feel his breath on her cheek, they were so close. His hand slid down to cup her chin, his gaze fixed on her, clearly searching for any sign of reluctance on her part. Her heart pounding, she leaned in closer, and then closer still, and closed her eyes. His lips touched hers. It was the briefest of kisses. His mouth was warm. He tasted of coffee. She felt the soft tickle of his beard, and then he lifted his head.

'Well?' he asked.

'I don't know what a proper kiss is, but that wasn't it.'

He laughed softly. 'How can you be sure?'

'I feel—cheated.'

'That makes two of us, then,' Jack said wryly. 'Unfortunately, it's all either of us can have here, or we'll not only make the scandal sheets, we'll be arrested.' He got up, pulling her with him, and then picked up the mugs. 'I'd best get these back and retrieve my deposit or I'll be a disgrace to the image of the tight-fisted Scotsman.'

Chapter Four

Jack was fully occupied overseeing preparations at the construction site, so Mercy set out to become better acquainted with London on foot, accompanied only by her guide book. This was a liberating experience in itself, for in the past, on the rare occasions when she had walked anywhere in the city, she had been accompanied by her maid, or more often by her husband, who had so heartily disliked the ordure of the streets that he made only the shortest of promenades.

There was a knack to keeping one's gown out of the mud, which became much worse as the frost began to thaw, looping the skirts up to allow her colourful petticoats to bear the brunt of the dirt. Spending so much time outside in the filthy London air also taught her the value of sturdy boots, and detachable collars and cuffs, as she had to send her laundry out—something she had never had to consider before.

Walking, she found, was conducive to thinking, and her thoughts constantly returned to the kiss she and Jack had shared in Regent's Park. It was preposterous that at the age of thirty-seven it had been her first proper kiss—only it had not been a proper kiss at all. She had felt cheated.

And as she wandered among the stalls of a local market in the early morning a few days later, she could feel her cheeks burning at the memory. Her lack of experience was embarrassing, but what astonished her, on reflection, was the candid admission she had made. She had always been reserved, even as a girl, but marriage and the constant threat of disapproval had made her habitually think very carefully before she spoke. Yet, from the first with Jack, she had been quite spontaneous.

The brandy… No, she wasn't going to blame the brandy again, nor was she going to explain it away on the grounds that he'd been a complete stranger or put it down to her mood that day. He was no longer a stranger, and the only thing she'd drunk in Regent's Park had been hot chocolate. She had kissed Jack, and she had enjoyed kissing Jack, and she wanted to kiss Jack again because—because he was Jack, she supposed.

He was like no other man she had met, and with no other interest—save her. He didn't care who she was, or what she had been, or what she might become. He thought she was *bloody gorgeous*—she smiled at that—but it wasn't her face or her figure that attracted him, or not only that. Jack liked her for herself. He was interested in her. He enjoyed her company. He desired her. And she desired him.

Mercy came to a halt in front of a shop selling porcelain and earthenware, sightlessly staring at the goods stacked in the window, platters and sauce boats, pudding basins and soup bowls. She had left her old life behind. She had no idea what her new life would look like, or even where she would be a year from now. This was a hiatus. An interlude from real life. A time to indulge herself, to enjoy herself and to make the most, if she dared, of the time she had with Jack. Whatever that might mean.

Three days later, they agreed on a visit to the Tower of London for their next outing, but when Mercy came into her drawing room to find Jack waiting for her, he immediately apologised.

'I had word last night that the first of my steam engines is due to berth at the docks today, and I need to be there to sign off the paperwork and make sure that everything is in order.'

'Of course you must be there. Your business interests take precedence over outings with me,' Mercy replied, swallowing her disappointment. 'You shouldn't have gone to the trouble of coming here first.'

'Actually, I wondered if you wanted to come with me to the docks. You could watch them unload, and then I'll bring you back home. You did say you wanted to know more about me. Or is that a daft idea? Aye, it probably is, never mind.'

'No! No, it's not a silly idea at all. I'd love to come. If I looked as if I didn't, it was simply because I'm worried I'll get in the way.'

'If I thought that, I wouldn't ask you. The thing is, Mercy, my time is going to be taken up over the next few weeks transporting the steam engines to the pumping station and overseeing the installation, so today's the only opportunity I will have to see you for a while.'

'It's a shame that Prue isn't in town. She would be a much more interesting companion for you to have than me.'

Jack shook his head, smiling. 'More interested, maybe, but not so interesting. I'd far rather have your company. It's going to be cold out on the river, though,' he said, eyeing her dress dubiously. 'And you're going to have to do a bit of clambering if we go on board.'

'I could change into my riding habit. Can you wait ten minutes? I promise, I won't be a moment longer.'

Mercy was already at the door when Jack nodded. She flew up the stairs, unbuttoning the paletot jacket which matched her gown, relieved to find that her maid was still in her bed chamber making the bed. The russet merino walking dress was quickly discarded, along with her petticoat and crinoline, and she quickly pulled on her blouse and the bottle-green skirt of her riding habit. The matching jacket was tightly fitting, buttoned up to the neck, with a velvet collar and cuffs on the wide sleeves. She changed her hat, but kept her fur-lined gloves, before swapping her velvet boots for a sturdier pair in brown leather. Then, muttering a breathless thanks, she rushed back downstairs.

'I'm impressed,' Jack said, getting to his feet. 'Practical and yet very fetching. Shall we go? I have a cab waiting.'

'I haven't actually worn my habit to go riding as yet,' Mercy said as they set off. 'I'm waiting on Sarah coming back to town to advise me on buying a horse. She is an expert horsewoman. I had a letter from her this morning. She will be in London within a week. Now that Parliament is back in session, the season will be getting underway.'

'I was under the impression that your friend wasn't fond of high society. I know next to nothing about her.'

'Lady Sarah Fitzherbert-Wright likes all society, high and low, provided it is interesting. She is thirty-two and likes to call herself a confirmed spinster. Sarah is considered far too vibrant for conventional tastes, and she has Titian-red hair which is not at all fashionable, but I think her quite lovely.'

'You said you had hoped she would marry your brother, didn't you?'

'They were extremely taken with each other when they first met, and both Prue and I thought they were growing close, but nothing has come of it. I tried to broach the subject with Sarah, and all she would say is that she is too set in her ways, which is precisely what Clement said about himself.'

'Are you looking forward to seeing her, or have things become awkward between you because of your brother?'

'It was a little awkward when we met in the country, but since Clement almost never comes to town I don't see that being a problem. It will be a novelty to be able to invite her to my house without worrying that she Sarah is extremely outspoken, you see, and she found it difficult to disguise her loathing of my husband. Needless to say, he hated her on first sight.'

'Then I'm pretty sure *I'd* like her,' Jack said. 'Unless she's one of those horsey types. You know, the ones who can't hold a conversation without boasting about some untameable beast they've mastered, or a fence as tall as a clipper they've jumped, or an epic ride to hounds where no one came back in one piece save themselves.'

Mercy giggled. 'Have you met many such types?'

'The only hunting done where I was brought up was by the teacher trying to get the weans into school when they were skiving off, and by the minister and the priest trying to round us up for church on Sunday. As for horses, unless you count the Clydesdales that pulled the brewery drays, no, I've not met too many equestrians.'

'Well, I can assure you that Sarah is not one of them. Why are we stopping?'

'We're catching a train,' Jack said, throwing open the door of the cab. 'Steam power, not horse power, is my preferred mode of transport. Shall we?'

They descended from the Great Eastern Line train at the new Custom House station, built especially to serve the Victoria Dock. Behind them stretched rows and rows of tightly packed terraced housing. In front of them, on the other side of the railway, was a long row of two-storey windowless buildings. The train screeched out of the station, leaving a thick cloud of black smoke in its wake, the freight carriages hitched behind the passenger coaches rattling on the rails. The road was jammed with traffic, tram cars and drays of all sizes, some drawn by a single pony, others piled high and pulled by outsize carthorses.

'This is London's biggest and newest docks, built

especially to accommodate the newer, larger steam ships,' Jack said, raising his voice to be heard over the noise. 'They have installed steam hydraulics for lifting heavy freight, though we won't be putting them through their paces.'

Extremely glad that she had changed, Mercy looped the long train of her riding habit over her wrist. 'What a shame,' she replied. 'That would have made my day.'

Jack laughed. '*You* have made my day,' he said, smiling warmly down at her. 'I hope you won't be bored.'

'Well, obviously I'm disappointed not to be seeing the hydro whatever-it-is being put through its paces,' she said, taking his arm as they set out on the precarious journey of crossing the very busy road. 'Tell me what I am going to see.'

'Warehouses, obviously,' Jack said, indicating the long rows of two-storey buildings ahead of them. 'Stay close when we're through the main entrance. It's a dangerous place, and can be a rough one. You'll hear some colourful language. It's not exactly a place for a lady, you know. Maybe I shouldn't have brought you.'

'I'm glad you did. Truly,' Mercy said, squeezing his arm.

They passed through the wide entrance way into a very different world. The noise of the traffic outside was muffled inside the warehouses and granaries, but it was replaced by the shouts of what seemed to be hordes of stevedores operating the hoists, with their bundles of goods in netting waving precariously in the air. The main basin was as big as a lake, divided up into four quays, each served by more warehouses. A railway bridge crossed the gap at the far end of the basin, and ships were already berthed and in the process of being unloaded at three of the quays.

Jack checked his watch. 'It's high tide now. Our cargo on the *SS Caledonia* should be coming through soon. Shall we walk down to the quay?'

The waters of the dock were thick with grease, and the air tangy, smoke from the recently berthed ships mingling with a myriad smells from the cargoes, and something much more acrid that made Mercy wrinkle her nose.

'That's coming from Silvertown,' Jack said, indicating the factories on the other side of the basin. 'They make waterproof clothing.'

'This is not your first visit here, then?'

'I make a point of checking out any docks before I use them. This place has a sound record of keeping out the pilferers. It would be pretty difficult for us to lose a forty-seven-ton beam or a fifty-two-ton flywheel, but boilers and compressors are another story.'

'I'm sure they are,' Mercy said, completely at a loss. 'I was about to say that I wished I had paid more attention to Prue, but it wouldn't have made any difference. My mind is simply not mechanical. I'm sorry, you could not have invited a less qualified witness to this momentous event.'

'Don't be silly,' Jack said, giving her arm a friendly shake. 'I'm not expecting you to get all excited over a few big lumps of cast iron, which is what it will look like. We're not even unloading here, that will be done at the pumping station. We're just berthing until they're ready for us, and picking up a few more components from one of the warehouses. And, if I'm not mistaken, that's the *Caledonia* arriving now.'

The ship was being guided in, a huge iron-hulled steam ship that seemed to Mercy far too big for the narrow opening. She stood with Jack on the dockside watching the complex manoeuvres. He grew noticeably more tense as the ship was eased into a huge turn, taking up almost the full width of the basin. His eyes were riveted on the signals between the two captains, one on the bridge of the ship and the other in the pilot boat.

The big lumps of metal that the steam ship was carrying represented his reputation and the future success of his business. Even Mercy understood from reading the papers that the eyes of the world were on London, the scale of Joseph Bazalgette's project to clean up the city's drainage being quite unprecedented. Jack had worked his way out of the Glasgow slums from nothing. Until now, she hadn't grasped just how impressive and determined he must have been to have done so, and to have made such a huge success of his business. He would surely not be here, conducting operations, were his company not one of the best in the country.

He was innately modest and, though extremely proud of his precious engines and his own role as engineer, he wore his success as a man of business very lightly. Other men who had come from his humble origins could become braggarts, forever boasting of how hard they had worked. Or they might erase those very origins from their history, claiming a very different heritage. Jack did neither. He saw no need either to boast or pretend. He must have suffered setbacks and disappointments, and he must have a core of grit and determination to have achieved his success, but that too he kept hidden. He didn't seek the admiration of others, nor did he care about the opinion of anyone he didn't respect. Which made his interest in her all the more remarkable.

'There, that's her berthed nice and safe.' Jack heaved an audible sigh of relief. 'Do you want to come aboard with me while I go through the papers with the captain? I don't want to leave you on your own here.'

'How do we get on board?' she asked, eyeing the gap between the ship and the jetty, with the dark, oily waters of the basin clearly visible in between.

'It's up to you. You can jump. Or we could put you in the cargo netting and have you hoisted on board,' Jack said, grinning at her horrified expression. 'Or alternatively you could just walk with me across the gangplank they're about to attach.'

It was late afternoon and dusk was falling, along with a mizzling rain, when they arrived back in Chelsea. Though he had a stack of work to do, and some hectic days ahead, Jack happily accepted when Mercy suggested he come in for a cup of tea. He never drank the stuff, but he was loath to end their day out.

'You and Captain McFarlane could have been speaking Greek for all I understood of the conversation. His accent is broader than yours. But I really enjoyed myself today,' Mercy said, handing him a dainty porcelain cup. 'You are obviously old friends.'

'We've known each other for years. McFarlane started out as an engineer on the Clyde paddle steamers. We used to go down the water for the fair every

absolutely nothing about the subject which is closest to your heart. I'm the opposite of all you respect and admire. Am I a specimen from another world that you are intent on studying?'

'No! What an odd thing to say. I don't think of you like that at all.'

'Then what am I? Why do you persist with me?' She turned back to the room, glowering at him. 'You are a hugely successful man. You are excellent company and cannot possibly lack invitations or the opportunity to indulge in one of your flings. You are also extremely taken up with a project that must mean an enormous amount to your company, and yet you let me hang on to your coat tails. Do you feel sorry for me, is that it?'

'Mercy, stop it.' Jack joined her at the window, taking her hands in his. 'I told you, you made my day coming with me, and I thought you enjoyed yourself.'

'I did. Very much.'

'Then what's brought this on?'

'I don't know. I saw you today for what you are, and I felt small and pathetic in comparison.'

'After what that man put you through, I'm surprised you're still standing, and you're doing a great deal more than that. You're fighting back, remember?'

'I'll show them,' she said, smiling faintly. 'I haven't shown anyone so far, though, have I?'

'I beg to differ. You chose to live here in Chelsea, and it was you who took the lease on this house and made all the decisions about your staff. And you've kitted yourself out anew too.'

'"Kitted myself out", as if I was a soldier about to go on a military campaign.'

'Wasn't that how you saw it, as a campaign?'

'I'd forgotten. It seems a rather pointless aim now. Perhaps that's what's wrong with me. You have such a sense of purpose, Jack. And so does Prue, and so too do Clement and Sarah. They all know what they want from life, and they're doing something about it.'

'You knew what you wanted too, and you've been through hell trying to achieve it. You've thought of nothing but that for years. Is it any wonder that you feel like you're in a state of limbo now?'

'Is that how I feel? Perhaps it is.' She pulled her hands free and turned back to the window again.

'Mercy, moving back to town, setting yourself up in your own house, in a place that is entirely strange to you, is daunting, but you've managed it.'

'That's true,' Mercy said, brightening. 'And I am enjoying living alone. But I am also very much enjoying notching up a host of new experiences with a very understanding and patient Scotsman who has pointed out the error of my ways. I shall do better, I promise.'

'You're doing a great deal better than you give yourself credit for. The only person you need to prove a point to is yourself.'

She heaved a sigh. 'You are quite right.'

He grinned. 'Of course I am.'

'Of course you are.'

'And I'll miss you, these next few days and weeks.'

'You'll have your boilers and compressors to keep you company. You won't give me a second thought.'

'I will, and a third thought too. In the meantime, talking of notching up new experiences, I believe we've one left half-finished. If you'd rather we left it that way?'

'I would not.' She met his eyes, blushing. 'I have been wanting to— I have been thinking a great deal about it.'

He put his arm around her waist, drawing her closer. 'So have I.'

'Really?'

'Truly.' He began with little kisses, encouraging her to return them, slowly at first, giving her plenty of time to change her mind. She put her arm around his neck and he kissed her again, teasing her mouth open.

'Oh,' she murmured, a sigh against his mouth that sent his pulses racing. But he forced himself to hold back, waiting for her to follow him, giving her every opportunity to call a halt.

She lifted her hand to his face, her fingers fluttering on his cheek, and he deepened the kiss just a little. She followed his lead, opening her mouth, angling her head, nestling in closer. He slid his hand down from her slender waist to the curve of her behind, and her breath quickened, as did his own. Her fingers were curled into his neck now and, when his tongue touched hers, she shivered. He thought he'd got it wrong, but she pushed herself right up against him, making that soft murmuring sound that went straight to his groin.

He ought to put a stop to it. He tried, dragging his mouth away, but one look at her face—her cheeks flushed, her eyes heavy-lidded and her lips soft and plump with their kisses—and he gave in to temptation again. And again. And again, until the pair of them broke apart, in need of respite.

'Are you all right?' Jack asked.

'Oh, yes.' Mercy smiled slowly. 'Very.'

He nearly kissed her again, just for that smile, but he managed to stop himself just in time. 'I'd better go.'

She made no attempt to disagree, following him out to the little hallway and waiting until he'd put on his coat and hat and picked up his gloves. 'Jack,' she said. 'I'll miss you too.'

He smiled at that, allowed himself one more kiss on her cheek, and then left before he changed his mind. It struck him as he walked quickly down the path that he was far more pleased than he should be at hearing Mercy would miss him. Almost as troubling was his own declaration that he would miss her.

Perturbed, he decided to walk back to his rooms while the fog remained at bay. His work was at a critical stage. If he got this contract right, it would establish his firm well and truly at the top of the engineering tree. He had every faith in his engines, but the whole process of installing them and having them play such a critical role in such a world-renowned project would set him up for life. Joseph Bazalgette's vision was going to make London a city fit for the future, for it wasn't only about redesigning the subterranean world of sewage and water supply. It was intended to redesign the whole of the river-front.

He wanted the name of Dalmuir Engineering to be part of the transformation. He wanted his engines to be what every other city wanted when they followed London's lead, and he wanted his firm to be the one that people mentioned when it came to innovation and reliability.

In other words, he muttered to himself, he should be far too taken up with work to miss Mercy. He couldn't

afford any distractions. By rights, he shouldn't even
have taken her along to the docks today, for there was
now a heap of things he still had to do. He'd never felt
inclined to share his work with anyone before. Mc-
Farlane had said nothing, but he knew the captain had
found her presence surprising. What was more surprising, Jack thought, was how much he had enjoyed
having her there, given how little she understood of his
business. He wasn't much of a one for talking about
his past either, but then, by her own admission, she
was the same.

They had nothing in common really, and shouldn't
have hit it off after their chance meeting, but they had.
Why not leave it at that? Life would conspire to pull
them apart soon enough. And, in the meantime, what
he needed to do was concentrate on his work and forget
all about her. Though there was no harm, he reckoned,
in letting himself dwell on what they'd just shared as
he completed his walk home.

The Morning Post, 15th February 1864

A Very Merry Widow!

*When Lord H A died suddenly last year, follow-
ing a brief illness, the world was shocked to hear
his allegations, delivered from beyond the grave,
branding his wife heartless, frigid and barren.
His widow, an established society beauty, retired
to the country to mourn the loss of her husband
and her reputation as one half of a model society couple.*

Formerly a peerless hostess, renowned for the elegance of her salons, the decorum of her balls and the exclusiveness of her country house parties, as well as the uxorious perfection of her marriage, Lady M A and her husband were the ideal couple, an example to all society of wedded bliss, until Lord H A belatedly and dramatically revealed the true state of affairs.

Our hearts were touched as we imagined his suffering as this most noble gentleman strove to conceal his wife's failings from public scrutiny. Lady M A deliberately denied her lord and master the son and heir he most naturally and fervently desired.

Had Lady M A followed the example of the Widow of Windsor, who has been mourning her most beloved Prince Albert for more than two years with no sign of emerging from her royal seclusion, we would perhaps have granted her the benefit of a little doubt, and credited her with a modicum of repentance. However, a mere year since her husband departed this life, Lady M A seems to be determined, on the contrary, to reinforce every one of those heart-wrenching accusations, emerging from her rustic hibernation to relocate to the Metropolis—though in a very different environment from her previous abode in Cavendish Square.

The widow has taken up residence in the artistic district of Chelsea, where she has formed a liaison with a mysterious Scotch gentleman, who has been observed to be a regular caller.

Seemingly determined to make a public as well as a private spectacle of herself, she was spotted by our intrepid reporter ice-skating in Regent's Park with the aforementioned Scotsman, with whom she seems to be on very intimate terms.

We have been unable to confirm a rumour that she had been hobnobbing with the Great Unwashed at a notorious casino in Holborn, where the polka is danced in a most raucous manner. However, we can confirm that her most recent escapade took place at the Victoria Docks, where a source confirmed that she had boarded a steamer and spent some time in the company of its captain, another Scotch man.

It seems the lady seems to have developed a penchant for our northern cousins. Could it be that the celts of North Britain prefer their women, like the greater part of their country, to be frozen wastelands?

Rest assured we will make every attempt to keep our readers abreast of developments—in the public interest, of course.

Chapter Five

When Mercy took on the lease of her Chelsea house, she had decided that she would not have any live-in servants and that those she employed would all be female. Prue's advice on the advantages of modern stoves, plumbing and hot-water boilers had proved invaluable, and meant that Mercy could happily bathe, make her morning tea and take her breakfast in solitude.

Eating sparingly under the watchful eye of her husband had made an endurance test of any meal in the past. She had come to believe her lack of appetite and indifference to food were innate. Even during her mourning period, while living with Clement, she had eaten sparingly and without enjoyment. Now, living alone, she had begun to explore her personal tastes. This morning she had eaten two baked eggs with bread and butter, followed by an apple, each thin slice eaten with a sliver of the crumbly cheese she had bought at the local market yesterday.

Sitting by the fire with her last cup of morning tea was her favourite time of the day. She relished the stillness and quiet of the house, secure in the knowledge that her day was her entirely her own. Outside, the weather remained grey, but the temperature had risen, melting the ice, making a muddy porridge of the roads. Jack would be pleased to see the building work recommence on the cavernous pumping stations and the chambers which would house his precious engines.

It was two days since she had last seen him, but the memory of those startling, astonishing kisses they had shared was vivid enough to make her lips tingle. She had forgotten her embarrassment at her lack of experience and had completely abandoned her apprehension that she would shudder with distaste or simply freeze. Those kisses had been a revelation, waking a response in her of which she'd had no idea she was capable. Even now, remembering the insistent pressure of his mouth, the touch of his tongue, the feel of his hands on her, made her quiver inside in a way she couldn't begin to describe, save that it must be addictive, for she craved more.

How much more? She knew all too well how lovemaking concluded, but she couldn't reconcile her experience with her husband with what she felt when Jack kissed her. But then, her husband had never kissed her. Were there other things he had neglected to do?

The one thing that was beyond doubt was that she did not have a body of marble! A slow smile dawned on her as this sank in. She wasn't frigid, but she was woefully ignorant. Jack, on the other hand, was clearly experienced. Dared she suggest, the next time she saw him, that he induct her further into the world of physical pleasure? She knew she would never dare say any such thing, but what if it happened naturally? If they kissed again...

The doorbell rang, making her jump. Who on earth would call so early? Nourishing a faint hope that it might be Jack, she was completely taken aback to be confronted by her brother, looking unusually harassed and clutching a newspaper.

'Clement, what on earth are you doing here?'

'I know, it's so early I haven't even had my breakfast.' He shrugged out of his coat, throwing it over the banister, and balancing his top hat on the newel post. 'Here,' he said, handing her the newspaper, 'you'd better read this.'

Mercy ushered him into the dining room, where he threw himself at the bread and butter. 'I'm starving. I wasn't even dressed when Sarah's telegram arrived.'

'Sarah sent you a telegram? What did it say?'

He pulled a slip of paper from his waistcoat pocket. '"Mercy in urgent need of support. See today's *Morning Post*. Go immediately to Chelsea. Will join you as soon as possible". I had no idea what the issue was, and caught the first train, forgetting all about the dratted newspaper. I had to buy it at the station when I arrived. I'll warn you now, it's a vile piece, Mercy. I'm sorry to be the one to bring it to your attention.'

With a cold sense of foreboding, Mercy did as he bade her, quickly scanning it, and then reading it more slowly a second time, disgusted at the glib jibes and foul innuendo.

'Someone has been following me,' she said grimly, folding the newspaper with shaking hands.

'It looks like it, I'm afraid. I take it you had no idea?

You haven't noticed any strangers loitering around here, anyone asking questions?'

'No, nothing like that. No, wait. There was a man at the ice rink in Regent's Park. I'd forgotten all about him. He said good day, and he stared at me as if he knew me and winked, but I haven't seen him since. At least, I don't think I have. He was completely un-memorable.'

'Well, he would be, wouldn't he, in his line of work? It's a very underhand sort of way to earn a living, if you ask me. The question now is what to do about it. If it were up to me, I'd ignore it, but Sarah wouldn't have urged me to come all this way just to administer sympathy. Should we sue for libel, do you think? I hate to pry, but *is* it libellous? I take it this Scotsman does exist?'

'Oh, he exists all right. His name is Jack Dalmuir. He's an engineer, if you must know.'

'I'm sorry.' Clement patted her arm awkwardly. 'You're upset, and no wonder.'

'I am angry that someone has had the audacity to follow me, but I refuse to be upset by such scurrilous mischief-making.'

Frowning, her brother scanned the article again. 'No one will give it any credence.'

'It doesn't matter whether it's credible or not, Clement. It is there, in black and white, and therefore people will *act* as if it's true.'

'Well, then, all you have to do is wait until it blows over, or something new comes along for people to gossip about. I expect that's why Sarah sent me hotfoot into town, to bring you home with me.'

'I'm not coming back to Hampshire with you. I am

not going to be shamed into leaving town, cowering in the country until this blows over. This is a call to arms.'

'Mercy, for heaven's sake, it isn't like you to be so melodramatic! What on earth do you mean?'

'Ever since I made my debut, I have been branded— yes, *branded* is precisely the word—as the most beautiful woman in society. Countless lines of print have been devoted to describing every trivial detail of my life, holding me up as the perfect society hostess and wife, with absolutely no encouragement from me.'

'But with a great deal of encouragement from Harry Armstrong, I'll wager,' Cement interjected sarcastically. 'I've never met a man so puffed up with his own consequence.'

'Very true, if that was all that was ever written, but it wasn't. The constant speculation about my—about my condition—or lack of, more accurately…'

'We needn't talk about that. I know how painful a subject it is.'

'Extremely painful. And, thanks to that codicil, everyone accepts my dead husband's views on the subject. They have never considered that I may have an alternative viewpoint.'

'I am sure you do, but you can't air it in public,' Clement said, looking appalled.

'I know, I know. Never question. Never explain. Our parents' mantra.'

'And a very sensible one.'

'So, instead of being heartless, frigid and barren, now I am to be labelled a harlot who hobnobs with dockers and sailors.'

'Well, I hardly think…'

'All of them *Scotch* men—which, let me tell you, isn't even the correct term. It is *Scots*, not Scotch. Scotch is whisky, as any woman with a penchant for that nation would know.'

'Mercy, I think you could do with a tot of that yourself at the moment. Or brandy, if you have that.'

'No, what I need is to take matters into my own hands. I am fed up with being told how to behave, and I'm absolutely sick to death of letting the world comment on me and judge me when I don't do what is expected of me. This piece is a blatant attempt to put me in my place, and I won't have it!'

'Did you really go to a dockyard?'

'Yes, I did, but why is that deemed to be more scurrilous than the fact that a complete stranger stalked my every footstep? You'd better be careful, Clement—if that reporter is still lurking outside somewhere, you'll be branded as my next beau. *The widow has expanded her borders and broadened her horizons to add the scalp of a devastatingly handsome Englishman to her collection.* As if I am some sort of siren, whose only purpose is to lure men into my trap.'

'I've never heard you— You don't usually— I have never heard you talk like this.'

'I have been saving it up for seventeen years.'

'What you need is Sarah's wise counsel. I wonder how soon she will be here.'

'I'm sorry, she should not have sent you on this wild goose chase. I am staying here. There is nothing for you to do.'

'Perhaps not, but I'm here now, and at the very least I can give you some moral support.'

'I went dancing. I went skating. I went to see a beam engine arrive at the docks. There is nothing immoral or indecent in a single one of those activities.'

'Mercy, it's not what you did—at least not entirely—it's the fact that you were alone with a man who is neither related to you nor quite decrepit. At least, I assume he is not?'

'He most certainly is not. Far from it.'

The doorbell chimed as Clement wrestled with this information. 'That will be Sarah,' he said, looking hugely relieved.

He was proved right a few moments later. 'Lady Fitzherbert-Wright, my lady,' Lucy announced, clearly taken aback to find her mistress already had company.

'This is my brother, Mr Carstairs, Lucy. I think we could all do with some tea, if you please. Sarah,' Mercy said, turning to her friend. 'It is lovely to see you but your rushing to town was quite unnecessary.'

'Nonsense. How do you do, Clement? It has been a while since our paths crossed.' Sarah nodded curtly at Clement before touching Mercy lightly on the shoulder, her usual embrace.

'He has come to town at your behest, but I fear it was a fool's errand,' Mercy said, surprising them both by hugging her briefly but tightly. 'It is good to see you, Sarah.'

Her friend smiled warmly, stepping back to study her. 'You are looking very well. Hobnobbing with low life and North Britons suits you.'

'Thank you, I believe you are right. It does.'

'Goodness, so it's true, then?' Sarah asked, stacking the breakfast dishes neatly at the end of the table.

Mercy shook her head, relieving Lucy of the tray of fresh cups and saucers she'd brought in and setting them out while her maid brought the tea.

'The Scotsman in question is apparently called Jack Dalmuir,' Clement informed Sarah, holding out a chair for her. 'He's an engineer.'

'An engineer? Did Prudence introduce you?'

'In a manner of speaking.' Mercy poured them each a cup of tea. Clement, she noted, had seated himself opposite Sarah, though the chair beside her was vacant. 'Jack went to see Prue's fountains. We met at the inn in the village.'

Sarah's brows shot up. 'Before you came to London, you mean?'

'You never mentioned him. At least, if you did I don't recall it.' Clement said, brows furrowed.

'Why keep him a secret?' Sarah asked. 'Unless, of course, there really is something in that story. Good heavens, Mercy, are you saying that you are having an *affair*?'

'Is that so very unlikely?'

Sarah stared at her in astonishment. 'Is it true?'

'Of course it's not true,' Clement said, getting to his feet. 'Enough of this. I am taking you home to Hampshire, my dear, just until the storm blows over.'

'I'm not coming with you. I meant what I said.'

'Which was what?' Sarah asked.

Wearily, Clement dropped back down onto his seat. 'She said it was a "call to arms", whatever that means.'

'More scandal? Isn't there enough in this rag?' Sarah said, indicating the *Morning Post*.

'Dancing, skating and an outing to the docks.' Clement shrugged. 'My sister assures me none of those activities are in the least scandalous.'

'Save that she was accompanied in each case by a man and had no other female with her to protect her honour,' Sarah said sarcastically. 'So one must assume, of course, that her honour was impugned, because she is incapable of protecting it herself. Of course, *we* all know that those inferences are arrant nonsense, but—'

'How can you be so sure?' Mercy demanded, riled by her friend's certainty.

'Because I know you,' Sarah said. Her eyes narrowed. 'At least, I thought I did. Is there something you wish to tell me?'

Yes! Mercy wanted to say. *At the age of thirty-seven I have finally discovered the pleasure of kissing. And I liked it so much, I would like to...* But, no, aside from the fact that her brother would be mortified, the kisses she and Jack had shared were private.

She shrugged. 'I simply wondered why it would be so wrong if they were true. I have completed my mourning period and am free to consort with whomever I choose. And, as for Jack, he has no ties. In addition, he's a perfectly respectable businessman.'

'If that's the case, he's not going to take kindly to being embroiled in this,' Clement interjected.

'He is not embroiled. The newspapers don't know his identity. And, besides, he knew as I did that it was a risk when we decided—' Mercy broke off, for both her best friend and her brother were staring at her in shock. 'When we decided to have some fun together,' she finished, glaring back at them. 'And you may make of that what you will.'

Clement's jaw dropped. 'Good Lord.'

Sarah, however, burst into a peal of laughter. 'Bravo!'

'Bravo? My sister more or less confesses that she has been—has been—'

'Having fun,' Sarah supplied. 'And I think you would agree, Clement, that, after seventeen years married to the odious Harry Armstrong, she has earned the right.'

'Yes, but are you seriously telling me that you are having—? Dash it, Mercy, I'm your brother. I can't possibly ask you... Are you sure you know what you're doing?'

'I am kicking over the traces a little, that's all.'

Sarah laughed again, then jumped up. 'I'm going to give you another hug,' she said, doing just that. 'We have a lot of hugging to make up for. My goodness, Mercy,' she said, sitting back down again, 'you are a dark horse and no mistake.'

'Are you saying you approve?' Clement asked, looking aghast at Sarah.

'I think Mercy is teasing us, but if it did happen to be true then I would assume that she knows what she is doing, and certainly does not require my approval.'

Clement coloured. 'I am merely concerned for my sister's welfare. Is there anything wrong with that?'

'Nothing at all, save that we both of us have been concerned for her welfare for years but have done nothing about it. I don't feel we have the right to criticise her now,' Sarah replied. 'What she needs most is our support.'

'I hope she knows that she always has my unwavering support.'

'I know you came here with the best of intentions, Clement.' Mercy stretched over to pat his hand. 'But I'm not coming back to Hampshire with you.'

'No, I understand that. But if this Scotsman has serious intentions…'

'Good heavens, I pray don't suggest that he should call on you and beg permission to ask for my hand!' Mercy exclaimed. 'Jack's only intention is to remain in London long enough to successfully complete his engineering project. And, before you start thinking he is taking advantage of me in the meantime, then I can assure you it is nothing of the sort. If anything, I am taking advantage of him by commandeering his free time.'

'Including having him escort you to a public dance hall, by all accounts,' Sarah said.

'Of course, the polka danced at a public casino is very different from the one danced in the ballrooms in Mayfair. And the refreshments too. I don't suppose you are familiar with a cocktail called a sherry cobbler?'

'No, I have never heard of it.'

'Afterwards, we bought a pie from a stall. Best British beef,' Mercy said, smiling reminiscently. 'Though it was more likely horse, Jack believed.'

'You ate horse meat? Now that,' Sarah said, 'I do find shocking. Good heavens, I feel as if I hardly know you.'

'I hardly know myself these days.'

'But you are enjoying your voyage of discovery, and you intend to continue it. Will the mysterious Mr Dalmuir continue to accompany you?'

Mercy's smile faded. 'I don't know. He said he didn't care about the scandal sheets, but it's easy to say that if one has never been the subject of something like that piece. I did warn him, but to be perfectly honest I thought they wouldn't be interested in me any more. I am back in London, but I'm not interested in returning to the London life I led before.'

'That's just as well, for I doubt you'll be invited anywhere now—leastways, nowhere respectable.'

'I don't care.'

'You don't mean that. I am sorry to be the voice of reason, but I'm not at all sure you know what you're doing,' Clement said diffidently. 'I understand wholly, my dear, why you wish to rebel. After living with that tyrant...'

'Bully!' Sarah said.

'That too. So I do understand why you wish to "kick over the traces", to use your own words, but I'm not convinced that you are strong enough to suffer the consequences. One more article like this one and you really will be shunned by polite society.'

'In other words, I should act contritely and promise to be a good little girl in future.'

'Really, Mercy, it is not like you to use such emotive language. Do you want to close doors that you might wish to remain open?'

'Oh, for goodness' sake, Clement, stop speaking like the pedant you are,' Sarah interjected. 'It won't come to that. Are you imagining that she plans to polka with her engineer in a Mayfair townhouse ballroom?'

'Don't put ideas in her head, for pity's sake.' Clement got to his feet once more. 'Since I've come all the way to town, I may as well make use of the day. I'm going to the British Museum. Sarah, I assume you and Mercy have a great deal to catch up on but, if you can bear to keep a fusty scholar company over dinner, I would appreciate your company later.'

Chapter Six

It was after nine when the rap Mercy had been anxiously awaiting sounded on her front door. She had all but given up on Jack, and was reading by the fire curled up on her favourite chair, still in her day gown but without her crinoline, as was her custom when she was alone in the evening. Looking out from behind the parlour curtains, she saw that Jack had stepped back onto the path to stand in the pool of light cast by the street lamp, and hurried to let him in.

'Thank you for coming. I know how busy you are.'

'Don't be daft. I'm only sorry I couldn't get here earlier.' Jack pulled off his hat and coat, draping them both over the banister, and followed her into the parlour. 'I'll admit, I didn't take your concerns about the papers too seriously, until I read that piece you sent me.'

'I know. I'm so sorry to have dragged you into this.'

'You warned me it was a risk.' He followed her over to the sofa and sat down beside her. 'Never mind me, I want to know how you are.'

'Defiant! My brother came here this morning, wanting to take me back to Hampshire with him. I refused. Sarah was here too. They were both utterly confounded, you know, when I told him that much of what was in that article was true. I enjoyed surprising them. I've always been so predictable, until I met you.'

'I'm glad you did. I've missed you.'

'Have you?' Looking into his eyes, she forgot all about the conversation. 'I've missed you too, Jack.'

Their kiss was the same as before, only better. More because she was confident in herself, and in his desire for her. She shivered with pleasurable anticipation as their mouths opened to each other, as their tongues touched, as she gave herself over to their kisses, not thinking, only relishing sensations. Relishing the taste of him and the tingles he set up on her skin as he brushed the nape of her neck, her cheek, her throat.

She inched closer to him and followed his lead, her arm around his neck, curling her fingers into his hair, stroking his cheek, his smooth skin and rough, close-cropped beard. He kissed her throat, kissed along the high neckline of her gown, and then their lips met again. His kisses aroused feelings she had never experienced before, dragging strange little pleading sounds from her.

Then, as he cupped her breast, she tensed slightly, and Jack immediately drew back. 'Do you want me to stop?'

'No.'

Even to herself she sounded entirely unconvincing. 'What, then?' he asked, obviously confused.

But she shook her head, unwilling to explain, pulling him back towards her.

He kissed her again, but her response was awkward now, self-conscious, and she was not surprised when he ended the embrace. 'You're tired, and no wonder. It's been a long and stressful day.'

'Yes,' she said, guiltily grateful for the excuse.

He studied her for a moment, obviously wondering whether to say more. 'You know I would never do anything that you don't want me to? That you don't like?'

She nodded, unable to meet his eyes.

'I didn't expect— Look, I don't know if you understand, but just because I touched you like that, I didn't expect...' Jack shook his head, looking deeply uncomfortable. 'I was making love to you, but I didn't expect it would lead to—that you and I would actually make love. Properly, I mean. Do you know what I'm trying to say?'

Completely mortified now, and equally confused, Mercy nodded, then shook her head.

'Never mind. It's late. Best leave it at that,' Jack said, looking quite defeated. He edged slightly away from her. 'Tell me how you left things with your brother'

It *was* late—Jack was perfectly right—and the conversation had made her feel as if there was a vast chasm in her understanding. 'Clement still thinks it would be best if I went back to Hampshire, but Sarah agrees with me that I shouldn't act as if I'm ashamed of what I've done.'

'So you're staying here?'

'Yes, and I'm going to prove that I won't be shamed into conforming or repenting.'

His brows rose. 'That sounds intriguing, and a wee bit risky.'

'It was actually Sarah's idea, though she meant it to rile Clement. She asked him if he thought I planned to polka with my engineer in a Mayfair townhouse ballroom.'

'Was she imagining me in a pair of overalls, smelling of the Thames, with my hair slicked back with engine oil?'

'I told her you were perfectly respectable.'

'I'd better see if I can hire something, then. Or maybe pick up something second-hand. Not too used, you know but, being a tight-fisted Scot and all, I don't want to be shelling out too much for something I won't get a good wear out of.'

Mercy laughed, partly with relief, for he was clearly trying to put her at her ease. 'I am perfectly sure you have an excellent wardrobe of formal wear, unless it is the fashion to don overalls for business dinner parties. But, as I said, it was a joke. I'm not expecting you to come with me.'

His brows shot up. 'Come with you where?'

'To a Mayfair ball. You can't come with me. If you did, everyone would assume that what was said in the *Morning Post* is true, and they will find out your name, and then you will be in the newspapers and your business will suffer and—'

'Hold your horses! Let me get this straight—you're planning to dress yourself up in your finest and flaunt yourself at some ball in front of the great and the good. Who presumably, having accepted that piece of rubbish as gospel, will duly turn their backs on you?'

'Not some ball. A specific ball, chosen for a very specific reason. And it's not so much about flaunting myself as showing them I don't give a hoot what they think of me.'

'What specific ball?' Jack asked ominously.

Now it came to the point, she was astounded by her own daring. 'It is customary to mark the reopening of Parliament with a grand ball at Cavendish Square. It is always the first crush of the season.'

'Cavendish Square? Where the Armstrong family townhouse happens to be situated?'

Her mouth was dry. 'Yes.'

'So these people, the ones you plan to demonstrate your contempt for, they are not just any people?'

'No.'

'Is it too much to hope that you at least have an invitation?'

'I suppose it could have been misdirected,' she said, making a pointless attempt to sound hopeful.

'Dear God. Mercy, you can't.'

The words immediately set her hackles up. 'I can do exactly what I choose.'

'Yes, you can. I apologise. What I meant was...' Jack stared at her hopelessly. 'I take it neither your brother nor your friend approves?'

'I haven't told them. I shan't tell them. They would only try to stop me. Besides, Sarah said she'd never cross that threshold again, and Clement never attends balls.'

Jack shook his head, smiling sardonically. 'You mean, you knew they'd tell you that you were off your head.'

'I am not *aff* my *heid*. I have thought this through, Jack,' Mercy said earnestly. She didn't need his approval, but she wanted him to understand. 'There will be no issue with my getting through the door, at least. It is my former home and, though I hated the place, it will still be staffed by servants who were in my employ for years, who I always treated very well.'

'So the servants won't throw you out, but what about the host?'

'George would be happy if he never set eyes on me again, but he won't cause a scandal by getting into an unseemly squabble in his own receiving line.'

'Hell's teeth! I beg your pardon, but I admire your guts. You're really thinking of braving the lion in his den?'

'George is a louse, not a lion.'

'A louse who took great delight in watching you being publicly flayed. Is that it, Mercy?'

'Yes.' She gave a huge sigh of relief, taking his hand and caressing it with her cheek. 'They will all be there at the ball. George, who is now Lord Armstrong, Frederick, his brother and their wives. All of them were there that day, and I am convinced they have all had a hand in making sure the contents of the codicil were made very public. I haven't heard from any of them since. What little communication there has been on legal matters has been through their lawyer. Poor man, he was mortified at having to read that codicil. He was placed in an invidious position—' Mercy broke off, shuddering.

Jack pressed her hand. 'Maybe you should rethink this. It's bound to upset you, seeing them again.'

'Perhaps it will. Perhaps it's time I let them see what it did to me. I barely said a word in my own defence, you know. Though Clement spoke for me, when he knocked George down.'

Jack gave a snort of laughter. 'Your brother, the classical scholar, punched someone?'

'I can see you have fallen into the trap of assuming that Clement is a bespectacled milksop.'

'Maybe, but never mind your brother for now. If you're determined to go through with this...'

'The more I think about it, the more determined I become.'

'I can see that, but I can also see it's going to be a real ordeal, facing down the very people who condemned you.'

'That's it!' Mercy exclaimed. 'You understand even better than I do. I want them to bear witness to my not giving a *damn* about them. I want to show them that their opinion is of absolutely no importance to me, and to show them and everyone else at that ball that I won't bow to their judgemen—that I refuse to be cowed.'

Jack whistled. 'That's no small ambition.'

'Do you think I won't be able to do it?'

'I think you'll do better with someone by your side.'

'Sarah...'

'I don't mean Sarah or Clement, I mean me.'

'No! I can't let you.'

'I beg your pardon?'

'Think of the risks, Jack.'

He wrinkled his brow and pursed his lips. 'I've thought of them. I'm coming with you. I don't need your permission any more than you need mine. I'm perfectly capable of weighing up the risks and making my own decision. If you're set on going through with this, you should have someone with you. It's not that I think you can't do it on your own, it's that I think you'll do it better if you know there's at least one person in the room on your side. Am I right?'

Mercy smiled crookedly. 'You know you are. It's not that I don't want you by my side but…'

'Do you honestly think that someone would baulk at buying the best beam engines in the world just because the man who owns the company is rumoured to be the lovely Lady A's lover?'

'There will be a number of extremely influential people at that ball, Jack. Peers and politicians.'

He snorted. 'And all of them with their own peccadillos, I'll bet.'

'You're probably right, but they don't flaunt them.'

'You're talking as if we are lovers. I'm a single man. You're a widow. What is there to object to in us keeping each other company?'

'Nothing, when you put it like that.'

'And that's how I would put it, if anyone asked me, but they won't. Look, if you're absolutely set on going yourself, I won't force myself on you. But if you think I can be a support to you…'

'Oh, I do, and I would be extremely grateful if you could come with me, if you are absolutely sure?'

'I'm absolutely sure.'

'Thank you. Thank you so much. I could kiss you.'

Jack smiled. 'Please, feel free.'

Her heart beating fast at her own daring, Mercy slipped her arm around his neck and kissed him. He kissed her back, but carefully, and she decided she didn't want to be cautious any more. She leaned closer, touching her tongue to his, and their kiss deepened. And deepened. And deepened, until she lost herself in the shivering delight his kisses roused, her fingers curling into his hair, her breasts pressed against his chest. More kisses, and he eased her back onto the sofa…and more kisses, on her neck again, and on the neckline of her gown.

She took his hand and placed it on her breast. He watched her carefully as he touched her, cupping it as before, but so gently. Even through the layers of her gown and her undergarments, she could feel her nipples tingling in response and the tension in her belly tightening. Then Jack kissed her again, and she kissed him back, arching up under him now as he touched her breasts. His tongue touched hers and their mouths clung. She wanted more, but she had no idea what, or how to ask for it, or what to do in response.

'Stop thinking about it,' Jack said, whispering urgently in her ear. 'Stop worrying.'

He kissed her again, and she tried to stop thinking and give herself over entirely to the sensations he was arousing. Sensations wholly new and wholly pleasurable that made her feel as if she was on the brink of something—though what? And what about Jack? Mutual pleasure, he'd said, but she wasn't sure how she was supposed to…or what she was supposed to…

'Oh!' He unbuttoned the bodice of her dress and slipped his hand down inside her underwear, and the sensation of his skin, of his palm on the highly sensitised peak of her nipple, switched her mind off. Pleasure seemed to course through her veins now and her mouth clung desperately to him. She was dimly aware of herself stretched out on the sofa with Jack fully clothed beside her, of the heat of his body close but not quite touching. Of the layers of clothing between them, a stark contrast to the constant, gentle, almost unbearable tingling response of her breasts to his touch on her naked skin.

And another sensation—a coiling pleasure low inside her that she had never felt but that was making her anxious as it mounted, making her body want to arch against his, to have what she thought she would never, ever desire. And, before this thought could ruin everything, her body seemed to gather itself into one single focus point and then explode. Waves of pleasure rippled through her, making her shudder, cry out and cling to Jack, her eyes wide open in shock until slowly it receded.

Jack gently kissed her again, then eased them both upright. His hair was a tangle. His coat lay on the floor. Her gown was crumpled and creased, the bodice almost completely undone. She should be embarrassed, but she felt stunned. 'I really didn't know.'

'I know,' he said with a crooked smile. 'And I'm extremely honoured—I mean that. And don't think for a moment that what you felt was one-sided. I assure you, the pleasure was mutual.'

She eyed him doubtfully for, while she knew nothing of the workings of her own body, she was not nearly so ignorant when it came to the male sex.

'Whatever you're thinking, I recommend you stop.' Jack got up, turning away from her to put on his coat. 'It's very late now, and I've got an early start.'

She scrambled up, hastily buttoning her bodice. 'I'm so sorry to have kept you from your bed.'

'I hope you're not, because *I'm* most certainly not.'

'Then I'm not either.'

He reached for her, then changed his mind. 'I don't want to, but I really do have to go. Will you let me know about this ball?'

Mercy nodded. 'Will you be too busy before—? No, don't answer that, I know you will. Besides, I have to make up for lost time with Sarah. I plan to accompany her to one of the lying-in hospitals which she funds. When Prue has her baby, I want to understand what she will be going through. I want to be able to help and, as I have no experience of my own to refer to, then I will need to find out from others.'

'That's a very noble thing to do.'

'Prue is my sister, and I love her. It's time I demonstrated that.'

They were at the front door. Jack put on his hat and scarf then pulled on his overcoat. 'For the first time in my life, I'm sorry that my work is getting in the way.'

He stooped to kiss her. Their lips lingered. He wrapped an arm around her. She stepped closer. Their kiss deepened. Then they both pulled back, smiling sheepishly. 'Goodnight, Jack.'

'Goodnight, Mercy.'

She watched him walk quickly down the path, turn around once and then wave, before striding off in the direction of the nearest cab rank. She closed the door and locked it, then set about banking the fire and dousing the gas lights before going upstairs and quickly preparing for bed.

Lying wide awake in the dark, her thoughts turned to the past. She had become so adept at banishing her husband from her memory that it was difficult now to recall what he had looked like. *Harry.* His name no longer evoked a shiver of distaste. He couldn't always have been so cold, so demanding, so possessive. There must have been a time, when they first married, when they had been happy, or at least not miserable. She had been filled with hope in the early years, so full of plans for the family she'd never doubted she would have. As had he. A son was all he'd been able to talk about. All he'd ever wanted.

His determination to get his son as soon as possible had brought him to her bed on a regular basis. Her only knowledge of what was required of her had come from nature, for her mother's advice had been so oblique as to be meaningless. He had covered her like a stallion did a mare, coming to her in the night, lifting her gown when she was on her knees and thrusting into her, usually without saying a word.

She'd borne it because she'd wanted to bear a child. As the years had gone by without success, he'd persisted and she'd never resisted—afraid, she saw now— about what would happen to them without this one bond to hold them together. Sometimes he'd failed to perform. He'd left, as he'd always done, pulling her nightgown down and muttering goodnight.

Tears leaked from her eyes. Had Harry been as ignorant as she had? *No ardour could awaken a womanly response,* he had said, which seemed to suggest that he'd known better—though he had lied, or he had been deluded, in imagining that he had attempted to awaken any response in her. He had taken his pleasures with other women, she must then assume, and found she didn't care. Ardour and womanly response made no difference to the outcome, or lack of it, and he must have known that. The accusations were those of a bitter man dying before his time, and without the son he had longed so desperately for to succeed him. Poor Harry.

And poor Mercy. He had made her life miserable, but it had not been entirely his fault. Would it have been different if she'd stood up to him, spoken her mind, rebelled at the constraints he had put on her freedom? But the process had been so slow, a creeping incarceration, and she had felt so permanently, deeply guilty at her failure—not only to provide him with a son, but her failure to love him, or even, in the end, to care for him.

It was over. She was alive, with her life to make her own now, and Harry was dead. If she had once been poor Mercy, she was no longer that woman. She might be barren, but she wasn't heartless, and she most certainly wasn't frigid. Jack had proved that beyond doubt.

Jack! Turning over in bed, she pulled the covers higher and closed her eyes, conjuring up the much, much more pleasant memory of tonight and her induction into the hedonistic world of sensual pleasure. She laughed softly to herself at her flight of fancy, as if Jack were a sorcerer and she his accomplice. But what had happened to her tonight had been magical, all the more so because it was so very different from anything she had experienced in the marital bed. At last she could begin to comprehend Prue's air of secretive satisfaction, the way she looked at her husband sometimes as if she wanted to devour him. Prue not only loved her husband, she desired him.

Mercy was not in love with Jack. She didn't want to spend the rest of her life with him, and she certainly didn't want to build her world around him—nor around any man, come to that. Not that he'd wish her to. Jack had very definite ideas about the woman who would eventually share his life, and Mercy couldn't be further from that ideal. But from the moment they'd met, even though she hadn't recognised it at first, there had been a physical attraction. It wouldn't last. Even Mercy knew that such things never did. But, while it did, she was resolved to make the most of it.

Chapter Seven

A crisis with the first installation at the pumping station forced Jack to rush back to Glasgow to oversee some changes to the specification of the boilers. He'd returned to London only last night. As a result, when he set out tonight for Chelsea in the town coach he had hired on the evening of the Cavendish Square ball, it would be the first time he'd see Mercy since having agreed to escort her to witness her public display of defiance.

He'd had little time to think about tonight, and maybe it was just as well, for his gut was telling him it was a madcap idea. It wasn't that he didn't sympathise with Mercy's desire to kick sand in the smug, self-satisfied faces of her former in-laws, but he wasn't at all sure she had considered the consequences. She'd be well and truly burning her bridges. As for him as a businessman, no—he was pretty certain he had nothing to worry about business-wise. As regards him personally, though, that was another matter.

Jack wasn't a man inclined towards self-delusion.

He knew he was long past the stage of having what Mercy called fun. His feelings had run far too deeply at their last encounter.

I really didn't know, she had said, with no idea of the way those words had made him feel. He was not angry any more on her behalf but, well he'd said it. He was honoured, though he wasn't sure she understood how deep went. The trust and faith she'd shown in him, after all she had experienced in her marriage. And he'd meant it when he'd told her the pleasure was mutual, even though she had hardly touched him. He had never been a selfish lover, but he'd never felt so fulfilled. He rolled his eyes at the word, but it was true.

What would become of the pair of them now, though? The answer to that was beyond him. They had no prospect of any sort of future together—that had been clear from the outset—but when he thought about never seeing her again, he had to admit it didn't sit well with him.

So once again he asked himself what he thought he was doing. Was it the novelty of the situation that appealed, and his own role as something between a consort and knight errant? Aye, right! It was neither of those things, nor had it anything to do with this upcoming encounter with high society. He'd never had any use for the entitled and useless—though, to be scrupulously fair, they were probably not all totally useless.

Mercy had been right when she'd accused him of being a snob. He was as ignorant of her world as she was of his. Anyway, the reason he was here in this fancy carriage, dressed up to the nines, had nothing to do with any of that. He was here for Mercy. After tonight, if all went well, she'd be well on the road to standing on her own two feet and he could happily let her get on with it.

He wasn't convinced, but the carriage drew up at Mercy's house before he was forced to contemplate an alternative plan. His ma would say he'd got himself in 'a right fankle', but it was too late to turn back now, even if he'd wanted to. Which, of course, he didn't, so there was only one thing to be done and that was to get on with it. Jumping out of the carriage, he walked briskly up the path and rapped on the door.

'Jack!' Mercy said as she opened the door, looking extremely relieved. 'It is so good to see you. I won't be a minute, will you come in and wait?'

'You didn't think I'd let you down, did you?' he said, following her into the parlour.

'No, I got your telegram last night. Have you resolved what you referred to as your technical problems?'

'I sincerely hope so. Time will tell. Look at you, all dressed up for the ball. You scrub up well.'

'As your ma would say?'

'You look absolutely breath-taking, and that's me talking.' Her hair was piled up on top of her head, showing off her long neck, and her low-cut gown revealed a great deal of creamy skin, the delicate lines of her shoulders and the swell of her breasts. Only a plain gold locket nestled seductively in her cleavage. He felt almost giddy looking at her.

'Do you like my gown? It is extremely unfashionable, as my dress maker informed me, being quite plain.'

'You don't need adornment.' Reluctantly, he dragged his gaze from her face to inspect her gown as she twirled for him. Silk or satin, he wasn't sure which, it was a blue that that perfectly matched her eyes. The skirt fell straight at the front and hung in deep pleats over her crinoline at the back. Fitted tightly at her waist, the bodice had a wide, pleated border that seemed to play the role of both collar and sleeve.

'How does that all stay in place?' he asked, fascinated not by the gown but by who wore it. 'Are you not worried that it might slip down when you're dancing?'

'The wonders of modern engineering,' Mercy quipped. 'Corsetry engineering, I should say.'

He wished she had not, for it set his imagination on fire. 'I'll take your word for it,' Jack said.

'May I return the compliment, and tell you that you scrub up well too, Mr Dalmuir?'

'Oh, this old thing,' he said, sketching a bow. 'Just something I happened to have lying around.'

'Your coat is cut to perfection, designed to fit no one but yourself.'

'So too are my overalls. If I rush back to my rooms, I'll have time to change.'

She laughed, as he had intended her to do. 'Are you still sure you want to accompany me?'

'It would be churlish of me to change my mind now, when you've gone to such an effort.'

'Oh, this old thing,' Mercy retorted. 'I just happened to have it lying about.' She grimaced. 'I can't pretend I'm not nervous, though. Perhaps a brandy might settle my nerves.'

'Tempting as that is, I think we would both be better keeping a clear head.'

Mercy frowned down at her wrist, where the pearl buttons of her long, white evening gloves were not yet done up, though she made no attempt to fasten them. 'George didn't have to have that codicil read out. He claimed it was necessary, and at first the lawyer backed him up, but when I look back on it now I think—I am certain—that it wasn't required by law. Which means that it was George's idea, and doubtless Frederick complied, because where George leads his little twin brother will follow.'

'Twins!'

'Identical twins, with identically mean, vicious natures. They hate me. I have always known that, and I've never known why. I have certainly done nothing to deserve it. They were neither of them particularly fond of Harry either, though at the reading, naturally, they claimed they were as devastated by my failure to provide an heir as my husband was. I called George out on that,' Mercy said with a grim little smile. 'I told him he couldn't wait to step into Harry's shoes. That was my one and only riposte.'

'I am really looking forward to meeting them,' Jack said sardonically, noting her use of her husband's name and wondering if it had been a slip of the tongue.

'Dominic, Prue's husband, came across George in the Crimea. "Entitled and arrogant" is all he would say of him, but in that tight-lipped way that means you know a person is trying to be generous.'

'What does your sister have to say about tonight?'

'I haven't told her. She has far too much on her mind

at present. I haven't told Clement either, as he'd only worry. And that doesn't mean I am falling back into my old habits of keeping everything to myself.'

'I didn't accuse you of any such thing. You want to make your own decisions. I applaud that.'

'Yes. I'm sorry. I am a little on edge.'

Teetering on the brink of a precipice, was how he would have put it. His instincts told him that the night had the potential to turn into a complete fiasco but, as she'd just made the point about wanting to make her own decisions, Jack hesitated to say so. Besides, if he didn't go with her...

'If you think it would be a mistake for us to be seen together,' Mercy said, pre-empting him, 'then I will completely understand. But, now that I've talked things through with you, I am quite clear that I must go through with this regardless.'

'Then I'll be right there by your side.'

'You might be better watching my back. I expect there will be quite a few knives sticking out of it. Would you mind fastening my gloves? It's one of the few things I can't do for myself.'

She held out her arm. There were six buttons in all, exposing the pale flesh on the inside of her wrist, and it was impossible to resist pressing a kiss there. When he felt her shivering response, he pressed another to taste the warmth of her skin and the scent of her—powder from her gloves, something floral. A mistake, for it set his body immediately on alert, aching for more. Concentrating harder than strictly necessary, he set about fastening the buttons.

* * *

The braziers had been lit and hung on the railings in the entrance way of the Armstrong town house. Seeing the footmen positioned in the square to ensure that the stream of carriages efficiently disgorged their passengers and moved quickly on, so as not to create a queue, made Mercy feel very mixed emotions. The use of servants to manage traffic flow had been her idea. The last time this ball, so firmly established in the social calendar, had been held, it had been she who was the hostess.

As they waited to descend and join the throng making their way through the wide-open front doors of her former home, she could imagine all too easily exactly what kind of manic activity was going on below stairs, and just how on edge her host and hostess must be feeling upstairs.

Their carriage had reached the carpet that had been rolled out to the edge of the road. Another of her innovations. 'We will be directed to separate retiring rooms to remove our coats when we get inside,' she informed Jack. 'Then we will meet at the foot of the main staircase and join the introduction line.'

'Don't worry about me. Just concentrate on yourself, and remember, I'm right at your side. And I'm watching your back too.' He lifted her hand to his lips, brushing a kiss to her fingertips just as their coach came to a complete halt.

The door was opened and the step unfolded. Jack jumped down, and Mercy followed, taking the footman's hand for support.

'My lady! We did not expect you tonight. It is a pleasure to see you here.'

'John.' Mercy smiled, extremely relieved to see that she had been right about the nature of her reception from the staff at least. 'How are you?'

'Very well, my lady. Mr Creggans has us following all your usual arrangements for the ball, as you can see.'

'Then we had better not detain you, or we will be guilty of holding things up. It is good to see you, John.'

'And you, my lady.'

'Who is Mr Creggans?' Jack whispered as they proceeded towards the door.

'The butler. He will be upstairs in the ballroom, supervising. This is James, on the door. Good evening, James.'

'My lady! What an—an unexpected pleasure.' The footman's smile faltered as he glanced towards the staircase, at the top of which the reception party would be assembled. 'I'm afraid we were not told to expect you.'

'No, I am planning to surprise His Lordship.'

'Indeed. I am sure he will be— Indeed. The retiring room…'

'Thank you,' Mercy said. 'I know the drill. I won't delay you further, James.'

'Good luck, my lady, you'll need it.'

The words were muttered under his breath. Mercy decided it was better not to acknowledge them, aware of the guests behind her listening avidly and not wishing to encourage disloyalty. 'I will see you in a moment,' she said to Jack, making her way towards the door on the right. A clutch of gentlemen awaiting their partners fell into silence as she passed, not one of them making a bow.

Taking her cue from them, Mercy steeled herself. She was out of practice, but she'd had years of experience in concealing her feelings behind a bland exterior. Tonight was a very different performance, but marriage had made her a consummate actor. She pushed open the door of the retiring room, imagining herself an actress walking onto a stage. 'Good evening, ladies.'

There was general jaw dropping and sharp intakes of breath. One lady started to sink into a curtsey, but was yanked firmly upright. Then, one by one, they turned their backs. Shaken, but determined not to let anyone see that they had affected her, Mercy untied her cloak and handed it to a maid she didn't recognise. She made a show of checking her hair in the mirror, frantically reassessing her situation. She hadn't really believed she would be cut dead, and consequently had not prepared her response, but a response was most certainly required.

She whirled around, taking the watching ladies by surprise, and addressed them directly. 'How many times have you each been my guest, I wonder? Too many to count, and yet you seem to have forgotten how well we are acquainted. I wonder if you will enjoy the new Lady Armstrong's hospitality as much as you appeared to enjoy mine in the past? I do hope she has arranged for a polka to be played. It is a dance I have recently become very fond of.'

An audible gasp greeted this remark but, though several of the familiar faces now bore red cheeks, still not one of them spoke. So be it. Fuelled by disgust, Mercy smiled her most sparkling social smile, dropped a very shallow curtsey and sailed out of the room.

The group of men was there, talking amongst themselves. Jack stood alone, casually leaning against one of the tall pillars, watching the new arrivals. His evening dress of black coat and trousers, white waistcoat and a plain-fronted shirt was extremely well-cut, obviously expensive, yet he wore it in the same way as he wore all his clothes—with a casual ease. He was not careless of his appearance, but he didn't invest much time or thought on it. She had never seen him check himself in a mirror, or inspect his coat for mud.

Mercy hovered unnoticed by a large potted palm, watching him for a moment. He was utterly lacking in pretension, title and pedigree, yet he attracted the interested glance of almost every new arrival, especially the women—something else to which he seemed quite indifferent. Then he turned her way, saw her, smiled and began to cross the hallway towards her. It was a perfectly ridiculous notion, but she felt as if his smile had bathed her in warmth. With Jack at her side, she felt invincible.

She smiled up at him as she slipped her hand into his arm. 'I am so glad you are here. I always loathed this house, it never felt like home, but it is stranger than I thought it would be, being back here. Like being a ghost at my own wake. I have just been given the cold shoulder by seven women who were my guests here two years ago. We are going to be well and truly shunned, Jack.'

'We can still leave. It's not too late to change your mind.'

'And show them that I care about what they think and how they are treating me? Absolutely not. Let us into battle.'

* * *

Jack had faced down hostile crowds before—workers unhappy with the pace of innovation, resistant to inevitable changes to long-standing working practices. He knew how to handle himself in such situations, knew never to show weakness, but he prided himself on his fairness, his ability to listen to grievances and to address those that needed to be resolved. That approach made him extremely successful in negotiating business deals in the face of demanding investors, bankers and hostile competitors. But tonight, as they ascended the sweeping staircase, was something beyond his ken. He wasn't in control, for a start, but deputy to the woman whose hand on his arm was trembling very slightly.

He couldn't imagine how she must be feeling. This mansion had been her home, the people who surrounded them her milieu. The interest in her was almost tangible, the air crackling with enmity. Everyone was looking but no one was meeting her eyes. Thus were the mighty fallen—he could just hear them thinking it. They were bloody loving it, these people who had for years been Mercy's guests, and who had doubtless called themselves her friend.

The heritage and privilege she had married into was crowding in on him. The huge clock that stood in the hallway chimed the hour. Portraits, which he assumed from their resemblance to each other must be Armstrong ancestors gazed sternly down from the walls. The servants all wore livery, the footmen with their hair powdered and tied back—to his modern eyes, a style both outmoded and demeaning.

He couldn't imagine the Mercy he knew being mistress of all this and the country estate she had mentioned, and heaven knew whatever other properties. It made him deeply uncomfortable, for it made her a stranger and reminded him of what he had always known but never felt before—that they were from vastly different worlds. He felt incongruous here by her side, not out of his depth by any means, but he didn't belong here. What was more, he didn't want to.

Mercy gave his arm a tug to attract his attention. 'We won't stay too long, an hour or so at most, but if at any point you wish to leave you must tell me.'

'Take as long as you like,' Jack said, kicking himself for having let her have even an inkling of his reservations. 'I'm here for you, for as long as you need to be here.'

'Thank you. We are about to come face to face with the foe,' she said as they reached the top step. 'Brace yourself.'

He felt her take a breath as she let go of his arm. Her smile was glittering as she confidently stepped forward. 'George.' Mercy took the hand, which had not been offered, in a firm grasp. 'You are surprised to see me here, I expect, for you did not send me an invitation. Did you think me still licking my wounds in the country? You will be very pleased to see that I am quite recovered, if that is the case.'

Lord Armstrong was a tall man, sparse of body and of hair which, he made up for as so many men did— mistakenly, in Jack's view—by growing a beard. The major had his facial hair trimmed in a frill, which drew attention to his very determined chin poking out above

it. With his aquiline nose, hooded eyes and a commend-
ably plain and extremely well-cut evening coat, he was
unmistakably an aristocrat, and one who would therefore be accorded the epithet 'handsome'. 'Arrogant and
entitled', Mercy's brother-in-law had described him,
and Jack could see that in the way the man was looking him up and down disapprovingly. It got his hackles
up enough, were it not for Mercy, for him to break into
his broadest and most vulgar Glaswegian.

'This is Mr Dalmuir,' Mercy said. 'Doubtless you
will have heard of his engineering company, which has
produced and is currently installing the beam engines
in the new London pumping stations that will be the
envy of the world.'

'How do you do?' Jack said, taking the man's hand,
which was once again un-extended, and squeezing it
mercilessly, hanging on to it just a few more seconds
when the man tried to yank himself free.

'And this is Lady Armstrong,' Mercy said, taking
the hand of the bemused woman standing next to her
husband. 'Georgina. This is Mr Dalmuir.'

George and Georgina! It almost overset him, but
Mercy had already moved on.

'And Frederick too. *What* a surprise. And Louise,'
she added, disappointing Jack, who had hoped for a
Frederica. 'We won't keep you. I know myself how
terribly busy you will be, though I understand you are
following my own arrangements, and so have no need
to wish you success. Don't worry, I know my way to
the ballroom. Shall we?'

Her hand was now distinctly trembling on Jack's

arm, but her smile was fixed firmly in place and her head held high. 'Well done,' Jack whispered.

'Save your congratulations for later. We've only just begun.'

Mercy entered the ballroom feeling quite sick. She felt no triumph or even pride that she had managed to storm the Armstrong citadel, only an almost overwhelming desire to escape. She had never believed all these people filling the ballroom were her friends, but she had never been anything other than polite to them, a generous hostess, a perfect guest. Some of them had known her since before she'd married, having come to Killellan Manor for the summer party and for Christmas. They had barely been acquainted with George, and yet they accepted his judgement of her unquestioningly. And the *Morning Post* version, of course.

The reality of her situation hit her hard. She was a widow, a woman whose influence had died with the husband who had stripped her of her reputation. Her year in mourning had given George ample opportunity to ensure that Harry's words were circulated and established as the truth, and the *Morning Post* had in all likelihood put an end to the thoughts of any who might have been inclined to support her, or at least give her the benefit of the doubt. She had no allies here. Thank goodness she had kept Sarah in the dark and spared her true friend the mortification of being shunned by association.

She wished she hadn't come. They didn't want her, and she didn't belong here. The orchestra was playing a march and the floor was filled with sets of couples sedately forming and reforming into columns as they walked through the prescribed moves, their faces set in the prescribed expression of polite boredom. None of the couples conversed. The ladies' biggest concern was protecting their trains from being trampled on, while the men simply looked as if they wished they were elsewhere. It could not be more different from the Holborn Casino.

'They look as if it would be more fun to go on a trip to the dentist,' Jack muttered, echoing her thoughts. 'I can't picture you living here.'

'Neither can I. It's as if that life was lived by someone else—or someone pretending to be me. It's the strangest thing. I was so accustomed to hiding my feelings, I never thought of it as acting until this evening, when I was in the retiring room and no one was speaking to me. I thought to myself, this is simply a different role I have to play.'

'You're playing it very well. No one in that line would have had a notion that you were shaking in those dancing slippers.'

'Except you! Knowing you were there, ready to land George another well-deserved punch, made all the difference.'

'I knew from the moment we arrived at the start of that line and you took that man's hand that you didn't need me. You should be proud of yourself.'

'Not yet.' People were becoming aware of their presence. Curious eyes were focussed on them. A space had been cleared around them. She sensed mutterings behind the flutter of fans and the backs that were being turned.

'You've made your point. Do you want to leave?'

'Hanging my head in shame? Certainly not.'

'If you're sure? We'll take a turn around the room, then, past that clutch of miserable old crones standing over there.'

'Dowagers, widows, chaperones and those past hope of securing a husband,' Mercy explained, taking his arm. 'It is known rather cruelly as Cat's Corner. I wonder if they will grant me a place among them. I am entitled to one.'

'What is the point of all this?' Jack asked, indicating the crowded ballroom. 'There's hardly a soul looks as if they want to be here.'

Mercy wrinkled her brow. 'They are here to prove they are entitled to be here, nothing more. It's like an exclusive club.'

'Your membership is going to be revoked, if your reception tonight is anything to go by,' Jack said as another couple leapt out of their way.

'It certainly looks like it. It's ironic, isn't it? I am the one who has been accused of being cold and heartless, yet here we are in a ballroom full of people in the very house that I used to live in, and not one of them has even acknowledged me.'

They had completed their circuit of the room. Mercy looked around her again, suddenly despondent. 'The heat in here is over-powering, I don't know why Georgina has kept all the windows closed, it's not as if there is a fog tonight. We will have one dance for form's sake, if you can bear it, and then we'll leave. That is a galop they are striking up now. Do you know it?'

'Excuse me, my lady. Lord Armstrong wishes to

see you.' The combination of her husband's butler and
the message he delivered hurtled her straight back to
the past. She had received just such a summons so
many times.

'Mercy? You've gone quite pale.'

'The heat,' she said, pulling herself together and
turning to face the butler. 'Creggans, I hope you are
well.'

'Lord Armstrong awaits you, my lady.'

'George. You mean George, of course. Very well.'

'Alone, my lady,' the butler said when Jack made to
accompany her.

'It's fine,' Mercy intervened when Jack made to protest. 'Wait here for me, if you please. I won't be long.'

Chapter Eight

The strength of his desire to follow Mercy out of the ballroom was another warning that Jack was getting in over his head, but he was too concerned about her to heed it. He couldn't fight her battles for her, but that didn't stop him wanting to. He couldn't go after her, but he couldn't bear to stay in the ballroom another second. The combination of the heat, the lack of air and the stench of perfume and sweat was making him feel nauseous. Some of the people here could do with a good wash.

'And it's not as if any of them have the excuse of having to cart the water up from the boiler house, six flights of stairs up a tenement close for a bath,' he muttered to himself. 'They've got servants for that.'

The reception queue was disbanded. Were both Armstrong brothers confronting Mercy? What were they saying? Jack pushed open the first door he came to and found himself in a huge drawing room. The gas jets were lit, and a selection of decanters had been set out on a table in the middle of the room, but it was surprisingly empty. He poured himself a tot of brandy and took it over to one of the three tall windows, fighting his way through a layer of red velvet braided with gold, and another layer of voile to push it open and take a few much-needed breaths of the cold, coal-tainted air. He'd give it ten minutes, and then he'd go and seek Mercy out.

He set the glass back on the table then, with one eye on the walnut and gilt clock on the mantel, he wandered morosely around the room. It was decorated in what he assumed was the height of fashion, but the net result was a confused clutter that offended his methodical and practical sensibilities. The wallpaper matched the curtains, dark red patterned with gold, and the sofas and chairs that were extravagantly scattered around the place were upholstered in the same colours.

You couldn't walk two steps without bumping into a table or a chair, and every surface was covered in *things*. Porcelain ornaments, glass vases, pierced silver boxes and, enamelled snuff boxes, carved figures... And all of it some poor servant would have to dust or polish. Terrified every day doubtless, that she would break something.

The paintings were all portraits in gilded frames, all of men wearing clothes from hundreds of years ago. Over the mantel hung two more in matching gilded frames. An elderly man with now familiar hooded eyes and determined chin, though clean-shaven, was on the right in the tight pantaloons and cutaway coat typical of the earlier part of the century. Lord Henry Armstrong, the plate informed Jack. And beside him, in a frock coat painted three-quarter-length, was Lord Harry Armstrong. Mercy's husband.

Jack's reaction was visceral. His hands curled into fists. The hair on the back of his neck stood on end. The man was facing away from the artist, looking haughtily off into the distance. Harry Armstrong had mutton-chop whiskers but no beard. His brown hair was parted at the side and combed flat over his head. His pate wasn't shining through, but it wouldn't have been long before it did, if his twin brothers were anything to go by, a thought which made Jack smugly satisfied, and then slightly ashamed. There was the same air of arrogance and entitlement in both portraits, a trait which the twin brothers had also had bred into them.

He stared at the portrait, trying to understand why Mercy had married such a man, but it made his bile rise, imagining her at his side. *Never mind—no, definitely never mind that.* The man was dead. She'd only have been, what, nineteen, twenty, when she married him? At that age he'd been barely formed, his head filled with engines and mathematics during the day and his nights… *No, never mind that either.*

The door to the parlour was flung open. 'Jack? Oh, thank goodness. Come quickly.'

'Mercy! What is it?'

'They are playing a polka. Hurry up, it's important!'

'What did they say to you?'

'I'll explain later. Please, Jack?'

Her colour was high, her eyes bright with anger, her mouth set. She looked magnificent. 'With pleasure,' he said, offering his arm.

She took it and they made their way quickly out

into the hall. He heard her name being called from downstairs, possibly by one of the Armstrong brothers, but she ignored it. When a servant dared to attempt to bar them from the doorway to the ballroom, Jack's glare was enough to hastily remove him from their path. Mostly unaware of the contretemps, the rest of the guests had packed the floor to dance a very sedate polka.

'I want us to dance it our way,' Mercy said, stepping into his arms.

'I wouldn't dream of doing it any other way,' Jack said, pulling her so tightly up against him that he lifted her off the ground, whirling her around before setting her down and launching straight into the dance.

Even in the Holborn casino, they would have been reprimanded for the wildness of their dancing. Time and again as he whirled her around, Mercy's feet left the floor. Long strands of her hair came loose. He was aware of the other couples stopping to stare, and then of the floor clearing until they had it to themselves. Finally, the music came to an abrupt halt. Jack picked Mercy up by the waist, birling her round one more time. There was a tense silence in the room as he made a bow and, beside him, Mercy dropped into a deep curtsey.

'Now that's what you call a polka,' Jack announced to their astonished audience before the pair of them strode out of the ballroom.

'You did it!' Jack said as the coach turned out of Cavendish Square.

'No, *we* did it!' Mercy said gleefully. 'Did you see the posse of servants George had lined up outside the ballroom to escort us off the premises? At least twenty of them, poor souls, looking deeply uncomfortable.'

'I suppose I should be flattered that he thought it would take that many. I noticed he made himself scarce.'

'Yes, but we had quite a crowd watching us when we walked down the stairs! I doubt that anything else will be talked about over supper. Poor George, his first ball as Lord Armstrong will go down in history for all the wrong reasons.'

'What did he have to say to you when he asked for a private word?'

Mercy's smile faded. 'We're here,' she said, as the carriage was slowing. 'Why don't you come in and I'll tell you how the conversation went?'

'Good idea, but I'll let the carriage go. I can get a cab later.'

She found her key and opened the front door. 'Wait for me in the parlour, I won't be long.'

Upstairs, she removed her cloak and gloves and, after a few seconds' debate, her crinoline. In the parlour, Jack was sitting on the sofa. She sat down beside him. 'Thank you for coming with me tonight. You were right. I don't think I could have managed without you.'

'You'd have got through it, I'm sure.'

'Not nearly so well.'

'Then I'm delighted to have been of service.'

'It was horrible, though, wasn't it? I knew we would be shunned, but to have all those people literally turning their backs on us, was vile. They were never my friends, but they have been my guests, eaten at my table. I would never be so cruel.'

'You're better than all of them put together.'

'I suppose it would have taken a great deal of courage for anyone to speak to us when everyone else was giving us the cold shoulder.'

'Or someone with a mind of their own.'

'Well, I'm finished with that life now. And it is clearly done with me.'

'I don't believe that punching the living daylights out of someone solves anything, but there were a good few faces I was sorely tempted to use my fists on tonight.'

'Really? You must be an even better actor than I am.'

'I'll confess, I near enough broke that weasel Armstrong's fingers when I shook his hand.'

'I wish you had. According to George, I have so besmirched the Armstrong name that he is going to investigate whether it's possible to have my right to use it revoked, or some such thing.'

'The man's a pompous arse.'

'You do have a way with words. I wish I had thought to tell him so.'

'Is that what he summoned you to tell you?'

'Amongst other things. Though I realised tonight that I had George all wrong.'

'If you are going to try to persuade me that underneath he's a thoroughly decent chap...'

'No! He is a pathetic creature who knows that he is out of his depth. I don't know if I did him a disfavour when I accused him of being desperate to step into Harry's shoes, but it was obvious to me tonight that he is a fish out of water. He wasn't raised with any expectation of inheriting, you see. He's actually third in line, for there was a brother older than Harry, so George has only ever known the army.'

'So he's struggling. A sensible man would look to his predecessor for advice, but I take it that wasn't why he wanted to speak to you?'

'The very opposite. He wanted to inform me that, if I ever attempted to trespass on any of his property again, he would have me arrested. He doesn't want his family *contaminated*—his very word—by my presence. When I pointed out that I was legally entitled to live in the Dower House, I thought he would have an apoplexy. Stupid man. It is in the grounds of Killellan Manor. As if there was any chance that I would ever wish to live there. So, obviously, I told him I would be moving in next month. That is when he told me that he was looking into stripping me of the right to call myself an Armstrong, but that he would refrain from also stripping me of my widow's jointure provided I did not betray any of the family history which my husband may have confided in me.'

'Which last,' Mercy said through gritted teeth, 'was a thinly veiled threat to ensure the Armstrong skeletons are kept firmly locked in the closet.'

'Are there many?' Jack asked.

'Plenty.'

'The man had a bloody cheek, then, accusing you of causing a scandal.'

'He used the same words he used when the codicil was read out. Called me a barren bitch. The first time, it hurt. Tonight, it simply made me furious. If you had been in the room with me—Harry's study, of all places too—then I think I might have kissed you to prove him wrong.'

'Instead, we desecrated the Armstrong ballroom by dancing your swan song,' Jack said.

'My swan song? I suppose it was.' Mercy felt as if a weight had been lifted from her shoulders. 'I thoroughly enjoyed it.'

'So did I. My only regret is that we didn't complete our little performance in front of our captive audience with a passionate kiss.'

His smile made her breath catch. Tonight's performance had been exhilarating, the truly scandalous nature of it adding to the thrill. She had never thought of herself as daring, but she had enjoyed every moment of it, and the night wasn't over yet. She smiled back at Jack and leaned into him. 'It's still not too late,' she whispered. 'Even though we haven't got an audience now.'

His response left her in no doubt that Jack also enjoyed the daring side of her. 'Even better,' he said, wrapping his arms around her.

This time, their kisses were different. Not careful, but teasing and confident. Then lingering, deepening, rousing the same sensations as before, the tingling tension she knew for desire. Jack kissed her neck, her shoulders and the curve of her breasts revealed by her evening gown. She wanted to touch him. She slid her hands under his coat, smoothing over the silk of his waistcoat, over the span of his back, but the cut of his coat defeated her.

He broke the kiss to stand and shrug himself out of it, dropping it heedlessly to the floor before pulling her up to wrap his arms around her, and they kissed again. He cupped her breast through her gown and, sensing his hesitation, she whispered, 'Yes,' reaching behind her for the lacing under the collar to loosen it.

The bodice fell over her arms. Jack dipped his head to kiss the exposed valley between her breasts and her nipples tightened inside her corset in anticipation. She flattened her hands over his waistcoat, feeling the heat of his skin beneath the fabric, feeling him shudder and his muscles clench at her touch, encouraging her to un-button his waistcoat, to touch him again, hands flat on his back, smoothing over his muscles, with his shirt the only barrier.

'Yes,' he whispered. 'Yes.'

He untied the strings of her corset to loosen it. The weight of the voluminous skirts of her evening gown dragged it down over her hips and onto the floor, but she lost interest in them as Jack's mouth fastened over her nipple and sucked delicately, making her cry out with delight.

Her knees buckled, or perhaps he eased her down onto the floor, and he lay down at her side. 'Tell me,' he said, his breathing harsh. 'Tell me if I do anything you don't like.'

'Yes.' But what he was doing was delightful—the soft tug of his mouth on her nipples, the scratch of his beard on her skin, and inside the drugging, dragging tension building. 'Yes,' she said again. 'Yes.'

He stroked down her belly, then cupped between her legs through her petticoats. The throbbing in-side her intensified. He kissed her on the mouth and cupped her more firmly, and her body arched up of its own accord. She forgot to think about whether this was right or wrong. Instinct took over. Whatever Jack was doing, she wanted him to keep doing it, so when he stopped she protested, only to cry out in shock when he touched her in the same way beneath her petticoats.

'Mercy?'

Her body had tensed in a far from pleasant way. The sweet delight which had been so close to enveloping her began to recede. Wanting to cling onto it, she put her arm around his neck and kissed him. She relaxed. Another kiss, slow and languorous, and she sighed with pleasure. Then he touched her in a very different way from how she had been expecting, and drew a long, shuddering moan from her.

He touched her again, his fingers sliding, stroking, sliding, and her entire body focused on the one spot where he touched her, desperate for more, not wanting it to end, and when it did, wave after wave of pure pleasure made her cling to him, kissing him wildly, pressing herself closer and closer until there was nothing but the layers of his clothes and her undergarments left between them. And the hard swell of his arousal pressed against her stomach.

Jack swore, immediately distancing himself. 'I'm sorry. I didn't mean— You mustn't think that I expect...'

'But I want to,' Mercy said, still caught up in the blissful aftermath, and only half-aware of what she was saying.

'So do I. Obviously.' Jack grimaced, pushing himself upright. 'But I can't. Won't. I didn't expect this.'

'Nor did I, but I want you to...'

'Mercy, I beg you, don't tempt me. You've no idea

how much I want to, and I can't tell you what it does to me, knowing that you want to. Because I know— But that's the problem, you see. I know what a big step it would be for you, and frankly it feels like a bloody big step for me.' He pushed his hair back from his face. His shirt was open at the neck, though Mercy had no memory of either of them taking off his tie. 'So I think that's enough for now, don't you? Besides, you've been through the mill today, and you've a lot to take in after what happened.'

'Do you think I don't know what I'm doing?'

'Do you?' He smiled crookedly. 'I know I'm not exactly thinking straight, and I won't be able to, either, with you sitting beside me like that.' He got to his feet, helping her up. 'We both got carried away. Let's leave it at that, will we?'

It was difficult not to feel rebuffed, but she knew in her heart he was right, so she nodded. 'Thank you, for tonight. For escorting me, I mean. And for dancing my swan-song polka with me. And for...'

He kissed her again. 'It was a pleasure. All of it was a pleasure.'

Mercy was exhausted but perversely, as soon as she extinguished her lamp and closed her eyes, sleep deserted her. Tonight had been momentous in almost every possible way. Once the elation had worn off, would she regret what she had done? She was too vastly relieved to believe that possible. The ball had shown her what her life had been, and proved beyond doubt to her that she had changed too radically ever to want any element of it back. Seeing that world through Jack's eyes... But no, that was the point, she was seeing it afresh with her own eyes, and it left her completely cold. Just as she had been, Mercy thought sadly, when she'd been part of it all.

She had been a very successful player on that stage for a very long time, however. She understood only too well how it worked, and how it could be manipulated. If she repented, if she retreated, she would eventually be able to return. *Yeah right!*, as Jack would say. And as for the Armstrongs? She wasn't going to give them another thought. None of them understood her, or cared to hear her side of the tragic story of her marriage. Their childlessness had been a tragedy for both herself and Harry, but it was history now.

The day she'd met Jack, she remembered telling him—rather pompously, thanks in part to the brandy—*Tomorrow is the first day of the rest of my life*. She hadn't known then that she'd still have to sweep up the debris of her previous life, but tonight that was precisely what she had done. And, at the end of it, she had taken another momentous step of a very different kind.

The fire in the bedroom had burned itself out and it was cold enough for her to see her breath. Mercy snuggled further under the covers. She was beginning to understand what was meant by love-making. Tonight's experience made her see that there was a great deal more to it than she had ever imagined. After she had—what? There must be a word for it, but she had no idea what it might be. Afterwards, though, when she had curled up tightly against Jack and felt his... He had been so hard but, instead of bracing herself for the intrusion, she had *wanted* him inside her.

Even alone, in the privacy of her bedchamber, this thought made her cheeks flush. And it awoke what she knew to be desire. What Jack had done to her made her want him. She wanted him now. She wanted to touch him the way he had touched her, and to kiss him as he had kissed her—not only on the mouth but to taste his skin, to see him. Naked. To feel him pressed against her. Inside her. Mercy shuddered, closing her eyes under the covers, and let her imagination run free.

Chapter Nine

Sarah called the next morning as Mercy was studying her map of London and contemplating a walk to look at the work on the new embankment. '*What* a commotion you have caused,' she said, hugging Mercy, pulling off her gloves and tossing her hat onto a chair all at once. 'I have had two notes from ladies asking me to pass on their best wishes, and one inviting us to tea, with the assurance that no other lady will be present. How are you?'

'As you see,' Mercy said, taking the tea tray that Lucy had hurried to fetch. 'I am extremely well.'

'I must say, notoriety suits you.' Sarah took a seat on the sofa. 'You do know that there is a full description of your "pugnacious polka" in the *Morning Post*?'

'Is that how they described it? I haven't seen it and have no desire to. Anyway, I prefer Jack's description of it as my swan song.'

'Ah, Jack. Who, as I predicted, has been unmasked as your Scot, "Mr D", who has an interest in sewage of every kind. I am afraid I am not joking. Here,' Sarah said, pulling a crumpled news sheet from her pocket. 'Read this.'

'Jack is an engineer, not a plumber, for goodness' sake,' Mercy said, after quickly and reluctantly scanning it.

'I'm more concerned at what that blasted rag said about you. Dare I ask how much of it is true? You don't have the look of a woman who has deliberately cast herself into the wilderness.'

'Yet that is precisely what I did, and I am glad. I only wish I'd done it sooner.'

Mercy quickly outlined events at the ball as she poured the tea. 'I also received a couple of notes this morning from "well-wishers", though neither of them invited me to tea. If you are about to suggest my taking Clement's advice to retire to the country until it all blows over, then you may as well save your breath to cool your porridge.'

Sarah arched her brow. 'That sounds like something a certain Scotsman might say. What will he make of having his name in the public domain?'

'I don't know. I doubt he will have seen it. He has repeatedly told me he doesn't care about the papers, provided they don't slander his engineering business.'

'I don't think that they are interested in his engineering business, frankly,' Sarah said, pouring herself a cup of tea. 'It is his business with you that they are interested in.'

'And that is nobody's business but ours!'

Sarah sipped her tea, frowning. 'May I be candid?'

'Aren't you always?'

'Not with you. Perhaps I should have been, in the

past. There have been any number of times when I have
wished to speak out and did not. I worry that I have
not been as good a friend to you as I could have been.'

'Sarah, you are my staunchest and truest friend.'
Mercy jumped up to give her a brief hug. 'You didn't
speak because I didn't want you to. And, let's be honest now, it wouldn't have made any difference, save to
confirm how miserable I was, as you were in no position to do anything to help.'

'It would be wrong of me to say that I'm glad that
man is dead, but I am very glad you are free of him.'

'I am, I promise you,' Mercy said, sitting back in
her own chair. 'Last night was like… I felt as if I was
cutting the last tie. I don't regret it, and I don't think
I will. Believe me, I have asked myself that question.'

'Then I am very pleased for you.'

'So pleased you are frowning.'

Sarah smoothed her brow. 'May I ask what your intentions are in relation to Mr Dalmuir?'

'I don't have any intentions. Nor does he. I told you
so.'

'I remember, but it seems to me… Mercy, forgive
me if this really is none of my business, but are you in
love with him?'

'In love! Good heavens, no.'

'But you are lovers?'

'When I suggested that we might be, you thought
it was a joke.'

'Because I thought the last thing you would wish
would be to— Because I knew how unpleasant you
found—' Sarah broke off, her cheeks scarlet. 'Marital
congress,' she concluded, wincing.

'Marital congress! Well, as a name for it, that certainly gets the pulses racing.'

Sarah laughed reluctantly. 'It's how my mother referred to it, and as you know, she found it very unpleasant too.'

'Perhaps because your father was as selfish or as ignorant as Harry. I am not sure which he was, most likely a combination of both, and it doesn't matter now save that it doesn't need to be unpleasant. On the contrary, it can be very pleasant indeed.' The effect of her declaration was enough to make her friend's jaw drop. Mercy laughed, her own cheeks now flushed. 'I was as astonished as you, but I assure you, it is the truth.'

'Well,' Sarah said, recovering. 'I have always known that for some women it is an enjoyable experience. Sadly, we see too many of them suffering the consequences at the lying-in hospital, but are you saying…? Actually, I'm not sure what you are saying?'

Mercy bit her lip, struggling for the right words. It would be very easy to end the conversation that even Sarah was finding difficult, but the lack of such frank conversations in the past had contributed to her own ignorance. 'I assumed that the fault was mine. That I have not a… That I am not amorous by nature. And, with Harry, it was always a means to an end.' She stopped, taken aback by this truth. 'With Jack, it has nothing to do with duty.'

'So you *are* in love with him?'

'No! I told you, there is nothing in the least bit serious between us.' Flustered, Mercy poured herself another cup of tea. It was tepid, but she sipped it, avoiding Sarah's gaze. 'He has been very kind to me. He is excellent company. We have fun together. I like him very much.'

She took a sip of tea. 'And I suppose I might be in *thrall* to him, because he has… Because I have learned… Because he has—he has shown me that I am amorous by nature. But I am not in love with him.'

'I am in love with Clement.'

'I beg your pardon?' Mercy set her cup down.

'I know. It's ridiculous. We could not be more different by nature or by inclination. He is happiest locked away with a stack of books, imagining himself in ancient Greece, while I like to be out and about in the world and doing things and seeing people. When we are together, it's true, we do find any number of things to talk about—and he makes me laugh, and he says that he admires my outspokenness—but I know he also thinks me very worldly, and hugely ignorant of everything that interests him.

'And, frankly, I have no desire to alter that. I tried to read a paper he was presenting at Oxford University, and it may well have been written in ancient Greek, for all I could make of it. So it's silly of me, and completely illogical too, to think myself in love with him. But I am and, though I've tried, I can't seem to make myself *not* be in love with him. I thought if I kept away from him…'

'So that's what you've been doing.'

'I thought it might wear off, but it hasn't. The other day, when he invited me to dinner—you remember?— well, I decided I wouldn't go. But then I did, thinking that I could prove to myself… But the only thing I proved was that I still love him.'

'I had no idea. You have not said a word.'

'I also haven't told you that he asked me to marry him, just after Prue's wedding.'

Mercy's mouth fell open in astonishment. 'And you call me a dark horse! Why didn't you tell me?'

'You had enough going on, what with Harry dying, and anyway, I turned him down.'

'May I ask why?'

Sarah picked up her tea spoon, stared hard at it then set it down again. 'Put simply, I got cold feet. It's an enormous change to make at my age, with no guarantees that it would make me happy, when I'm already perfectly happy with my lot, as is Clement. I am afraid that, if we marry, we might lose what we already have and discover that we don't actually make each other happier after all. We might even make each other miserable.'

'Like I was, you mean?'

'And my mother. What if I am like her, Mercy, and find the whole process of marital congress disgusting?'

'With Clement— Oh, goodness, I hate to ask this, he's my brother... Have you...?'

'I've kissed him. I enjoyed it. But kissing isn't—it's not kissing that frightens me.'

'It's an excellent start, though.'

'Really?' Sarah sniffed, wiped her eyes and handed Mercy back the handkerchief. 'I told him that I couldn't be a scholar's wife. The other evening, over dinner, he told me that he thought we should discuss the possibility of us both "making compromises", but I panicked and told him there was no point. I doubt he'll ask me again.'

'Do you want him to?'

'It doesn't matter. He won't.'

'Well, then, perhaps you could tell him that you've reconsidered and that there might be merit in at least having the discussion.'

'I'll think about it. Perhaps what I need to do is follow your lead and discover first if I am, after all, of an amorous disposition,' Sarah said, with her wicked smile. 'Then, if I am, and Clement proves to be a satisfactory lover...'

'Sarah!' Mercy put her hands over her ears. 'That is my brother you are talking about, and Clement is far too honourable a man to make love to you until you are his wife.'

'By which point it will be too late for me to change my mind. Do you know, Mercy, I think you have stumbled on a much better way of making such a momentous decision.'

'I am not going to marry Jack. Aside from the fact that he has very fixed ideas about what he wants from a wife, and I am the opposite of every one of them, I am not in the least bit interested in marrying again. I have only just obtained my freedom. It was hard-won, so I'm not giving it up that easily.'

'Ha! And yet only a few moments ago you were counselling me to do just that.'

'I wasn't. I said...'

'That I should try Clement out as a lover first.'

'Sarah!' Mercy dissolved into shocked giggles. 'You are absolutely outrageous.'

'I know. Isn't it fun? And liberating. I wish I had started long before now.'

* * *

Mercy spent the afternoon visiting the lying-in hospital with Sarah, whose mother had helped to establish it. The women being cared for were all in an advanced state of pregnancy, but their circumstances varied widely. There were wives of tradesmen who had fallen on hard times, and wives of soldiers and sailors whose husbands were either serving abroad or had deserted the marriage, if not the military.

Some of the women had simply borne too many children, and could not afford to pay for a midwife or other medical assistance. Some women had experienced traumatic births and required specialist attention. Some of the women were not married, but the lying-in hospital provided them with sanctuary and assistance: servants whose masters had taken advantage of them, young women whose betrothed had had second thoughts once their condition had become known and some young women who had been too ignorant or lacking in caution to care about the consequences until they became apparent to all.

Mercy was pleasantly surprised by this apparently non-judgemental approach, until she discovered that an unmarried woman could only avail herself of the hospital's services once. Twice-fallen women were sent to the Magdalen Hospital for Penitent Prostitutes.

Next to the General Lying-In Hospital was an asylum which provided temporary sanctuary to the neediest mothers and their new-born babies. All too soon these mothers were obliged to leave to free up beds, and forced to decide whether or not to take their baby with them. Painfully often, the child was left behind to be given into the care of an orphanage or a work-house. The addition of one extra mouth to feed in an already large family was frequently one too many; a servant returning to work which required her to live in would not be permitted her to bring her child with her, whether she was married or not. A sailor or sol-dier's wife waiting on a husband who might or might not return could not risk the financial burden of a child.

Mercy listened to the women's tales with horror and pity. No matter what the circumstances, whether it was a first child or a twelfth, the decision to give up a baby was heart-breaking and final. The ties were cut irre-vocably. The child could not be taken back once it was given into the care of another, nor could it be visited.

'It is for the best,' the matron informed her. 'For both. A clean break for the mother and a fresh start for the baby.'

Was that true? According to Sarah there was no alternative, but as they made the journey home—to her friend's astonishment suggesting they take the omnibus—she began to wonder if finding an alterna-tive might be her calling. Her own sister would have been raised in an orphanage if their parents had not taken her in.

She descended the omnibus at the stop nearest her house, having said goodbye to Sarah, and was still deep in thought when she heard her name called.

'Jack! What a lovely surprise!'

'My senior engineer arrived this morning from Glasgow, so I finished early. Thought I'd let him find his feet without me looking over his shoulder. You were miles away.'

'I have been planning a new career as the old woman who lived in a shoe.'

'And had so many children she didn't know what to do?'

Mercy smiled. 'Yes, but I would have a plan.'

'You do like to have a plan, don't you?'

'Now that I have completed my plan to disestablish myself so successfully, I am turning my mind to what to do now. I have spent the afternoon with Sarah at the General Lying-In Hospital in Lambeth.'

'Lambeth!' Jack stood back while Mercy opened the front door. 'And how was your visit?'

'Heart-breaking, but not in the way you are thinking. There are so many little ones being given up to orphanages and workhouses because their mothers simply can't care for them.'

'And so many bairns who've run away from both places wandering the streets because the orphanages and workhouses don't care for them either,' Jack said grimly. 'Are you thinking of taking some of them in? You'll need a bigger house.'

'I haven't got a plan yet, only a glimmer or an idea. Go into the parlour. It's after five, so I have the house to myself. Would you like some tea?'

'No, thanks.' Jack took off his coat and hat, set his gloves down on the hallstand and decided it would be best to launch straight in. 'Look, there's something I need to talk to you about.'

Mercy's face fell. 'You've seen the *Morning Post*?'

'It was brought to my attention. I take it you've seen it too?'

'Sarah brought it this morning. It implied you were a plumber.'

'With "an interest in sewage of all kinds". They want to get their facts straight.'

He sighed, sitting down on the sofa. 'It wasn't exactly unexpected, and when I looked at it, to be honest, my first thought was that your man Armstrong had had a word to make sure it was slanted the right way—to make sure he came out of it as the poor victim.'

'I didn't think of that, but you're right. I don't care though, Jack. I have absolutely no regrets about last night.'

'No more do I. And, as to that piece, as far as I'm concerned it's pure drivel, but unfortunately there's some who don't agree with me and think that I've been attracting "all the wrong sorts of publicity", as it was put to me today.' His hackles rose at the memory. 'A man who claimed to represent the Metropolitan Board of Works came to see me at the site today.'

'What did he say?'

'There are plans to build four pumping stations in and around London. I'm supplying the engines for two, and I gave them a good price on the understanding that, if I make a good job of it, I'll be awarded the contract for the others. There's no question but that I'll make an excellent job of it.'

'But there is the possibility of them reconsidering if you continue to get your name in the papers for all the wrong reasons—is that what this man implied?'

'More or less.' He had been a bit more specific than that, referring to the dubious choice of company Jack was keeping, but Jack decided to keep this information to himself for now.

'He was one of those who speak in a roundabout way so as not to incriminate themselves and, like I said, I'm not convinced he was even speaking for the Board. They might be preparing the ground to get me to cut my price, rather than to cut me out altogether, but they've been very fair with me up till now. I'm not sure what his agenda is. Anyway, I made it crystal-clear that I don't take kindly to having anyone tell me how to run my life. He left with his tail between his legs.'

'What are you going to do about it?'

'I don't know yet,' Jack said, which was the truth. 'A bit of digging, to start with. I find it difficult to believe they'd award the contract to someone who will charge them more for engines that don't work so well and who hasn't the experience of building the first two.'

'So you don't think it's a risk, then?'

'It's a possibility, but if it is I'll manage it,' Jack said, sounding less certain than he should be. 'I confess it has me a wee bit jittery.'

'I thought you were going to tell me that you couldn't see me any more. I would understand.'

Her voice wobbled and, there it was, the obvious solution staring him in the face. That was exactly what he should tell her. He shouldn't be taking any chances. 'Like I said, I haven't decided what to do yet,' he said.

'You've done so much for me, Jack. I couldn't bear it if I was responsible for damaging your prospects.'

'You won't. I can take care of myself.'

'And you have taken care of me too.'

'I've enjoyed every minute of it.'

'So have I. But if the time has come…'

'No.' His protest was instinctive. 'Unless you're saying that you think…?'

'No!' She sounded even more vehement than him, and looked every bit as taken aback. 'Unless you think…?'

'Not yet, at any rate,' he said, knowing fine and well that he was procrastinating but completely unable to stop himself.

Mercy nodded. 'Not yet,' she said.

But soon. The words lay between them unspoken, and then, because there was nothing more to be said, he kissed her. And because she responded so completely, melting into him, wrapping her arms around him, he kissed her more deeply and forgot about work, his strange encounter, everything, save the need to kiss her again. He could kiss her for ever and it wouldn't be enough. He wanted to savour every moment, to kiss every inch of her skin, to watch her face reflect her pleasure as he touched her, the surprised delight of her as she climaxed.

'Jack.' Mercy broke the kiss, panting, pushing herself upright. 'I want you to make love to me. Properly.'

There was nothing at this moment he wanted more, but he knew almost as well as she did what an enormous step this was for her.

'I don't want to wait any longer. I *want* you to make love to me. I mean it, Jack,' Mercy said, smoothing her hand over his cheek. 'I'm sure.'

He caught her hand, kissing her palm. 'At any time, if you want me to…'

'I'll say. At any point. I promise.'

Whatever he saw in her eyes, as he gazed seriously into them, reassured him. He smiled at her and pulled her to her feet and picked her up, holding her high against his chest, and made for the stairs.

She hadn't planned this tonight but, as Jack carried her up the stairs as if she weighed nothing, Mercy was absolutely certain that the time was right. Everything had been leading to this moment. Yesterday she had cast off the last vestiges of her old life. Talking to Sarah today had dispersed any remaining fears she had about love-making and tonight, though neither of them had said so, both she and Jack were aware that their time together was coming to a natural ending.

She wanted him to make love to her but, as he set her down in her bedroom, kicking the door closed behind him, the sight of her bed and its unpleasant connotations gave her pause, making her wish they had remained downstairs. There was no gas supply upstairs in the house, so Jack was turning up the bedside lamp.

'I want to see you when I take your clothes off, but if you'd prefer I can put it out again.'

She forgot about the bed. '*All* my clothes?'

'I hope so. Are you worried you'll be cold? I'll do my very best to keep you warm.'

Looking at him was already making her hot. Naked. With the lamp on. She pushed the last tendrils of fear away, wrapped her arms around him and decided to let her kisses speak for themselves.

He undressed her slowly, pressing kisses to every bit of flesh revealed as he unbuttoned her jacket and then the blouse she wore underneath. Her skirt was next, and then her ruffled petticoats and her crinoline all fell to the floor, leaving her in her corset, sky-blue with dark-blue ribbons, and her white silk drawers and stockings. The way he looked at her, his eyes dark with desire, a slash of colour on his cheeks, left her in no doubt that he relished what he saw, giving her the confidence to enjoy him looking and appreciate what nature had given her.

He kissed the tops of her breasts, unlacing her corset, and her nipples were already tingling in anticipation. His coat and waistcoat were on the floor with her gown. Mercy tugged his shirt free from his trousers and smoothed her hands over his chest, feeling him shudder in response. She wanted to see him, wanted to look at him, to taste and to touch him in the way he was tasting and touching her. Pushing his shirt higher, she kissed him, feeling the swell of his chest muscles, her hands on the dip of his waist tracing the line of his rib cage, feeling the shallow breaths he took.

He yanked his shirt over his head and her corset fell to the ground, leaving only her chemise. 'You are so lovely,' Jack said, his voice harsh, 'so lovely.'

He took off her chemise, leaving her naked apart from her drawers. She shivered, not with cold but with anticipation, and then gave a long sigh of delight as he kissed her breasts, his tongue tasting her nipples. The rhythmic throbbing inside her intensified.

When he eased her back to the bed she hesitated, only for a moment, but his eyes locked on hers reassured her, and his hand slipping between her legs, sliding inside her, drew a long moan from her. She barely noticed that she was lying on the bed, was aware only of Jack lying beside her, stroking her, touching her, until she cried out, surrendering to the waves of pleasure pulsing through her body.

This time when she instinctively turned to him he pulled her closer, kissing her deeply. Her breasts brushed against his naked chest. His hands smoothed over her bottom, then around to her waist, tugging at the strings that tied her drawers. She wriggled free of them, refusing to let herself think about all the things she didn't know, the things she had known utterly banished in the moment. She followed his lead, smoothing her hands over his rear, his hard muscles clenching at her touch, his breathing harsh, muttering her name, kissing her, cursing as he tried to kick off his shoes.

'A minute,' he said, rolling away to remove the rest of his clothing.

She watched him, sitting up. It didn't occur to her not to watch, dimly conscious of never having watched, of never having seen a naked man like this, so unashamed. Jack had a hard stomach and muscled thighs and between them…

Mercy stared, fascinated, her hand reaching out before she snatched it back. 'Sorry.'

He sank onto the bed beside her and kissed her, then took her hand and gently wrapped it around his aroused manhood. It was smooth and hard, like silk, when she had expected roughness. She looked up, met his eyes and smiled. They kissed slowly. 'Yes,' she said, before he could ask her. 'Please.'

Kissing. Side by side, skin to skin, kissing. Then he came closer. His body covered her, easing her legs apart.

'Are you sure?'

'Yes.'

He entered her slowly, sliding in so easily she cried out in surprise, making him hesitate until she tilted towards him, encouraging him and discovering at the same time that she liked it. He pushed higher, waited, then slowly began to move rhythmically. His eyes were on hers, watching her. When he moved, her body moved too, arching upwards to pull him in deeper, making her tighter inside with each thrust he gave. Still he watched her, until his powerful thrusts sent her over the edge, her body clinging tightly to him until with a deep, harsh groan he reached his climax, burrowing his head in her shoulder as he spent himself inside her.

'Did I hurt you?'

Mercy smiled hazily, shaking her head.

He kissed her. They were still joined, their limbs slick with sweat, and he showed no desire to free himself, kissing her again, pushing her tangle of hair back from her face. 'You're bloody gorgeous, do you know that?'

'Thank you. You're pretty bloody gorgeous yourself,' she said.

His laughter rumbled against her chest. He ran his hand down her body to rest on her bottom. 'I'll ask you just one more time. Are you sure you're all right?'

'I'm not all right. I couldn't be any further from all right. I am—I am in a state of bliss,' Mercy said. 'I would even go so far to say that I have never been so contented.'

'I would go so far as to say that I feel the very same

myself,' Jack said, kissing her again before gently rolling onto his side.

'Thank you, Jack.'

'My pleasure,' he said, smiling wickedly.

'I meant thank you for—for taking the time to make this so wonderful. I feel as if it's my first time. I know that's silly,' Mercy added when his smile faded.

'No. It's not silly.'

They lay in silence for a while then Jack sat up. 'I don't know about you, but I am suddenly ravenous.'

Mercy giggled. 'Now you come to mention it… Shall I…?'

'No, wait there. I'll go and rustle something up.' He got out of bed and pulled on his shirt. 'I won't be a moment.'

Jack padded downstairs in his bare feet. He hadn't been in Mercy's kitchen before, but he wasn't surprised to discover that it was spick and span, with the kettle, filled and set to one side, gently simmering on the impressively modern stove-top. The cups and saucers were where he expected them to be, as was the teapot, sitting with the a silver water-jug on a tray in readiness. A peek in her larder made him smile, for it was neatly stocked and regimentally ordered, and he reckoned owed nothing to the maid and everything to the mistress.

He found some bread and cut it, buttering it and putting it on the tray with a wedge of crumbly white cheese she was fond of, then waited for the kettle to come to a boil, trying to ignore the niggling feeling he had that something was not quite right. Everything about what they'd just shared had been perfect. Nothing he'd ever felt compared to this. He'd never felt so contented, to use Mercy's words. What was wrong with any of that?

The kettle boiled. He warmed the pot and carefully measured the leaves from the caddy. Another first, he thought, smiling to himself, bringing a woman tea in bed.

I feel as if it's my first time, Mercy had said.

His smile faded. It was far from his first time, but he had nothing to compare to this. He'd never met a woman like Mercy, mind you. Perhaps it was taking such care with her, knowing how much she'd been hurt, and wanting... Ach, who was he kidding?

Jack set the kettle back on the stove and picked up the tray. He was in deep, and who wouldn't be, with a woman like Mercy? But he'd be a right eejit if they started thinking this was anything more than a fling. No, it didn't sit well with him to call it that, but that was what it was at the end of the day. Mercy had made it very plain she wanted nothing more, and he most certainly didn't. It would be a wrench when it came to saying goodbye...

He set the tray down again, for the very thought of that was like a kick in the gut. He'd never felt like that before. His flings had always been fun, and they'd always ended without regrets. This... No, he refused to call it a fling. He was in pastures new here, and he didn't know where it was going to take him.

There, another first, and not one he liked. It was the uncertainty of it. How many times, since he had first met Mercy, had he asked himself what the hell he was doing? And had he once come up with an answer? No, not once. Was she any wiser than he was? He couldn't imagine how she could be. This whole situation was pastures new for both of them.

He picked up the tray again and made for the kitchen door. He was thinking too much. There was a beautiful woman lying naked in bed, waiting for him, so what was he doing here? He elbowed open the kitchen door and made his way back up the stairs.

'Did you think I'd run off?' he said.

'Dressed like that?' Mercy was sitting up, the sheet pulled over her, her hair tumbling down over her shoulders. 'You'd have been arrested.'

Jack set the tray down carefully on the bed at her side and climbed in beside her.

'Thank you,' she said, accepting the cup of tea he poured for her and taking a slice of the bread and butter. 'This is very decadent.'

'Bread and cheese and tea! You've led a very sheltered life.'

She giggled. 'The sad truth is that if you'd brought me champagne and caviar I wouldn't have been nearly so pleased. I've grown addicted to that cheese they sell at the market.'

He cut her a sliver and offered it to her. She took it, her tongue brushing the tip of his finger, and he dropped the knife, clattering it onto the tea tray, leaning in to kiss her. She wrapped her arms around his neck, pulling him close, and the sheet slipped. He dipped his head, kissing the valley between her breasts.

Her tea cup fell with a thud to the floor. Cursing, he lifted the tray, leaning over the bed to drop it onto the floor. He was already hard. When he leaned over to kiss her again, she moaned, pushing herself up against him. He pulled her upright, easing her onto his lap, feeling her hot and slick against him, and then hot and slick around him as he slid inside her. He was struggling to keep control of himself as her face showed her delight, and she kissed him hard and began to move.

He tried to restrain himself, tried to take it slowly, but she wouldn't let him, her kisses wilder and wilder as she took him, sending them both out of control, crying out and clinging as they came together, clinging to each other at the end and still clinging as he fell back, taking her with him, wordless, spent, sated.

Chapter Ten

Jack left very reluctantly as dawn was breaking, to head back to his rooms and change for work. Wearing only her robe, Mercy saw him to the door for one last, prolonged kiss, watching as his figure disappeared into the hazy fog of the winter morning.

They had spent the night making all sorts of love, dozing, talking about anything save the subject that now loomed large in her head as she made her way back up the stairs, banked up the fire in her bedroom and wrapped her quilt around her. Her bed and her body were both in a state of wild disarray that bore very obvious testimony to how she had spent the night. She would need to remedy both before her maids arrived.

Listlessly, she washed and dressed, then set about putting the room straight, trying to reassemble the bed into some sort of order, shaking out her pillows and feather quilts, tucking the sheets in. She opened the window, but the fog was curling thicker outside, so she immediately closed it again. The room was cold, the intimacy they had shared dispersed. She gathered up the tea things onto the tray and took them down to the kitchen, hurrying now to make a fresh pot while she was still alone.

Her appetite deserted her. Her mood became as grey as the day outside. Sipping her tea in the parlour, she wondered if Jack was thinking of her, if he too was suffering from this odd melancholy. Was it usual, after a night of passion?

I feel as if it's my first time, she had said to him. Her toes curled at the memory, at how naïve she had sounded. Now she had proved beyond doubt that she was neither frigid nor cold, there was no logical reason why she should not take another lover when Jack inevitably left her life, as he must. Save that she didn't want another lover, any more than she wanted to think of Jack with another woman.

At least not yet, Mercy told herself. Not while she was *in thrall* to him. She smiled wryly, recalling the conversation with Sarah—goodness, had that only been yesterday? So much had happened that she'd barely given her friend's confession a thought.

Sarah was in love, and Clement had asked her to marry him, yet she had turned him down. Practical Sarah, independent of spirit as well as financially independent, did not want to turn her world upside down in order to marry. Did Sarah wish for children? She had never said so, only that she didn't wish to go through the experience of having them. And as for Clement... Mercy frowned. She couldn't remember him ever expressing an opinion on the subject. Did he have one? Was he indifferent or, like Prue, too aware of Mercy's unfulfilled longing to be a mother to broach the subject? She had never asked him.

What a selfish sister and friend she had been. It had been over a year since Clement asked Sarah to marry him. A year when Mercy had shared his home, once again too caught up in her own miseries to notice whether her brother was lovesick. Yes, she'd asked him and he had dismissed her, but she hadn't persisted. Would it have made any difference? Sarah really did seem very entrenched in her ways, but after a year of waiting for her feelings to diminish she was still in love. Whatever that meant. She wasn't exactly sure that Sarah had described it and, thinking back over the conversation, she was even less sure that she had dispensed any helpful advice. Sarah would be better speaking to Prue about such matters.

Mercy had never been in love. At school, she had never had what the other girls called 'a pash'. Was that what she had for Jack—a passion? It certainly described last night. Intense and all-consuming while it lasted. But the point about passions was that they didn't last.

The thought was consoling. Mercy poured herself a last cup of tea and forcibly turned her thoughts to the future that was entirely hers to shape.

It was late afternoon, but the fog had grown so thick that it was quite dark outside. Mercy had cut short her walk and was writing a letter to Prue when there was a sharp rap at the door. She heard Lucy crossing the hall to answer and a familiar voice utter a gruff greeting, then a moment later Jack strode into the room, still in his coat and hat.

'Lord George Armstrong was behind it!' His voice was clipped. One look at his face told her he was furious.

'What…?'

'That man who came to see me yesterday, purporting to be from the Board of Works? It was Armstrong who put him up to it.'

'George sent him! How did you discover that?'

'It took a bit of digging but I'm not without contacts in high places myself.' Jack threw his hat onto the chair and pulled off his gloves and scarf. His coat was sodden. His boots were mud-spattered. 'It's a filthy afternoon out there. I've trailed mud all the way through your hall.'

'Never mind that. What made you suspect George?'

'It was what the man he sent said to me, that the company I have been keeping could be severely detrimental to my future prospects,' Jack said, looking deeply uncomfortable. 'Since the only company I've been keeping outside of work is—'

'Me,' Mercy interrupted grimly. 'So what he meant is that *I* am detrimental to your future prospects!'

'I'm not having anyone tell me what company to keep, and when I should stop keeping it—not George Armstrong, or anyone else, and so I told him.'

'You confronted George?'

'I did indeed.' Jack smiled grimly. 'That butler tried to set two of the footmen on me to try to stop me getting in, but they had the sense to lay off me when I made it clear I meant business.'

'And George?'

'Ach, I wiped the floor with him. The eyes of the

world are on this project, I told him, and the dates for getting the first two pumping stations up and running are fixed, with the proposed dates for the second two already published. All of which is the truth. My firm's work is crucial to meeting those target dates. I told him if he tried to interfere with the contract process I'd pull my men out—quite literally pull the plug on the whole thing—and I'd make it clear who was to blame.'

'You would never do that.'

'Of course I wouldn't, but he doesn't know that. I called his bluff and, like the lily-livered coward he is, he crumbled. It worked a treat, so you've no need to worry.'

There were shadows under his eyes. There was stubble growing where he was usually so meticulous about trimming his beard. 'You don't look like a man who isn't worried.'

Jack shrugged. 'He's a pathetic weasel of a man and a pompous arse.'

'He may be both, but he is not without influential connections, and if he is set on making the point that I am poisonous company, and anyone connected with me will be contaminated, then he will find another way to make it.'

'I reckon he's got it in for me too, considering the part I played in our floor show at Cavendish Square.'

'I warned you several times over about the possibility of your name being dragged through the mud along with mine.'

'And I told you each time it was a risk I was prepared to take.'

'Because you thought it wouldn't harm your business!'

'It hasn't harmed my business. Not yet, any road.'

'Precisely! It still might happen.'

'I'm all too aware of that. What bothers me is that, when I went rampaging over to Cavendish Square today, I cared a lot less about putting that man right about my business than I did about putting him straight on interfering between you and me.' Jack gazed at her, helplessly pushing a hank of damp hair back from his brow. 'God's honest truth, Mercy, I know I should have told you my suspicions last night, but I didn't want to face up to what it might mean.'

Her anger fled. She took his hands. They were like ice. 'I wanted last night to happen.'

His fingers tightened on hers. 'So did I.'

A lump rose in her throat. She bit her lip fiercely, determined not to make the inevitable any more painful than it had to be. 'So our fling is over.'

'Don't call it that!'

'It would probably have burned itself out anyway. We have too much *not* in common, and we never intended... So you must not think that I'll be... What I'm trying to say, Jack, is that I have already been thinking about my future, only today, and so I was prepared—I was expecting this. I'm ready to say my goodbyes.'

'I'm not.'

'This has been a—what do they call it?—a warning shot across the bows.'

'I know, and I'm not planning to ignore it, but I was thinking— Look, tell me if this is a mad idea, or if I've got you wrong or I'm being selfish or whatever… Ach, maybe it is a mad idea.'

Despite herself, she began to feel hopeful. 'I can't tell you if I don't know what it is.'

'Last night was like nothing I've known before. I know all you've said about us going our own way and having nothing in common is all true, and I know besides that the whole point of our spending time with each other was to help get you on your own two feet, and we've done that—or rather, you've mostly done that.'

'With your help. I couldn't have done it without you.'

'You could, though maybe a bit slower.' Jack smiled. 'Let's not go round the houses on that one again. My point is, Mercy, I know this can't last, but I feel like we've only just begun and I'd like us to have just a wee bit more time together.'

'You know I feel the same, but how can we?'

'We can, just not in London.'

'I'm not sure…'

'I have to go back to Glasgow again for a few weeks—that's why my second in command is down here. I thought—and here's where you must tell me if I'm off my head—I thought I'd take a few extra days— I mean a real break—and you could join me.'

'For a holiday? In Glasgow?'

Jack laughed. 'No. I'm thinking we might go *doon the watter* to Dunoon.'

Chapter Eleven

It was the beginning of March. The weather was becoming milder, the fog was lifting and the dormant winter grass and shrubs in the London parks were showing early signs of growth. The London season was in full swing, the popular shopping streets jammed with carriages, the theatres and operas playing to full houses and a stream of debutante balls was being held in the Mayfair town houses prior to the official court presentation at Buckingham Palace.

Though this had been her life until Harry had died, Mercy missed none of this. Jack had left for Scotland the day after he had confronted George Armstrong. Mercy tried to set her mind to planning her future. She visited the General Lying-In Hospital several times without Sarah, helping out on the wards and attending a number of births. She surprised herself by discovering she had a talent for such work. She found the miracle of birth entrancing, and was neither disgusted nor horrified by what the women endured, wishing only to alleviate their pain and share in their joy.

But she didn't imagine herself becoming a full-time nurse. Her future remained obstinately hazy, and her focus, when she was alone, wandered rather too often to Jack. Until her passion for him had burned itself out, she couldn't help feeling she was in a state of limbo.

They had arranged to meet in Glasgow in five days' time. On impulse, she decided to leave London early and visit Edinburgh. She had never been to Scotland, and she had never travelled alone before. She would prove to herself that she really was an independent woman of independent means.

Excited by the prospect, she telegrammed her change of plans to Jack, took a first-class ticket and boarded the Scotch Express, which left King's Cross station at ten in the morning and arrived at Edinburgh Waverley promptly, ten and a half hours later. Three days spent seeing the sights of 'the Athens of the North', taking rooms in a hotel and dining there alone buoyed her confidence, and the time passed in a whirl.

It was not until she was ensconced in a first-class carriage on board the Edinburgh and Glasgow Railway train that she began to have doubts. She was really looking forward to seeing Jack again, but it was possible that in their weeks apart, weeks when he had been extremely busy, his passion for her had faded. And, even if it had not, would they be awkward with each other?

She had no idea what arrangements Jack had made for their trip *doon the watter*. Would they stay in a hotel? Goodness, would they have to pretend to be married? Her resistance to this was so strong it disconcerted her. As the steam train powered on through mile after mile of farmland and heath, she began to panic and forgot to crane her neck, as the hotel porter had suggested, for a view of the ancient Linlithgow Palace as they passed through that small town.

The train pulled into Glasgow's Dundas Street station far too quickly for her peace of mind. She had barely noticed the other passengers in the carriage, a middle-aged man and his wife who nodded a polite goodbye and a young man in a very new suit who blushed fiery red when she bid him good morning.

Mercy shook out the folds of her dark-blue travelling skirt and smoothed a wrinkle out of the sleeve of the matching jacket. Jack had warned her it would be cold, so she had brought a warm cloak, but this morning, inspecting herself in the mirror of the hotel bed chamber, she had given way to vanity and had it packed. The braided jacket with its row of silver buttons fitted snuggly, drawing attention to her figure. The lace-trimmed blouse she wore beneath her jacket showed off the length of her neck. The little hat artfully perched on her carefully arranged hair was frivolous and her gloves and buttoned boots matched. She couldn't remember Jack ever commenting on her clothes, but knowing she looked well boosted her confidence.

As she finally descended from the carriage, clutching her travelling bag, she was surprised to find the platform almost empty, and a porter already waiting with her trunk.

'He'd gie'd you up for lost,' the man informed her, nodding at the figure standing beside the engine, wreathed in smoke and steam.

Her heart skipped a beat. It was with difficulty that

she restrained herself from running towards him, and impossible to stop the smile spreading across her face as he came towards her with his distinctive, loping stride, his own smile lighting up his eyes.

'You got here, then,' he said, taking her hands in his.

'I did.'

'It's good to see you, Mercy.'

She nodded. 'It's good to see you too, Jack.'

They laughed at that, for they both knew what an understatement it was. Then Jack gave instructions to the porter and offered his arm. 'Welcome to Glasgow, the fairest city in the whole, wide world. I thought we'd take a wee cup of tea at the station buffet before we head to Gourock to catch the ferry.'

It was a Saturday, and though it was only March the sun was shining a combination which meant Glasgow's Central Station was packed with excited day-trippers, mostly women and their bairns getting a head start, the working men to join them later. Jack kept a careful hold of Mercy, who was wide-eyed and, as ever, completely unaware of the effect she was having on people. Heads were turning to gawk at her, and no wonder, for she was looking particularly beautiful. Or maybe he'd just forgotten in the last few weeks quite how lovely she was.

As if he had! One of the things that had bothered him had been his inability to forget about her, no matter how busy he'd been. It wasn't that he ever lost his concentration when it mattered, but his mind had a tendency to drift when it wasn't fully occupied—during the most tedious parts of his many board meetings, or when one of his draftsmen was having to explain a particular feature for the second or third time for the sake of someone less quick on the uptake. Then he'd find himself wondering what Mercy was doing, and if she was thinking of him.

They joined the throng on the Gourock train and, though he found them a seat in First Class, the carriage was packed. Mercy gazed out of the window, entranced, bombarding him with questions, asking where was his townhouse from here, where was the tenement he had grown up in, where were his yards. As they roared out of the station and over the Clyde, where the throng of boats further down river on the Broomilaw could be seen, he tried his best to answer her.

This wasn't a fling that they were having. A passion was what she'd called it, and in the crowded carriage he was aware of her sitting closely beside him, of the body he could picture all too clearly beneath the blue suit she had on. He'd never in his life lost himself in a woman's body they way he'd lost himself in Mercy. Fling, passion, whatever they called it, they were both determined it was temporary. If so, then the coming few days would surely quench their thirst? He tried to believe it but could not, and that worried him. Did she feel the same? If so, where would it leave them at the end of this trip?

As ever, when he asked himself any questions about Mercy, he had no idea of the answer. When she interrupted his thoughts, asking him what town they were approaching, he was happy to be distracting, pointing out the imposing and impressive Paisley Cathedral. It was strange, making this familiar journey again after so long and seeing his life marked out by their progress as the train left Paisley behind and the tracks skirted along the banks of the iver Clyde heading for the port. Answering Mercy's eager questions brought up so many memories of his youth and his apprenticeship that he'd long forgotten.

The main channel of the river was narrow, and chock-a-block as usual with cargo ships and passenger steamers, puffers loaded with coal and a few old-fashioned clippers under sail. Across the water, the huge granite plug of Dumbarton rock and the castle dwarfed the ever-growing spread of the whisky bonds. As they neared the port and the sprawl of the shipyards, he could have sworn he could hear the clatter and clang, the cacophony of noise that rang in your ears long after the whistle had blown and the yards emptied for the day.

When the train pulled into Gourock and Mercy and him joined the crowd streaming out onto the platform, he was assailed by different memories of his much younger self. The steamers were tied up, their funnels already puffing, in a line along the long quay, the wooden gangplanks tied and ready with the gold-painted signs showing their destinations: Rothesay and Brodick, Largs, Lochgoilhead, Dunoon.

'So many people,' Mercy said, clinging to his arm.

'This is nothing. During the fair, it's standing room only on deck,' Jack said, commandeering a porter for their bags and pointing at the *PS Dunoon Castle*. 'I remember when I was wee, we had to run for it, my ma and her friend Cathy, me and Cathy's three, and all of us carrying baskets and boxes tied up with string, for we'd not a trunk or even a travelling bag between us.'

'Did you stay in a hotel?'

He laughed. 'We boarded in one of those huge houses on the sea front—you'll see what I mean when we get there. A couple of genteel sisters down on their luck—I remember thinking them ancient, though they couldn't have been more than forty—who took in summer lodgers. They fed us breakfast and dinner.' He shuddered theatrically. 'They could cook none! Mind and hang on now,' he said to Mercy, for they had reached the gangplank. 'These things shift about a bit and it's a long drop.'

The wind was getting up as they reached the deck, but the sun was shining and the sky was unusually blue. 'There's a passenger lounge,' Jack said.

'Oh no, I don't want to miss anything, let's stay outside.'

'You'll be freezing.'

But she shook her head, so he found a place on the starboard side where they'd get the best view of their destination, and stood behind her to give her what little shelter he could. They rounded the point at Gourock and the wind hit them full on. Mercy shivered, but when he suggested they go below she shook her head vehemently. A cloud scudded over the sun, and then another, darkening the sky and all but clearing the decks. Jack unbuttoned his coat and wrapped it around her. She leaned back against him with a sigh.

'On the train from Edinburgh this morning, I worried you might have changed your mind,' she said.

He had to bend in to hear her, for she was still facing out to the water. Her cheek was icy cold. 'I was counting the hours.'

Mercy laughed, turning to face him. 'You'll be counting the hours from now until you are reunited with your precious engines.'

'Right now, I couldn't care less about my precious engines.'

Her smile faltered. 'Jack…'

'Right now, and until we board the steamer back again, is what I meant. All we've got is these few days.'

She reached up to touch his cheek. She nodded. 'Then let's make the most of it,' she said.

She kissed him. She tasted of salt. Her lips were icy. The deck was not actually deserted. But he put his arms around her regardless and kissed her back.

The sail on the steamer was every bit as exciting and revealing as the train journey had been for Mercy. She bombarded Jack with questions and, seeing the way his face softened when he answered, listening to his self-effacing tales, she gained a new insight into just how far he had come and what drove him.

He must have been tough to thrive in such a world as he described. He must have had to use his brawn as well as his considerable brain. He had joked about using his fists on George but until now she hadn't understood the restraint a man like Jack would have had to exercise not to lash out. And what he called his Glasgow stare wasn't so much about the menace in his direct gaze, but his unquestionable ability to put it into practice if required. That was what made it so effective. He never had, as far as she knew. It was testament to the man standing behind her that he didn't have to.

The steamer rounded the dog leg of Gourock, that

Jack informed her was the tail of the bank, into the widening firth of Clyde, and again a different man answered her question. In his tone now was the excitement of a child on holiday pointing out each landmark and bringing the journey to life for her. The village of Kilcreggan which straggled along the shoreline gave way to the long, narrow stretch of Loch Long and, looming above them, the majesty of the mountains at Arrochar marked the start of the Highlands.

'What beautiful scenery,' Mercy said, enchanted.

'And only twenty-five miles from Glasgow,' Jack replied.

The piers which peppered the peninsula jutted out at regular intervals, from Blairmore to Strone and Kilmun, where a pretty church rose up on the banks of the Holy Loch. At Sandbank there were two boat yards and a dock for shipping the gunpowder which was milled nearby.

The steamer turned parallel to the shore and they made their first stop at Hunters Quay, stopping only briefly, with barely time for the few passengers who were leaving to run down the gangplank before it was pulled away and they set off again. 'This next stop is Kirn,' Jack told her. 'That's when I knew to get back up on deck from the engine room and get ready to disembark, else Ma would send someone down to find me.'

The paddle steamer approached Dunoon pier at a terrifying rate, and Mercy was convinced they would ram straight into the wooden jetty. But at the last minute the captain pulled the *Dunoon Castle* parallel, put the engines into reverse and berthed.

The castle after which the steamer was named stood

directly opposite the pier, a disappointing ruin consisting of a grassy hill with crumbling ramparts on the top. The town itself looked slightly bedraggled in the drizzle that had come on as they berthed. The wide promenade and the crescent beach of pebbles and dark sand was quiet, as the boarding houses that lined it were shuttered because it was low season for anything other than day trippers.

'That's the West Bay,' Jack said. 'And that house there was where we stayed when I was wee. It looks as if it's seen better days.'

'Where will we be staying?'

'I've rented a cottage a bit out of town and hired a gig to take us out and about. That looks like it over there. Let me sort our luggage out.'

Mercy waited, watching the other passengers heading mostly in the direction of the beach to the left, though some were making for the town on the right where a street filled with shops and cafés ran parallel to the shore. The slats of the wooden pier were barnacle-encrusted and slippery, smelling ripely of seaweed and brine.

Mercy was nervous again, her mind dwelling on the practicalities of sharing a cottage with Jack. Was coming here a mistake? It occurred to her for the first time that she might be setting herself up for heartache at the end of it. She wasn't in love with him, but whatever she did feel for him was showing no sign of abating. It would be a wrench.

'I thought we agreed to live for the moment,' Jack said, startling her.

'How did you know what I was thinking?'

'Your face was a picture. Are you having second thoughts?'

'My face is not usually a picture, as you put it. I must be out of practice.'

'Is that not a good thing?'

Mercy smiled reluctantly. 'Not if I ever need to lie to you.'

'Then don't ever try. You haven't answered my question.'

'I'm not having second thoughts. I was only wondering about practicalities—dinner, for example.'

'There are no servants. I've arranged for fresh supplies to be delivered every morning. I didn't think we'd want to have to go to the bother of explaining ourselves. Did I do wrong?'

'No, you did perfectly right. I don't want to have to pretend to be Mrs Dalmuir. Or anyone's wife,' Mercy added hurriedly. 'Shall we go? It looks like the rain is settling in, and I'd rather not arrive soaked through.'

'I warned you about the weather.' Jack helped her up and climbed in beside her. 'We don't call this the *Wet* coast of Scotland for nothing.'

'I think you just invented that.'

'I might have done.' To her relief, he smiled. 'I know it will be a bit strange, just the two of us, but I thought if it turned out that you were a crabbit besom in the mornings then I'd be glad to see the back of you by the end of the week.'

Mercy burst out laughing. 'Let me try to translate... If I happen to be a bad-tempered harpy in the mornings, you'll be looking forward to waving me goodbye at the end of our holiday?'

'I'm impressed.'

'So, I better cook you perfect scrambled eggs, beam at you across the breakfast cups and regale you with snippets of poetry while you eat?'

'That would be a sure-fire recipe for having me head for the hills first thing. And there are plenty of those round here.'

'You prefer me to be a "crabbit besom"?'

Jack turned to smile at her. 'Do you know, I'm oddly tempted to see you try. I certainly don't expect you to be cooking me eggs of any description, though. I'm used to fending for myself.'

'Don't you trust my cooking?'

'Can you cook? It's odd that I don't even know that.'

'Not really, apart from rustling up a simple breakfast for myself. I confess, I've been relying on Lucy's mother to cook my dinners and leave them for me to heat up. What about you, can you cook?'

'I've a limited repertoire.'

'What a lot we don't know about each other.'

'And what a lot we do.'

His smile—that particular smile—had the same effect it always had on her. She leaned into him, smiling back, and felt the sharp intake of his breath. She barely noticed that he let the reins fall, caring only that his arms went around him and that they kissed, and all she could think of was that it was this she had missed so much, this that she wanted, this that had brought her five hundred miles north. It was the taste of him, the way his mouth clung to hers, the way he knew exactly when to deepen the kiss and the touch of his tongue, and the scent of him, and the tickle of his beard and, the smoothness of his cheek, and the clamour he set up inside her.

The pony put an end to it. Having had enough of the sodden grass at the verge of the road, he set off, jerking the gig forward. Jack swore, grabbing at the reins and laughing. Mercy grabbed at the door.

Their cottage had once been the gatehouse of a large estate. The main house at the end of the long, overgrown carriageway was a burnt-out shell, and the grounds had been left to nature to take its course, but the gatehouse was kept habitable by the family and used during the summer as a holiday home. It was a charming building, with a small dining room facing out to a sandy bay with a small stone pier.

'That's Cumbrae,' Jack said, pointing to a wedge-shaped island in the distance. 'And behind it is the seaside town of Largs on the Ayrshire coast. Over there, the craggy big island is Arran, and beside it, that's the Isle of Bute.'

'Where your ma liked to holiday?'

'It is indeed. On a clearer day than today, if you look due south you can see Ailsa Craig, which is a granite outcrop that rears out of the sea and looks like a loaf of bread. It's uninhabited, apart from thousands of seabirds. If the weather's kind to us, we'll get some lovely sunsets, but I wouldn't count on it. This area has the reputation of being one of the wettest places in Scotland.'

The parlour faced into the grounds, overlooking what once must have been a park but was now an overgrown field. They had no neighbours, the nearest village being two miles away. Food appeared at the front door every morning, and Mercy joked it must have been delivered by fairies, for she never saw it arriving.

In tune with the food, the week was magical, even if the weather was not. When the rain lifted, they walked through the grounds of the house, discovering the ruins of an ancient castle, a walled garden and a water garden cut into the hills that rose up behind the house. Three small ponds had been cut into the hill, connected by arched bridges that reminded Mercy of the willow pattern on the tea set she had bought when she'd taken the Chelsea house. Silver lichen grew on the camellias that were coming into creamy-white bloom. Reeds grew tall at the sides of the ponds. Sitting together, perched on the edge of one of the bridges, they watched huge silver fish darting through the feathery green algae.

They kissed on the bridges. They kissed in the grotto they'd discovered, a small cave decorated with thousands of shells. They kissed in the walled garden, where the cherry trees were budding, and in the ruined succession house where a gnarled vine had spread its tendrils through the wrought iron, breaking almost every pane of glass. With no one to see them but the birds and the roe deer that had taken over the park, and who watched them from the overgrown rhododendrons which had once formed a border along the carriageway, Mercy and Jack wandered hand in hand, borrowed galoshes on their feet and borrowed gaberdines over their clothes to protect them from the almost perpetual rain. When it wasn't raining, it was almost certainly about to.

In the cottage, they made love in every room. They made frantic love, passionate love and slow love. They made love in the morning then watched the sun rise in the eastern sky across the water. No matter how dull the day, it found a way to peek through the clouds, spreading golden rays out over the dark grey water.

In the evenings, when the sky always cleared and the waters always calmed, the sun sank invisibly in the west and they watched from the bay as the reflections filled the sky with pink and gold, the light tracking at speed over the hills across the water from Gourock down to Inverkip, Wemyss Bay, Largs and south over Cumbrae, Aran and Bute. They ate dinner in the little dining room, looking out to the dark waters and the sky, which every now and then was filled with stars. And then they made love again.

They slept in the same bed, a novelty for both of them, they discovered. Mercy tried not to count the days, but every morning when she woke with Jack's arm loosely round her waist, his breath soft on her bare back, she could feel it creeping towards her. Their inevitable parting of the ways.

They were due to sail back to Gourock on the Saturday. On Friday, Jack took Mercy a trip down memory lane, as he called it. She had assumed it would be a tour of the town and the haunts he remembered as a child. In fact it was a tour of the piers from Toward, the nearest to their cottage, all the way round the peninsula to Ardentinny, where they ate a picnic of bread, cheese, smoked venison and poached salmon on the beautiful sandy beach. The sun wasn't shining, but it wasn't raining, and the wind was a gentle breeze which counted, Jack assured her, as a perfect spring day. So they sat on the beach for a while longer, with a blanket wrapped around them, and pretended that this wasn't their last outing.

The return journey was silent. Back at the gatehouse, they watched the sunset from the dining room window. It was a poor effort, for the rain had set in again, and the clouds remained stubbornly gathered, depriving them of the show. As darkness fell, they retired to the little parlour at the back of the house.

Their kisses started gently, but soon they became desperate, their lips clinging, stopping only for breath and then kissing again, storing up kisses for the time soon, far too soon, when there would be no more. They made love slowly, tenderly, knowing each other so well now that they could eke out every stage of it, take each other to the brink and then draw back. And, when they finally toppled over the abyss together, Mercy found tears streaming down her face. She wiped them away, not wanting Jack to notice. If he did, he said nothing. At daybreak they made love again, frantically this time. Then they bathed, dressed and took breakfast in silence.

Mercy fastened her cloak and pulled on her gloves. She felt sick. Why had they agreed to part? The logic of it eluded her. It felt wrong. In the hallway, the gaberdines they had borrowed hung side by side, the galoshes positioned underneath. In the scullery, the dishes had been washed and put away. In the bedroom, the sheets had been stripped from the bed and placed in the hamper which the unknown servants would take to launder, the quilts folded and placed in the cupboard. In the parlour, Jack stood at the window, gazing morosely out at the parkland.

'It's raining,' he said. 'We'll wait until it passes, or you'll get soaked.'

'The steamer...'

'We can get the next one.' He turned away from the window. 'On second thoughts, better not wait. The weather might deteriorate.'

'Shall we go—grasp the nettle, so to speak?'

He nodded, but made no move. 'I don't get it. There's nothing sensible about my wanting to prolong this—this whatever it is we have together. The one thing I know, it's not is a fling. If this was a fling, I'd have no problem at all with it ending. It doesn't matter what it's called. What matters is... Like I said, I don't get it, Mercy.'

She could see what it cost him to speak from the way he clenched his jaw and from the coldness in his tone. 'We agreed that...'

'I know what we agreed, and I know why we agreed it, and nothing's changed. I'm not suggesting that we—I'm not suggesting that it changes anything. All I'm saying is that this is a bloody sight harder than it should be.'

'I know.' Seeing Jack struggle gave her the strength she needed to quell her own desperate desire to beg for a reprieve. She couldn't bear to see him suffer. 'But we can't risk making it even more painful for ourselves.'

'Because we've no future together, have we?' he asked roughly.

'You know that we don't, as well as I do. Your business...'

'Aye, my business. Do you know, right at this moment I don't give a flying f—' He broke off, shaking his head furiously. 'But I know that's not true. I care just as passionately as I have ever done. Anyway, it's not just about me. The livelihoods of hundreds of my employees and their families depend on me.'

'Let's say, just for the sake of argument, that we continued with our affair—and that is how the world would describe it—what then?'

'What do you mean?'

'How long for? A few more weeks? Or months? Or until you decided it was time to settle down with your helpmeet?'

'I don't know. I haven't thought. Are you telling me that you're finding this easy?'

'No, but I'm trying not to make it any harder than it needs to be for either of us.'

'What if we never got sick of each other?'

'Don't be ridiculous.'

'But what if we didn't and I eventually asked you to marry me? Well,' Jack said, as she instinctively recoiled, 'I already know the answer to that one but that just confirms it.'

'You can't possibly have been serious.'

He stared at her for along moment, then shrugged. 'No, you're right, I can't. I'm not ready to settle down yet. I've a business to look after, and once I've made my name with this London contract the world truly will be my oyster.'

'If you're intent on conquering the world, perhaps you'll never be ready to settle down.'

'Maybe not. Look, forget I spoke. I'm not thinking straight. You're right about not drawing this out any longer than necessary. If we hurry up, we'll still be in time for the steamer.'

* * *

Jack was furious with himself as he loaded their luggage onto the gig and closed up the gatehouse. What the hell had that pointless and embarrassing outburst been about? And what had it achieved, save to make things awkward between them and put Mercy on her guard?

'Marriage, for the love of—' He broke off, cursing under his breath. Just when he was starting to smell real success! Bloody fool thing to suggest, even hypothetically. He was finding it difficult because everything this week had been perfect, and it had been perfect because they were hiding away from the real world. Time to get back to reality. He'd realise soon enough what a fool he'd almost made of himself. But before that he needed to put things straight with Mercy.

'I'm sorry,' he said gruffly after he helped her up into the gig and sat down beside her. 'Can you forget everything I said in the last half hour? I didn't mean any of it.'

'We have had a blissful time, but harsh reality awaits us the minute we leave here,' Mercy said, unconsciously reflecting his own thoughts.

'Exactly.' He leaned over to kiss her gently, felt her hand flutter against his cheek and then forced himself to end it and took up the reins.

The rain turned to mizzle as they reached Dunoon, and by the time they were turning down towards the pier the sun was weakly shining. The *Duchess of Argyle* had just docked and was disgorging a fresh horde of passengers. Jack brought the gig to a halt just before the pier and waved at a lad hanging about waiting for an errand.

'You can look after this until Black's turn up to collect it,' he said, throwing the boy a shilling. 'And get a porter for me, will you?'

Mercy had climbed down. She was staring at the steamer, not knowing Jack was watching her, a look of anguish on her lovely face that wrenched at his gut. But when she turned back to him it was gone, and she was smiling bravely. He recalled that first time they'd met, admiring how stoic she'd been about what she'd been through, admiring the way she'd refused to feel sorry for herself. Seeing her do it again felt like a door slamming in his face. He couldn't bear to watch her struggling to sustain the performance for the rest of the journey.

'I'll see you onto the boat,' Jack said. 'But I've decided I'm not coming with you. I'll get the next one. It's better all round.'

She flinched but she didn't argue. He walked up the gangplank with her. The steamer was quiet for the return journey to Gourock, but what passengers there were stayed on deck to wave and watch the departure. The ship's funnel blasted. Mercy clung to his hand, lifting it to her lips, pressing a kiss onto the back of his glove. The funnel blasted twice more. 'Goodbye, Jack,' she said, giving him a shove. 'Be happy.'

His feet felt as if they were glued to the deck. Leaden when he picked them up. They had already untied the gangplank. He leapt across the gap, getting a frightening glimpse of the grey sea churned up by the paddle. The *Duchess of Argyle* gave one more blast then the rest of the ropes were untied and thrown onto her decks.

Mercy was clinging to the rail, her eyes trained on

him. He stood rooted to the spot, then the steamer took off. Mercy lifted her hand to wave. He watched her as she became smaller and smaller, and when he could no longer make her out, he watched until the steamer was out of sight, and the waves from her wake had rippled into shore, and the *boom, boom* echo of her paddles had grown silent. And then he turned, forgetting all thoughts of boarding the next steamer, which was already coming into sight, and walked slowly away.

Chapter Twelve

Killellan Manor, Hampshire, April 1864

'I brought you some tea. Is she finished feeding? Let me take her.'

'Thank you,' Prue said. 'I don't know what I'd have done without you.'

If she had not been a widow, Mercy thought, setting the tray down on the bedside table, Prue would have been forced to rely on someone else, for Harry would never have permitted her to spend so much time away from his side.

She took her little niece carefully from her mamma, smiling tenderly down at her. The baby had arrived suddenly and traumatically almost a month before she was expected, but three weeks after her birth the wrinkles at her neck, tiny wrists and ankles were starting to fill out and she was thriving. The same could not be said for her mother, who was still so poorly that she had not yet left her confinement bed, but her reliance on Mercy had brought the sisters closer than they had ever been.

Sharing the tears and fears, the stresses and strains of the past few weeks, had made the barrier that Mercy's marriage had placed between them a distant memory.

The baby was already sleeping. Mercy kissed her velvet-soft cheek then laid her down in the cradle. 'I'm just glad that I was able to help, and I'm delighted to be able to spend so much time with this darling little one. I'm making the most of it, for she won't want her auntie when she has her mamma to cosset her and look after her.'

'You're wonderful with her. So much more confident than me.' Prue dabbed at her eyes. 'Sorry. I have become a complete watering pot. I don't know what's wrong with me.'

'It's the baby.' Mercy drew up a chair, poured her sister a cup of tea and put a slice of bread and butter on her plate. 'It is quite common and perfectly natural. I learned that at the Lying-In hospital.'

'I hope so. Poor Dominic, I cry almost every time I see him, and he thinks it's his fault.'

'Well, it is, in a way.'

Prue chuckled. Then sniffed, dabbing at her eyes. 'Oh, dear. I'm so sorry. Seeing you with Verity...'

'Oh! You've chosen a name at last.'

'We decided this morning. I wasn't so sure, for I've always thought our names a little ridiculous, but it was because they lost poor little Verity that our parents adopted me. And Dominic thinks it's a lovely name. Mind you, Dominic thinks Prudence is a lovely name.'

'It is, compared to Mercy, and Mercy is a lovely name compared to...'

'Clement! I know. Poor Clement, the only thing worse would be if he had chosen to be known as Clem.'

'Good grief, do you know I've never even thought of that?'

'He picked Verity up yesterday for the first time when he visited. She was in her cradle and he was studying her, you know that way he does?'

'As if she was about to explode,' Mercy said, giggling.

'Exactly! I thought he might drop her, but he picked her up properly, supporting her head and everything. Unfortunately, she was wet, and made a damp patch on his coat. He asked me when they become trained, as if my baby was a puppy, and you should have seen his face when I told him it would be a year or two. He looked utterly appalled, and started muttering about civilisation not having developed very far in two thousand years.'

'I expect those clever Ancient Greeks he so admires managed to get their children out of napkins when they were two weeks old.'

Prue chuckled. 'That's exactly what I said, and do you know what he answered?'

'That he'd investigate the matter?'

'Precisely! But his questions made me wonder, do you think he is contemplating marriage? I know matters had cooled between him and your friend Sarah, but he let slip that he had been for a drive with her the other day.'

'Did he? He hasn't said a word to me. And Sarah...' Mercy frowned, remembering their last conversation. She had been so sure that Sarah's confession of being in love would lead her to the altar. 'Actually, I haven't seen Sarah myself for a while. She is at her country house, where her cousins are staying. Some family emergency. I have been very lax in writing.' Mercy topped up their tea and placed a second slice of bread and butter on Prue's plate. 'Eat.'

'Yes, Nurse.'

Verity grunted. The sisters both visibly held their breaths until the baby sighed and went back to sleep. 'For someone so tiny, she makes a lot of noise,' Prue said. 'I lie awake listening to her breathing.'

'No wonder you're so tired. I can take her cradle into my room tonight, if you like, so that you can get some proper rest.'

'No, you've done more than enough. Besides, she's my daughter. If she's going to keep anyone awake, it ought to be me. Not that I mean to be ungrateful, or imply that an aunt is any less important than…'

'Prue, be silent.'

'It's just that you're so natural with her, so much more confident than I am. I can't help think that you would have made a—' Prue broke off, covering her mouth with her hand. 'I am *so* sorry.'

'Here.' Mercy handed her a fresh handkerchief and took her tea cup and plate away.

'I'm really, really sorry.'

'Don't be.' Mercy took her sister's hand, rubbing it against her cheek. 'I'm more confident because I made sure to have some practice with other people's babies at the Lying-In hospital, I told you that. And it's easier for me too because—because Verity is my niece, not my daughter.' Tears rose in her eyes, and her sister's cheeks were wet but, now the subject had finally been broached, she wanted to clear the air.

'I can't have a daughter of my own, and that's my tragedy, but that doesn't make me wish everyone else was barren—especially not my sister, who I love very much. Even more than I love my niece.'

Prue burst into tears. 'Oh, dear, I am so, so sorry. I promise these are happy tears,' she said, laughing and sobbing. 'You've changed so much—I mean for the better. Not that you weren't—I mean before—but since, you know, since you were widowed? What I mean is you are so much more yourself! And it's such a relief to see you happy. If you *are* really happy, because you are very good at hiding your feelings. And I can't help but wonder, because sometimes when you think I'm asleep I see you holding Verity and looking so sad.'

'Oh! It's not Verity who makes me sad,' Mercy said, taken aback by this. 'I mean, I'm not sad.'

Prue dried her eyes and poured herself another cup of tea. She sipped it slowly, saying nothing, but making Mercy deeply uncomfortable with the way she was scrutinising her. Her sister had worn a veil over her face for many years in order to hide her facial scars from the world, but it had allowed her to study people at length unobserved, a habit she maintained.

'You're very good at it,' Prue said finally. 'But not so good as you once were. Pretending, I mean,' she said. 'If it's not Verity, then what is it?'

Mercy bit back the denial that rose automatically to her lips. She had given up Jack, but she must not give up on what she had learned from her time with him. 'I am not sure I wish to discuss it. There's not much to discuss. There was—there was a man in my life. For a short time. Now it's over. As I said, there's nothing left to discuss.'

'Jack Dalmuir? Clement told me.'

'What exactly did Clement tell you?'

'Don't be so prickly. His name, and not much more, but like everyone else I saw the articles in the *Morning Post*, Mercy.'

'Why didn't you mention it?'

'I've been waiting on you to bring the subject up, but you never have. I wish I'd been at the ball at Cavendish Square. I'd have loved to have seen your "pugnacious polka". I don't know what that awful Armstrong said to you to make you do it, or if you planned it or acted on impulse but, however it came about, it was perfect. His first ball as Lord Armstrong, and the ball which *you* made your own, and you own it still.' Prue chuckled. 'I *wish* I could have been there.'

'I haven't really thought of it in that light before. I didn't plan it to turn out that way, but I'm glad it did. I have washed my hands of all of them now.'

'I'm proud of you, Mercy. That must have taken a great deal of courage.'

'I was terrified, but once I was there I was so angry, and then I saw them all for what they were, and I was angry at myself for letting them matter. As I said, it's over now.'

'So this Jack Dalmuir, was he merely your—I don't know—partner in crime?'

'How odd you should use that expression. That's how it started.'

Prue gave her hand a squeeze. 'So he was more than that?'

'Yes. Much more.'

'Are you in love with him, Mercy?'

'I'm not interested in marrying again.'

'That's not what I asked you. Do you love him?'

'No. I don't think so. I can't let myself. There's no point.' A tear escaped her. She scrubbed it away. 'I'm never getting married, and Jack needs a good, practical wife.'

Prue burst out laughing. 'You are both good and practical, but neither are solid grounds for marriage. Marriage is the biggest upheaval, the most difficult, testing, trying… It is frankly hard work. And if you don't love each other then it is doomed. Oh, dear heavens.' She put her hand over her mouth, looking utterly appalled. 'I will not blame poor Verity for my complete lack of tact. I am so very sorry.'

'Don't be. You're tired, and you have been through a very difficult birth.'

'That doesn't excuse…'

'It does.' Mercy got to her feet and picked up the tray. 'Dominic will be back on the evening train, and if you want to persuade him that you are capable of getting out of bed for a few hours tomorrow then you should follow Verity's lead and get some sleep.'

'I'm truly sorry, Mercy.'

'Don't be.' She stopped at the bedroom door. 'I thought a child would make everything right. I see now that it would quite possibly have made things a great deal worse. Harry and I—the marriage *was* doomed. Get some rest, Prue. I'll see you later.'

* * *

Mercy handed the tea tray over to Mrs McNair, Prue's housekeeper, and decided to take a walk in the gardens. The sun had come out. Since her marriage, Prue had installed several more of her distinctive water features at Hawthorn Manor, though none were as elaborate as her original design in the fernery. They reminded Mercy painfully of Jack, and so she made instead for the walled garden that Dominic had transformed to emulate his farm holding in Greece. At this time of the year, all his tender crops required the heat of the glass houses, though the ground had been dug over in readiness for them, and his precious herd of goats that wintered here transferred to the meadow at the front of the house.

The conversation with Prue had made Mercy feel queasy, or perhaps it was the tea. Had the milk been off? Prue hadn't seemed to notice, but yesterday her sister had eaten a whole portion of cod in parsley sauce before she remembered that she loathed both. She was much better today, though. Able to sustain an entire conversation without once losing track of her thoughts, unfortunately. At least she hadn't lied to Prue and, though it was painful, she had tried to be honest about Jack—as far as it was possible for her to be honest about Jack.

Frank, Dominic's large ginger cat, came trotting towards her, his ringed tail standing straight up, and brushed himself against her crinoline before heading over to his favourite bench that sat against one of the glasshouses. Mercy followed him, and when she sat down the cat leapt onto her lap, kneading her skirts and circling before making himself comfortable. Mercy scratched his forehead and Frank began to purr, a strange throaty, rasping noise peculiarly his own.

Lifting her face to the sun, she closed her eyes. It was three weeks and four days since she had left him on the pier at Dunoon. Arriving in Glasgow that evening, on impulse she had decided to stay for a few days, to explore the city and the surrounding area. When she had arrived home, a three-day-old telegram from Dominic requesting her urgent presence at Hawthorn Manor had been waiting for her at Chelsea, and she had not returned to London since. She had made no attempt to contact Jack, and he had not tried to contact her. She knew him well enough not to imagine he couldn't have tracked her down if he'd wanted to. He had not tried, which had spared her having to rebuff him. They had agreed to part, they had parted and they had remained apart, which meant, surely, that the decision had been the right one? Even if it didn't feel right.

Sighing, for she was heartily sick of going over this same ground again and again, Mercy stirred and Frank leapt to the ground, giving her an offended look before prancing off. She began to wander aimlessly along the paths that separated the garden into neat squares. She wasn't in love with Jack, but she missed him terribly. There were times when she missed him so much, she tried desperately to persuade herself that there was some way for them to resume their affair. She longed to make love to him again. If it was only that... But it wasn't only that. She missed Jack. She was lonely without him. She was far from unhappy, but there were times when his absence made her miserable, and it was those times that made her determined never to see him again.

Her independence had been too hard won for her to surrender it. She would rely on no one else for her happiness except herself. And one day, when Jack was a distant memory, she would be truly happy. In the meantime, she had a sister who needed her, a new niece to dote over and a future that remained obstinately difficult to define.

Four weeks later, Prue was completely restored to health and, though she and Dominic begged Mercy to stay on, it was obvious that they wanted to spend some time alone with Verity. And who could blame them? She was leaving the next day, returning to Chelsea, and after dinner she retired to her bed chamber to complete her packing when Prue appeared.

'I brought you this,' she said, handing her a twist of paper tied with a ribbon. 'It's a lock of Verity's hair. Not much, since she barely has any yet, but I thought you might wish to put it in Mamma's locket.'

'Thank you, Prue.' Mercy gave her sister a hug. 'I shall treasure this.'

'You've been wonderful. I shall miss you.'

'Chelsea isn't the other end of the world.'

'No.'

Mercy finished folding a blouse and placed it in her trunk. Her sister was frowning down at her hands, biting her lips. 'What is it? You've obviously got something on your mind.'

'I've been trying to decide whether to speak to you

about it or not. I could be completely wrong. I hope you won't be offended if I am.'

'Prue? It's not like you to beat about the bush. What on earth is it?'

'You didn't tell anyone that you were taking a holiday in Scotland.'

'No. It was a spur-of-the moment idea. I told you that.'

'If Verity hadn't arrived early, we may never have known you were away.'

'I made no secret of it, when you asked me.'

'No, but you didn't tell me you were going. Were you with Mr Dalmuir in Scotland?'

Mercy stiffened. 'If I was...'

'It is none of my business, I know.' Prue plucked another blouse from the pile and deftly folded it. 'Dominic and I did not wait until we were married to make love together. I'm not telling you this to shock you...'

'You have, all the same.'

'Really? Oh, well, never mind that. What I'm saying is, that I know what it's like, to be overcome with... When you are in love, it is perfectly natural to want to make love.'

'I'm not in love with Jack.'

'Oh. I see. Actually, that wasn't what I was asking.'

Her sister was looking deeply uncomfortable. 'Good grief,' Mercy said, astonished. 'Are you asking me if Jack and I were lovers?'

'Were you?'

'Yes, briefly, if you must know. It's over now, so if you're imagining that I might wish to *marry* him—' Mercy broke off in astonishment as Prue winced. 'Have you gone mad? After the experience I had, you cannot possibly think that I would want to get married again?'

'It's not that. Mercy, I'm worried that you may have to, whether you wish to or not. I'm concerned there may be unintended consequences,' Prue added, as Mercy stared at her blankly.

'Consequences?'

Prue pointed at Verity. 'That kind of consequence.'

'A baby? You think I might be expecting a baby? I think maybe that real little baby over there has affected your judgement. I can't have children, Prue, remember?'

'You don't know that for certain. What if you are mistaken? The early signs are all there. You said that your tea tasted like iron, and three times now you've told me you felt queasy.'

'Once because I had not eaten all day. Once because the milk in my tea had turned.'

'It hadn't.'

'Stop it. Please don't. I am not expecting a child. That I am incapable of bearing a child has been proved conclusively for it was never, I promise you, for want of trying. I thought you understood that.'

'I did. Of course I did,' Prue said, dabbing at her eyes and looking quite wretched. 'And it never occurred to me that the problem may lie with *him*.'

'It didn't ever occur to me either.' Could it be true, though? Mercy dropped onto the bed, wrapping her arms around herself.

'That's something else I've noticed about you,' Prue said. 'You do that a lot. You never used to...'

She immediately unfolded her arms. 'Next you will

be telling me that mothers who have just given birth have a sixth sense about such things.'

'Actually, I think that might be true. You look different to me.'

'I look different because—because— Oh, I don't know why. Honestly, Prue, that is the most unscientific thing I have ever heard you say.'

'Let us examine the science, then. When did you last have your monthlies?'

'I don't know!' Mercy exclaimed, completely flustered. 'Since Harry died, there has been no need to take note. In fact, it's been a huge relief not to take note. Besides, I will be thirty-eight next birthday...'

'Oh, yes, ancient.' Prue reached for her hand. 'Dearest Mercy, I am so sorry to have given you such a shock. I could be quite wrong, but I felt I couldn't not mention it.'

'I don't want you to be wrong. I mean, I think you are wrong. But if you are not and I am expecting a child... Oh, my goodness, Prue, what a turn of events that would be!'

'It's a possibility. Only time will tell. Think now, this is important. When was the last time?'

'March? No, perhaps February.'

'And can you recall the date when you first...? Oh, but of course you can, what a foolish question.'

'February,' Mercy replied, blushing.

'So you could be as much as two months late. Have you truly no sense that you might be with child?'

'I can't be.' Mercy laid her free hand flat on her stomach. 'Two months is nothing. One can only really tell after three or four.'

'I knew within days.' Prue smiled tenderly. 'In a completely instinctive way. I simply knew.'

'But I don't feel any different. Do you really think it is possible?'

'I wouldn't have spoken to you otherwise. I almost decided not to, for I had no idea how you would react. I know how much you long for a child, but under the circumstances…and it is early days yet. Perhaps I shouldn't have spoken?'

'No. I'm glad you did. I can't believe it. I'm scared to believe it might possibly be true.'

'Here.' Prue handed her a handkerchief. 'I carry several on me at the moment.'

'Thank you.'

'I don't suppose you have the slightest notion of what you are going to do, if it is true?'

'Do?'

'With regards to Mr Dalmuir?'

'Jack?' Simply saying his name made her feel as if she was standing on the edge of a cliff. 'I can't,' Mercy said.

'Can't what?'

'I don't know. Think. Talk about it. Anything. I can't. Not until I know for sure. It's too much to contemplate.'

'Much too much for the time being. You're quite right.' Prue levered herself up from the bed. 'I could be wrong, but you'll know for certain one way or another in a few weeks. Then will be the time to make some big decisions.'

Life-changing decisions, in every way, if it was true,

and not only for her. Not yet! 'Don't look so guilty. I am glad you spoke up.'

'Are you? You know that you can talk things over with me any time. I'm not going anywhere any time soon. And, whatever you decide, Mercy, you're my sister and I'll stand by you.'

'Thank you.' Mercy got up, giving her sister a hug. 'Right at this moment, I'm feeling a bit exhausted. I've got a long journey in the morning.'

'Of course. I'll see you before you set off.' Prue kissed her cheek. 'I am so sorry…'

'Don't be daft. I mean, silly,' Mercy corrected herself. 'I am glad we had this chat. Now go, and let me finish packing so I can get to bed.'

But, as the door closed softly behind her sister, Mercy sank onto the window seat to gaze out at the darkened garden. Packing and sleep were the furthest thing from her mind. She felt sick at the prospect. She felt giddy. She wanted to jump up and down and shout with glee. She wanted to go to sleep for a month and wake up to find—what? She dared not hope. But if it was true—a child! A child of her own to love and to care for. At last, after all these years!

She must not get her hopes up, though. Prue could be wrong. But until Harry had died she had always been, sadly, as regular as clockwork. How could she have missed such an obvious sign? Because she had not been counting. Because she was convinced that the problem lay with her. Harry had made certain of that. Now there was the distinct possibility that it did not. Wrapping her arms around herself, she closed her eyes, resting her forehead on the cool window pane. A baby. Her own baby. And Jack's.

Her eyes flew open again. Jack! She jumped up from the window seat. She was having Jack's child. Jack didn't want a child. He had been very clear about that. He had a plan. To expand his business. To find a suitable helpmeet. To get married and have a family. In that order. That very logical, very conventional order. If she told him that he was about to be presented with the family first, he would be horrified. She would ruin his life. She couldn't do that to him.

Mercy picked up a skirt and tried to fold it, but her usual skill had deserted her. She dropped it in a heap on the floor and returned to the window. It was quite dark outside, and the first tiny stars were beginning to appear. If she told Jack he was going to be a father, he would almost certainly offer to marry her. If he married her, their child would bear his name, and so would she. They would legally belong to him.

No! No, no, no. Never, ever again. Jack was different, he wasn't Harry, but he was a man, and if she was his wife... No! She had left the past behind. She had left that world behind. She never wanted to return to it. Even if Jack was different. Very, very different. So different, she couldn't imagine him trying to rule over her as Harry had. But if he wanted to, if she was his wife, that was what he could do. And, even if he didn't mean to, circumstances would force him to take over for she'd lose her widow's jointure and she'd be completely reliant on him to put a roof over her head, and to feed and clothe her. And if she wanted to buy even a piece of her favourite crumbly cheese she'd have to ask him for the money, and where would she buy her favourite crumbly cheese if she wasn't living in Chelsea?

'No, this not about cheese!' The hysteria in her voice shocked her out of her panic. If she didn't tell Jack, he wouldn't feel obliged to ask her to marry him. She didn't want him to feel *obliged*. She didn't want him to propose out of a sense of duty. She didn't want him to propose at all! But if she didn't marry her child would have no father. The stigma attached to that didn't bear thinking of. She would go somewhere where no one knew her and say she was a widow, which was true. And Jack would never know...

But that too felt wrong. He had a right to know. If she was expecting a child... *If!*

Nothing was certain. Nothing had to be decided. She had a month, a whole month, to wait and to ponder. And then, when she was certain, *if* it turned out to be true, then she would be obliged to make some difficult choices.

Chapter Thirteen

London, one month later

It was almost three months since Jack had watched Mercy sail off on the *Duchess of Argyle* and, though she'd been constantly on his mind, he hadn't seen her since. Then today, standing on the deck of a steamer heading down river to the pumping station, he'd looked up as they'd passed under Waterloo Bridge and there she was.

His heart had leapt at the sight of her, dressed in her favourite shade of blue, gazing out towards the embankment works, and he'd stopped himself just in time from waving and calling. Seeing her had overset him out of all proportion, for he'd decided, for his own peace of mind, that she had left London.

He got through the day in a daze and left early to return to his rooms. Sitting in front of the empty grate, his dinner untouched, all the memories he'd been working so hard to push to the back of his mind came crowding back. The many different ways she smiled. The way she bit her lip when she was pondering a difficult decision. The stubborn tilt to her chin. The gleam in her eyes when her hackles were up. The way her tongue tripped over itself with questions when she was interested in something, and the way she made no pretence of being interested if she was bored. The way she laughed. The way she made *him* laugh when she used his coarse phrases, making then sound so much more shocking in her own very proper English accent. The uninhibited way she kissed him, and the way she made love with him. The trust she put in him, and the unabashed delight she took in what he did to her and in what she did to him.

And after love-making, the way they lay together, her head tucked under his chin, her body curled into his, their skin damp and clinging. These were the sweetest and most painful memories of their time in Dunoon. They would wake in the night in the gatekeeper's cottage and talk, laughing so hard at something one of them had said, and they'd never remember in the morning what it had been.

Enough! Resolutely, Jack turned to the stack of correspondence that needed addressing but, after an hour staring blankly at an inventory, he gave up, took a tot of whisky and retired to bed. It was worse there, for his thoughts returned to that last morning and refused to be banished. He remembered the rain. The desolate feeling he'd had, with their luggage standing ready to be loaded onto the gig, the hearth swept and cleaned and those two gaberdines they'd been wearing hanging side-by-side on the pegs in the vestibule, spurring

him to make that pathetic, clutching-at-straws proposal
that had nearly ruined it all.

He pulled the pillow over his head and screwed his
eyes tight shut, but the scene played out for him again
regardless. Bloody fool. How many times had he reminded himself since that he'd been a bloody fool?
He was lucky that Mercy had retained some common
sense, even if the horror on her face had been like a
kick in the teeth. It still hurt thinking about it, even
though he agreed with her that his half-hearted proposal had been a terrible idea. He hated being linked
in her head with that man she'd married. He was a very
different man from Harry Armstrong. He and Mercy
would have had a very different kind of marriage. She
ought to know that, at least. He'd have gone out of his
way to make her happy.

And how, precisely, did he think he'd do that? Jack
flung himself upright, throwing his pillow to the
ground, then followed it, pulling on his robe and making for his parlour again. Turning up the gas, he sat
down once again at his desk, pulled a blank sheet of
paper towards him, picked up his pen, dipped it in the
ink pot and drew a firm line down the centre of the
page. It worked a treat when he was trying to make a
tricky business decision, listing all the reasons for, and
those against.

For, he wrote. He missed her. That was hardly a reason. *Against,* he scribbled— then threw his pen down
in despair.

Mercy wasn't a business proposition. She was a
woman who couldn't possibly live up to his memory
of her. Thanks to them having put an end to their time

together before they had grown tired of each other, he had no bad memories of her. He hadn't had time to grow bored, or irritated by one of her habits, and all the fears he'd had about her getting in the way of his business had been unfounded.

Because he'd given her up.

Before he'd been ready.

Jack sighed. It had been a mutual decision, and the fact that Mercy had also stuck to it should be telling him that it had been the right one. The work here in London was going well, and the contract for the other two pumping stations was about to be signed. He was already starting to expand his workforce back in Glasgow. After that was done and the first installation was complete, which it nearly was, he would be free to follow up on a few other prospects, including the one in Germany. Exciting times. He'd be able to give more men much-needed work, and apprentices too. This was no time to be thinking of anything other than what he'd always been happy to spend every waking minute on.

If only he hadn't seen her today. He checked the clock. Yesterday. Wearily, he pulled his correspondence towards him and began methodically to work through it. By the time he rang for his shaving water, he had cleared the lot.

'A telegram for you, Mr Dalmuir,' his man said, setting down the jug of hot water. 'It came just a few moments ago. I hope it's not bad news.'

Mercy checked the clock. It was five minutes later than the last time she had looked, and still at least half an hour before she could reasonably expect Jack to call on her. If he did decide to call. She couldn't be certain he had seen her yesterday on the bridge but if he had, and he'd ignored her, then the chances of him calling were—what? She never had understood gambling odds. This wasn't a game.

She picked up the teapot and started to pour her tea, only to realise that she had already poured it. Tea slopped onto her saucer. Calm was needed. Calm and a clear head. This was going to be one of the most difficult conversations she had ever had. If not *the* most difficult. She had to tell him about the baby. Of *that* she had been certain almost from the beginning, though it was only when she'd seen him yesterday that she had decided she couldn't wait any longer. She had to tell him. He had a right to know. And then?

Mercy picked up her over-full tea cup and took a sip. It rattled against her teeth. The tea was cold. She took another sip and forced herself to take a small bite of her bread and butter.

Knowing Jack, he would do what convention dictated was the right and honourable thing and ask her to marry him. And then she would explain why she would not. Could not. Why it would be wrong for them both.

Yes, that was it. She would remind him why his almost-proposal in Dunoon had been a mistake. And then she would confess her situation. And then she would tell him her plan to take care of the child herself, to move elsewhere, to pose as a widowed mother. It was a sound plan, even if it lacked a great deal of detail, but he needn't worry about the detail. He'd be too relieved to worry. He didn't actually want to marry her. She didn't want him to take her on out of a sense of duty. She didn't want to become his responsibility. She didn't want another husband who wanted her only as the mother of his child. She didn't want Jack to turn into that man. She wanted Jack to remain Jack, in her memory.

The doorbell rang, making her jump, even though she had been expecting it. She hurried to the parlour, and was trying to adjust her rigid smile as Lucy showed her visitor in. Jack! She almost forgot the occasion, almost rushed towards him, her hands out, eager for his embrace.

'Jack. Thank you for coming. I am sorry to have sent such an early telegram, but I wanted to catch you before you left for work. Would you like some tea?'

'No, thank you.' He had taken off his hat and gloves, but he still wore his coat. 'How are you? You look very well.'

'I am, thank you. And you, you look well.'

'As you see.'

He made no attempt to touch her. Mercy waved him to the sofa and took the chair opposite. 'I saw you yesterday. I was on Waterloo Bridge and you went past on a little steamer.'

'I spotted you too.'

'Oh. I thought you had, but then you didn't wave.' She had no idea whether this was a good sign or a bad one. He looked exactly the same. She felt sick— not the mild queasiness that came over her most afternoons now, but the terrified kind, as if she were tied to the rails in front of an oncoming train. This was Jack, Mercy reminded herself, but that only made it worse because, whatever she said and however she broke the news, he was going to be angry, and possibly even hurt. 'My sister Prue had her baby.'

'I saw the announcement in *The Times*. I trust all is well?'

'It wasn't for a while, but it is now. I was in Hampshire, staying at Killellan Manor until last week, helping out. Is your business—?'

'Going well,' he interrupted her curtly. 'The second contract is all but signed.'

'That's wonderful news. You have had no more trouble since…?'

'If that's what you wanted to know, then no. Armstrong has not tried to interfere again.'

'He is probably congratulating himself for having successfully achieved his objective.'

'Mercy, I couldn't give a damn what he's thinking or doing. He can give himself all the credit he likes for putting an end to our liaison. He may have pre-empted it, but we knew from the first that it would end, one way or another.'

Liaison? The word the papers had used, she remembered. She didn't like the sordid overtones. What did it matter, now that it was over? 'Yes,' Mercy said. 'I know that. We never intended anything—we always knew it would be temporary, and I for one don't regret it.'

Her tone was slightly too defiant. Jack frowned. 'You didn't have to ask me here to tell me that.'

'No, but I wanted you to understand that I have no regrets.'

'Nor do I.'

'Are you sure?'

He coloured, crossing his ankles, then uncrossing them. 'If you are referring to my foolish suggestion that we consider marriage…'

'You didn't mean it. You said you were not ready to settle down, that you have a business to look after.'

'And, once I've made my name with this London contract, the world will truly be my oyster. I know what I said, Mercy, and the fact remains that my business is at a critical juncture. I don't know what I was thinking even suggesting marriage.' He got to his feet, unbuttoned his coat and then sat back down again. 'I suppose I was simply looking for an excuse to extend our...'

'Liaison.'

He winced. 'Whatever. I spoke without thinking, in the heat of the moment. Even if I had been serious, your expression was enough to inform me of how repugnant you found the idea.'

'Of marriage,' she said. 'Of giving up my freedom. I don't find you in the least repugnant. Quite the opposite. I thought I'd demonstrated that very clearly. Many times.' An image of herself sprawled naked beneath him, crying out in utter abandon, flashed into her head. She glanced over at him and their gazes held for just long enough to make her certain his mind had gone down the same path. Mortified, she looked away.

'The point you are so eloquently making,' Jack said dryly, 'is that we neither of us wish to marry. I think we have established that fact beyond reasonable doubt.'

'Yes.' She nodded several times. 'Never, in my case. But at some point in the future, when your business has no more room to expand, you will settle down with your helpmeet.'

'For heaven's sake, Mercy, I wish you would stop throwing that word back in my face! You make me sound like a...'

'Pompous arse?'

'Aye.' He smiled reluctantly. 'Something like that.'

'You're not. You're a good man, and I am so glad to have met you.' She stopped, for now tears were clogging her throat that she dared not let fall. Calm, she reminded herself. She must remain calm. But what she wanted to do was run. Or find a way to jump back in time for just an hour, to be able to throw herself into his arms and lose herself in his kisses and forget.

But there was no going back, and she had known since yesterday that this conversation had to be endured if she was to move forward. She had never lied to Jack, but being honest with him was proving horribly difficult. She hadn't been prepared for the effect Jack's presence here in her parlour would have on her. The room was too redolent of happier times. She should have arranged to meet him somewhere else, somewhere neutral. Yet how could she possibly say what had to be said in a public place?

'Mercy.' His voice had gentled. 'What is it that you want to say to me? You didn't send me an urgent telegram in order to tell me you're glad you met me.'

'No.' She steeled herself. 'I am glad too, that we cleared up the matter of—of not wanting to marry each other.'

'Each other?' Jack jumped to his feet again. 'So what—are you planning to marry someone else? Is that what this is about?'

'Good grief, no! I've no intention of marrying anyone.'

'Then, for the love of God, will you stop dithering and tell me what this is all about?'

'I am with child.' She wished it hadn't sounded so cold.

Jack dropped back onto the sofa as if he had been shot, staring at her in disbelief.

'I'm sorry. I didn't mean to blurt it out like that, but I can't think of any other way to say it.'

'You said you couldn't have children.'

'I thought I couldn't. I am very sorry.'

'You're *sorry*?'

'No, not sorry to be expecting a child. I could not be more pleased to be expecting a child. I thought— well, as you know, I thought I couldn't. But it seems I can.' *Shut up, Mercy!* Jack was still staring at her as if he couldn't understand what she was saying. The urge to comfort him was confusing. She was trying to protect her baby, but it was very difficult to see Jack as the threat. This was Jack!

'I can't believe it,' he said, shaking his head. 'When? I mean, when will the baby...?'

'In about six months, as far as I can tell.'

'Six months!' He looked horribly shaken. 'So you have known... How long have you known?'

'Not long.' It wasn't a lie, but it felt like one. 'It was my sister who guessed, about a month ago, but I have only been certain for the last week.'

'And was it seeing me yesterday that made you decide I ought to know?'

'No. I admit that I did consider keeping it from you, but—'

An explosive curse made her jump. 'You *admit* you thought to keep it from me? I'm going to be a father, and it actually crossed your mind not to tell me?'

'Yes. I'm being honest with you. It did cross my mind.' She'd thought she was prepared for his anger, but Jack had never been angry with her. It hurt. It made her think that she didn't know him. It made her think that, after all, he might be like any other man. Any other husband. She crossed her arms, forcing herself to glare back at him. She was *not* that woman any more. 'I considered keeping it from you because it would be simpler, frankly, if you did not know.'

'Simpler!'

'Simpler, less trouble, and a great deal less painful for you. You don't want a child—or at least not this child, and not any child just yet. I want a child, Jack. I want *this* child and I won't let anyone take it away from me.' She was on the verge of tears, and it was vital that she remained calm, that she *explained*. 'But it would be wrong for me not to tell you. I've always been honest with you, right from the start, and that matters a great deal to me. I was always going to tell you. Seeing you yesterday simply made me realise that I couldn't put it off any longer.'

Jack stared at her, his expression rigid. For once, she had no idea what he was thinking. 'So now you know,' Mercy said, deciding to plough on, wanting it over and him gone. 'I can understand you're angry, but you must know it was never my intention to mislead you, and you need not fear I expect anything from you.'

He broke his silence with a roar. 'What?'

She clasped her hands tightly together. She would not allow him to intimidate her. 'I am perfectly aware that this child is my responsibility. You are an honourable man. If you had believed there to be the least chance of my conceiving, you would not have—you would have taken measures to prevent it.'

'Bloody hell, Mercy, I'm afraid your idea of honourable and mine are poles apart. In my book, honourable men take responsibility for the consequences of their actions. They most certainly don't take to the hills when they discover they're going to become a father.'

'You don't want to be a father. Not yet. You said so yourself.'

'It is *our* child. And it will bear my name.'

She shrank back in her chair for, though she had expected this, she had hoped to avoid it. 'No, Jack.'

'It's not what you want, it's not what I planned, but this changes everything. We're getting married, for the child's sake.'

'Absolutely not! Five minutes ago, you agreed with me that you don't want to get married.'

'Five minutes ago, I had no idea that I was going to become a father.'

'It makes no difference. I'm not marrying you.'

'I'm not Harry Armstrong.'

'It doesn't matter. I'm not—I don't want—I won't marry you.'

'So you'll give birth to a bastard and bring it up without a father? Is that what you're planning?'

'Don't use that word.'

'It's the word everyone will use. What name will it have—Armstrong? I'd like to see their faces at Cavendish Square when that birth is announced in *The Times*.'

'It won't be announced in *The Times*, and I am certainly not letting my child go by that name.'

'So what, then? Smith? Jones? Anything but Dalmuir, I take it!'

'Not Armstrong. Never.' Yet that was her name. A new, horrendous possibility occurred to her. What if George laid claim to her child?

'So what?' Jack continued ranting. 'Are you going to tell people you found it under a mulberry bush and adopted it?'

'I'll say I'm a widow. It's the truth.' She tried frantically to remember her plan for how this conversation was supposed to go. 'I will take another name. It doesn't matter which.'

'It doesn't matter! For f—' Jack broke off, striding across the room to the window, and turning his back on her. 'We need to calm down.'

'There is nothing more to discuss.' Her mind churned with new fear. Panicked and shaken, all she wanted was to have Jack gone.

'You're right,' he said, turning back to face her. 'There is nothing more to discuss. We're getting married.'

'No, we are not.'

'You don't like it, but when you think about it you'll see that I'm right.'

Which was exactly what she'd expected he would say. She'd prepared herself for it, and she'd prepared her calm, logical rejection, but it was the determined way he spoke, that air of implacability, that cut the final ties of her temper. She would not allow the past to repeat itself. 'How dare you tell me what to think?'

Jack recoiled. 'Mercy, for heaven's sake.'

'Do not tell me what to do.' She spoke through gritted teeth. Her fists were clenched.

'I'm only saying…'

'Well, stop saying it. You have said more than enough.'

'Mercy…'

She pushed him away. 'I thought you were different. I thought you understood. I had seventeen years of being told what to do, what to wear, who to court, who to snub, what to think! I am never, ever going to put myself in that position again.'

'How dare you compare me to that man you married? I am not a tyrant.'

'"There is nothing more to discuss. We're getting married",' she flung at him. 'Forget that you can think for yourself, Mercy, and let me decide for you, in other words. I am not your puppet.'

'You're being completely irrational.'

'Get out, Jack.'

'I'm not going anywhere. We've things to discuss.'

'Get out, Jack. And don't bother coming back.'

He took a step towards her and she shrank away from him. There was a long, painful silence as they stood frozen. Jack looked stricken. 'You really thought I was going to hit you? I was trying to…' He stared at her for a moment, his throat working. 'I thought you knew me.'

It was an agony to say nothing. It cut her to the quick, seeing how she had hurt him, but further discussion could only lead to more pain.

Jack buttoned his coat. 'You'll be hearing from me,' he said curtly.

Mercy shook her head. He turned his back on her. The parlour door closed softly behind him and, a few moments later, she heard the front door close. Shaking, she let out a huge sob and crumpled onto the rug.

Jack strode down the path and on past the cab rank, all thoughts of going to work forgotten. Furious with himself, he dug his hands into the pockets of his coat and made instinctively for the river, cursing himself under his breath. The white heat of his temper shocked him. That Mercy could think he would hurt a hair on her head, when all he'd wanted to do was pull her into his arms and tell her...

What? Tell her exactly what she didn't want to hear—that he'd take care of everything? Sickened, his pace slowed, and to his shame he found himself on the edge of tears. He tipped the brim of his hat lower over his head and huddled deeper into his coat. The sun was shining, the sky was doing a London impression of blue, but he had never felt so bloody grey and miserable. A clutch of weans were playing a game of football on a scraggy patch of grass, the goal posts marked out with their coats.

Morosely, he stopped to watch them. When he'd been wee, they'd played kickabout on the wasteland where the worst of the tenements had been pulled down. They'd had a proper football made of stitched leather that had weighed a ton when it got wet and would give you a right dunt if you tried to head it. He couldn't remember how they'd come by it.

They'd taken turns to keep it safe, he remembered. The two sides had been made up of whoever had turned up, starting with a clutch of skivers dodging school, the teams increasing when the schools came out. Some would leave for their dinner then come back again, some had skipped their dinner, some had played on because they wouldn't have been getting any dinner. They'd stopped when it had got too dark to see, and they'd used to argue over the final score. Was is sixty-eight to fifty-three, or forty-one to thirty-five? He couldn't remember there ever having been a draw.

The ball that landed at his feet was a sad-looking specimen with the stitching falling apart. He kicked it back to the waiting lad, resolving to get a new one delivered tomorrow, when doubtless the game would have resumed. On a Sunday, in the Gorbals, the fathers had joined in the game. Jack had never played on a Sunday.

Shoulders hunched, he walked slowly down to the river and turned towards Vauxhall. His ma had always been cagey about how his dad had died. She'd lost him, she'd always said, and Jack had wondered on and off as he'd grown older what she'd meant by that. She'd been touchy about it when he had asked, and eventually he'd given up.

It had been the same on the one occasion he'd asked her why his granny and granda didn't want to see him. He must have been eight or nine, because it was something at school that had set him off, a story that had long faded from his mind. *Why not?* he remembered whinging. *Why don't they want to see me?* And, the more he asked, the more tight-lipped she'd got, until she'd packed him off to bed. The next day, she'd told him she was too proud to go grovelling, and surely they didn't need anyone, did they, when they could get by themselves? He'd squared his wee shoulders and agreed with her, and had never asked again.

He'd repeated Ma's version of events when Mercy had asked him, he remembered now. Was it a tall tale or the truth? Had his da, the charmer, died or run off? Had his ma been too proud or just ashamed? It was too late to ask now, not that he would even if he'd had the chance. It was done and dusted. But still, though he'd never let his ma know, he felt the lack of a father. He had felt it.

Jack kicked a stone, sending it flying in the air to land in the oozing mud of the river bank. If he could explain to Mercy why it was important... But he shouldn't have to explain himself, and he couldn't bear her to pity him—the poor wee tyke whose da had run off and never given him another thought. All the same, he couldn't bear to think of his own child asking questions that Mercy wouldn't answer. He didn't want his own child to grow up doubting, thinking his father wanted nothing to do with him.

He cut into a small public garden and slumped down on a bench beneath a cherry tree that was in full bloom, dropping his head in his hands. Mercy was expecting his child. He was going to be a father. Bloody hell, he was going to be a father! He stretched his legs out and gazed up at the cherry blossom, a stupid grin spreading across his face. The news had somehow got lost in the complete fiasco that had played out this morning.

In six months Mercy was going to have their child. An actual baby. Probably a wee girl, with Mercy's blonde hair and heart-shaped face, but maybe with his eyes and an interest in mathematics. *Bonny and blithe and good and gay.* He smiled, recalling the childhood rhyme. That was the Sabbath child, and he could easily imagine that was Mercy. Needless to say, he was Saturday's child who worked hard for his living. His daughter wouldn't have to work hard, though she'd not be shy of it. He'd send her to a good school, not one of those ladies' academies that taught stitching and French, like his ma had gone to.

I had a very similar education myself, Mercy had said, laughing at him, that first day they'd met. Mercy was having a child. He'd been so consumed by his own reaction that he'd not even considered properly what that must mean to her. All her life, all she'd wanted was a family of her own, and it was the one thing she thought she could never have. Barren, her husband had labelled her, and she'd never disputed it. But she wasn't. How must she be feeling? He hadn't even taken the time to ask her. All those years of being blamed, and feeling so guilty, convinced it was her fault. All the sacrifices she had made, and the misery she had endured, and it hadn't been her fault. Squeezing his eyes shut, she tried to remember if she'd said a word about it and came up with nothing.

Instead, what came back to him was his own words, his high-handed demand that she marry him, refusing to listen to her refusal or to consider what lay behind it. Behaving, in other words, exactly like the man she had married. Jack groaned. He had spoken from the heart, but he couldn't have handled it worse.

She must be ecstatic, but in he'd launched with both feet, demanding his rights as if the bairn was a piece of land and not a human being. She was carrying a tiny new life, and it was down to her to bring it into the world, and he was already laying claim to it. No wonder she'd turned on him. It wasn't like him to be so heavy-handed. And then compounding the error by pointing out that it would be a bastard. Which it would, mind, and there was no getting over the fact that that would be a huge hurdle for any child to overcome.

Not one his child would have to overcome. Which meant that he and Mercy would have to get married. Realising he was about to go round in another circle, he got to his feet and began walking again. The fact of the matter was it was a complete tangle. Mercy didn't want a husband. God's honest truth, he wasn't in any way prepared for a wife, as he'd spent much of last night telling himself. Had that only been last night? Where would they live? If he was to be a father, he couldn't be away from home too much and, for his business at this exciting stage in its development, that meant there would be no new stage—which meant his plans to create more jobs would have to go down the drain.

And Mercy didn't want to get married. He couldn't force her up the aisle. He wouldn't want to force her up the aisle. He didn't want a reluctant wife. But, now he thought about it, the idea of having Mercy as his wife was growing on him. He'd missed her, and the missing her had shown no sign of diminishing with time, no matter how hard he tried. Marriage hadn't been part of his plan, not yet but, looking at it in this entirely new light, he reckoned it had a great deal going for it. Mercy was not his bloody *helpmeet*—and thank the stars for that! Why would he want to come home to a helpmeet when he could come home to Mercy? When he could go to bed every night with Mercy and wake with her in the morning?

Unless the bairn woke them first. The child that had provoked his declaration, that he'd quite forgotten for a moment. His second declaration. He'd proposed—or almost proposed—the first time because he wanted Mercy. He still wanted Mercy. How many more declarations must he make before she accepted him? Would she ever accept him? She wouldn't be pushed. On the contrary, the more he pushed, the more she'd dig her heels in. Had *she* thought of the practicalities of having a bairn and no husband? She probably had. It was one of the things he'd admired about her from the first— the way she got her sleeves rolled up and got on with the hand fate dealt her.

And let's not forget, he told himself, *this hand is a winner as far as she's concerned.*

Despondent once more, Jack shook his head, swearing under his breath, though not so violently. What a mess. If ever there was a time to get lost in a bottle of malt, it was now. Save that drink never solved anything. If fact, it only caused more problems. He'd seen plenty of evidence of that growing up in the Gorbals. He'd have to find another solution to his conundrum. Did one even exist?

Chapter Fourteen

'So, for the sake of argument,' Mercy said, 'in such an eventuality there would be no prospect of the child being taken from the widowed mother by her dead husband's family?'

Across the desk, the lawyer tapped his finger on the blotter, frowning. 'We are talking hypothetically, Mrs Carstairs?'

'Of course.' There was no reason to panic. The man had no idea who she was and, even if he did, she was his client. He was obliged to protect her confidence. He would not go rushing round to Cavendish Square, demanding to speak to George. Mercy relaxed her shoulders and attempted what she hoped was a reassuring smile. 'I am merely trying to establish the legal niceties.'

She waited, tapping her foot anxiously, but the lawyer was determined to take his time, pursing his lips, tapping his pen on the stack of folders which lay on the blotter in front of him and then pushing his pincenez up the bridge of his nose before clearing his throat. 'Hypothetically speaking, then?'

She gritted her teeth. 'Yes.'

'Well, then. Hmm. If a widow has a child out of wedlock, the child will bear its mother's name, which will therefore be her dead husband's name. Of course, if the dead husband was still alive, the child would be deemed his property, even if he was not the father, and would therefore be his to…er…dispose of as he saw fit. Removing it from the mother, for example. I'm sorry, did you say something?'

She shook her head, with difficulty swallowing the rest of her indignant protest. 'But in my case—' She broke off and took a steadying breath. 'In this hypothetical case, the woman is a widow, therefore her husband is dead. So surely, sir, the case is straightforward? The child belongs to her and no one else?'

There was an edge of desperation in her voice. She dared not say more. Clasping her hands over her stomach under cover of the desk, she waited like a prisoner in the dock, for judgment to be delivered. It took an excruciatingly long time.

'Hmm.' The lawyer removed his pince-nez, scrutinised them carefully, then took out an ink-stained handkerchief to polish them before returning them once again to his nose. 'When it comes to the law, nothing is straightforward. Which is fortunate for me, eh? Forgive my attempt at levity. It is a very interesting question, though I confess, I find it difficult to think of a circumstance in which the dead husband's family would wish to lay claim to such a child.'

'For spite!' she exclaimed, unable to stop herself. 'Because they knew how much the widow longed for a child.'

'Aha!' The lawyer's brow cleared. 'I have it now. You are a lady novelist researching a plot, is that it? My wife is an avid reader, though her tastes, I am afraid, tend to the low and the highly coloured. I am forever suggesting that she raise her mind a little with some of Mr Trollope's novels. *The Chronicles of Barsetshire* cannot be bettered, in my humble opinion, for their realistic rendering of the English countryside and the gentle way of life which prevails there. Yet she prefers Mr Collins' sensationalism. *The Woman in White* is her particular favourite. I presume it is a novel of this nature that you are writing, Mrs Carstairs?'

One of Jack's oaths was on the tip of her tongue. Mercy gave something that might or might not pass for a nod and smiled tightly. 'I would be very much obliged if you would answer my question.'

'Well now, spite? No, if you would accept a suggestion, would not a more credible motivation be that they simply wanted to care for the child? Think about that, Mrs Carstairs. Assuming that the husband's family are respectable, and this widow is clearly not given her situation, then I for one can perfectly understand that they may want to remove the child from her clutches, so to speak. To give it a better life, as it were.'

She stared at him incredulously. 'A better life without its mother?'

'A mother who gave birth out of wedlock!' The lawyer looked outraged. 'Come, Mrs Carstairs, even in a sensationalist romance that must be condemned.'

She knew that! She had gone over and over what Jack had said, that awful word he had used. 'It seems wrong to me,' she said, 'to condemn anyone without understanding the circumstances—and very wrong, in my opinion, to remove a child from a loving mother.'

'I will leave it up to you, my good lady, to resolve the moral issues in your novel. I can speak only for the law, and on balance I think that it would favour the mother.'

'Really?'

'A legal ruling could go either way, but I believe so.'

'Thank you!'

'You are welcome. I do hope, however, that in your novel the poor woman puts her child before her own wishes and surrenders it of her own accord.'

'I am sorry to disappoint you, but it is my intention to take this particular story in a very different direction. Thank you for your assistance.'

'I hope I have given you food for thought,' the lawyer said, getting to his feet.

'Abundant.' What he hadn't done was allay her fears. The Armstrongs could attempt to snatch her child from her if they knew. They might not succeed but they could try.

'Excellent. I am glad to be of help. I shall look out for your novel, Mrs Carstairs. I may even purchase a copy for my wife. Good day to you.'

The note from Jack was waiting for Mercy when she returned home. Her heart leapt at the sight of his handwriting, then plummeted when she remembered the terms upon which they had parted three days ago. It made no mention of their previous conversation except to say that they had a great deal to discuss and might be better served doing so with cooler heads and in a place less redolent of the past. Neutral territory, so to speak. The day after tomorrow, he suggested, and would assume she was amenable unless he heard from her. He was, as always, her obedient servant, the letter concluded.

Was he being ironic? Or was he using the formality of his language to distance himself from her? Or perhaps he wished to indicate that he was still willing to aide and abet her in whatever way she required? No, that was reading far too much into it.

She spent the rest of the evening reading more and more into those few words, however, and only as she prepared for bed did it occur to her that she had not for a moment considered refusing to see him. She wanted to see him. Arguing with him so furiously and bitterly had left her drained and depressed. Neither of them had shown themselves to their best advantage. If she had seen another side of Jack, then she was pretty certain he must have witnessed a very different side of her. She didn't want him to remember her that way. She didn't want her own memories of him to be tainted. Though it would be inevitable, wouldn't it, if what Jack wanted from tomorrow was to persuade her to change her mind?

It was almost certainly what he was going to do. Marriage was the only solution to their problem in the eyes of almost everyone but herself, as the lawyer she consulted had inadvertently made crystal-clear. No matter how she railed at it, or felt it to be unjust, if she didn't marry Jack her child would be a bastard.

Their child. It was wrong of her to deprive her baby of its father, and wrong of her to deprive the father of his baby. Her instincts told her that Jack would be a good father, but her instincts were also telling her that it would be wrong to allow him to sacrifice himself at the altar of duty and marry for the sake of their child.

How to reconcile all of this? It seemed impossible, but she would have to find a way. They had created this child together. She had told Jack of her own accord that she was pregnant, and in retrospect it had been ludicrous of her to expect him to walk away and forget both of them.

Her head hurt. Mercy pushed herself up in bed. Any other woman would stop asking herself these questions. She would put her baby first and accept Jack's proposal. But would marrying a man who had proposed out of a sense of duty really make their child happier? And what about Jack? She had married Harry for the sake of a family, and look how successful that had been. Would she and Harry have been happier if they'd had a family? She couldn't answer for Harry, but for herself, it was an unequivocal no.

She remembered when Prue had first told her she was expecting little Verity. Her sister had been so concerned about upsetting her that she had tried to repress her own joy. She remembered telling Jack, that first day they met, that having a child with Harry would have been wrong. While this child—her hands automatically flattened possessively over her stomach—this child felt right. Unlike Harry, Jack would never take her child away from her. If that had ever truly been a threat, she wouldn't have told him about the baby. It wasn't only that she had been honest with him from the first, she had trusted him with her mind and her body. He wasn't a tyrant. He had never, save on that one occasion, tried to direct her thoughts or her actions. Jack wasn't Harry, yet in the heat of the moment she had spoken and acted as if he were.

She had to make amends. She would put it right when she saw him tomorrow. When he would probably propose. Mercy groaned softly for, despite the fact that being married to Jack would, she was sure, be very, very different from being married to Harry, she could not convince herself that it would be right to accept him. They would both be sacrificing hard-won independent lives, entering into a bond that would tie them to each other for ever, forcing them both to compromise, to change, to reshape. A huge upheaval, as Prue had said, and Prue was deeply in love with her husband.

Do you love him? Prue had asked.

I don't think so, Mercy had answered. *I can't let myself. There's no point.*

Her answer stood. Love would be one more unnecessary complication, because Jack didn't love her. And marriage, according to Prue, was doomed without it. She trusted her sister, and she had her own doomed marriage to stand testament. She didn't love Jack, but she cared for him, a great deal too much to allow him to sacrifice his future happiness by marrying her.

A tear trailed down her cheek. She didn't love him, but she missed him so much. She missed the man who understood her. The man who believed in her. The man who supported her, even when he didn't agree with her, and who didn't try to change her mind even when he was convinced she was wrong. She missed that Jack. And the Jack who thought she was *bloody gorgeous,* and who made love *with* her and not *to* her. She missed that Jack. She hadn't forgotten about him, but she had been so taken up with the news that she was to be a mother, she had forgotten the woman Jack had awoken.

She was tempted to close her eyes, to forget everything, to slide back down under the covers and to remember. But what good would it do, save to make her yearn for what was already in the past? She had a future to sort out, and the one thing it did not contain was a husband. Jack didn't understand that. She had hurt him with her blank refusal, and it mattered to her more than ever that he understood her motives. When tomorrow came, she had better be sure this time that she could explain herself.

The sun was shining the next morning when Jack arrived in a cab at Mercy's house in Chelsea. He had himself well under control, absolutely determined not to let this conversation turn into another fiasco, for he was fairly certain she would give him short shrift if it did. He had rehearsed everything he wanted to say, although some of it, when he thought about it, made his guts roil. But if he needed to flay himself to get her to understand, then flay himself he would. He wouldn't lose his temper. He wouldn't demand and command. He'd explain, and he'd put his case, and hope to hell and high heaven that she'd listen.

He was expecting Lucy to answer the door, so when Mercy opened it herself he was immediately on the back foot. She looked so lovely, he found himself momentarily lost for words and struggling with the urge to kiss her. Not once during their last meeting had kisses been in his thoughts. It was disconcerting to discover that in those first few seconds he forgot all about the child in whose future he was so determined to claim a stake, caring only for the woman he had lost.

She was wearing something summery he hadn't seen before, pale green patterned with sprigs of blue flowers. On top of her hair sat a preposterous confection of straw and ribbon that wouldn't serve in the least to protect her from the sun. Her figure betrayed no sign of her condition. He must have been staring at her a tad too long, for she adjusted the silk scarf she had draped over her shoulders to cover her stomach instead.

'Good morning,' Jack said, giving himself a shake. 'Are you set?'

'If you mean, am I ready to go, then the answer is yes. May I ask where we are headed?'

'Brighton.' He opened the door of the cab and she climbed in before he could offer his hand. 'On to London Bridge station now,' he instructed the driver, and climbed in beside her. 'I thought you'd appreciate some sea air.'

To his relief, she smiled. 'I would, very much. Spring seems to have given way very quickly to summer this year. I don't think I have ever spent the summer in town before.'

'Never?'

'Last year I was in Hampshire with my brother. Before that I was a slave to the social season,' Mercy said sardonically. 'One could stay on in town for the regattas at Henley and Cowes, but generally once Parliament went into recess one went to the country. Or abroad— to a spa, in my case.'

To cure her of her inability to have a child, Jack recalled. What had she endured, in addition to the humiliation? He couldn't begin to imagine. 'Do you not wish...?' he began, then stopped himself, for what would be the good in drawing attention to all that pointless suffering? 'Ach, never mind.'

'Do I not wish that I could have discovered earlier that it was all a waste of time?' Mercy said, after a moment.

'I don't want to drag up the past. I'm sorry.'

'No, I don't either, but it was seventeen years of my life, and I can't pretend it didn't happen. Of course I've thought about it.'

She was wearing white gloves of cotton lace. Frowning, she pulled the left one off, splaying her hand to examine her fingers. Her nails had been allowed to grow, he noticed, and they had been buffed, the skin around them showing no trace of her former nervous habit. The small gesture touched him to the heart. 'Look how far you've come,' Jack said. 'You should be very proud of yourself, Mercy.'

She shook her head, then nodded, smiling faintly before pulling her glove back on. 'All those years of treatment *were* pointless, I know that now, but at the time what could I have done to break the vicious cycle? It is not, sadly, possible to prove scientifically that one is incapable of bearing a child. Until one is too old, there is always hope.'

And hope was the killer, he saw clearly and painfully. It hadn't killed her. She had endured—no, more than endured. She'd put on a front, she'd played her part, fooling almost everyone, and she'd atoned in the only way she could by bending herself to her husband's will. He could never have done what she had. 'You are some woman—do you know that?' Jack said, the words wholly inadequate but all he could think of.

He made no attempt to hide the emotion in his voice. Their eyes met. She smiled at him, that crooked, disparaging smile. 'A truly Jack-style compliment.'

'I mean it.'

Her mouth quivered. She looked away. 'I know.'

The train to Brighton was extremely busy, their carriage full. The journey to the south coast, through the rolling green downs and farmland of England, was very different from the journey they had taken together on the west coast of Scotland. Mercy longed to lean into Jack, to recall that other journey, to recapture the magical feeling of escape they'd had, of being together in their own world despite the crowds around them. But today was about the future, not the past.

She was dreading the discussion to come, more torn than at any time in her life, and less sure of her own mind than she had been since Harry died. The temptation to accept what Jack was almost certainly going to offer, to surrender her reservations to what convention decreed would be best for their child, was almost overwhelming. It was such an enormous decision, affecting not one but three lives. Marriage would be easier in so many ways.

But it would be wrong. Jack would not even be considering offering for her if it was not for their child. She would not ruin his life in order to protect the life that she was carrying. He didn't want to marry her. If he'd loved her... But Jack didn't love her.

She slanted a look at him. He was studying his hands, his face grimly set. There were shadows under his eyes. His hair was cut shorter than usual. His nails were trimmed to the quick, a habit he'd acquired from when he'd been an apprentice, he'd once told her, for otherwise the grease stained them, making his hands look dirty no matter how hard he scrubbed. He had a puckered scar in the shape of a jelly fish at the top of his left arm from an accident involving a steam jet. He didn't like apples, but he could cut them into paper-thin slivers that melted in the mouth. He could swim like a fish, but he couldn't guarantee to stay on a horse at a gallop.

She had known him less than six months. The time they had spent together could be distilled into a few weeks. There were years and years of things he had done, places he'd been, friends he had made, lovers he had taken, that she knew nothing about, yet she knew him. She *knew* him, and he knew her. It was why their last meeting, their only argument, had been so deeply painful.

She didn't want to lose him. She couldn't bear it. But she had already lost that Jack. He was gone, and in his place would be Jack the father, possibly Jack the husband. No, not that. She began to panic. It was easier to think logically when he wasn't here.

It was stifling inside the carriage. And as the train slowed, the brakes making the wheels screech on the track, black steam belching from the engine pouring in through the carriage door that the young man in the seat opposite had flung open, even though they were not yet at the platform, Mercy began to feel nauseous.

Jack grabbed the door, pulling it shut again, glowering at the man. 'Hang on,' he said quietly to Mercy. 'Only a few more minutes.'

She nodded, concentrating completely on keeping her breakfast down, allowing herself to be helped up when the train came to a halt. The other passengers, cowed by Jack's Glasgow stare, waited until he had helped her disembark.

'Would you like a cup of tea? There's a station buffet by the ticket office.'

'Thank you. That would be lovely.' Reluctantly, Mercy detached her hand from his arm. 'I'm already feeling better.'

Jack had the waitress escort her to the ladies' convenience, and when she returned, feeling considerably better, there was a pot of tea and a plate of bread and butter on the table. He drank his own tea silently, allowing her to do the same. He did not make a fuss of her, or repeatedly ask her if she was feeling well, or suggest that she lie in a darkened room.

Half an hour later, they emerged from the station into bright sunshine in a pale-blue sky. 'You've lost your peely-wally look, but if you start to feel unwell again you must tell me,' he said to her. 'Straight away, mind.'

'Peely-wally.' She smiled. 'Much more descriptive than pale. I promise, I will tell you. Thank you for looking after me.'

He flinched. 'I suppose I should be glad you'll take a cup of tea from me. Will we walk down to the front? It's not far.'

'I'm sorry,' Mercy said, cursing herself for her lack of tact.

But Jack shook his head. 'Don't be. I'm over-touchy. You've made it obvious that you don't need looking after.'

She didn't need looking after—she'd have managed without him, but not nearly so well, today and on several other momentous occasions. He'd never said that. *You're quite a woman,* was what he'd said, or, *You're stronger than you think.* True, she had consistently surprised herself, but Jack had been consistently there to witness it, a silent support who had never stepped in without her permission. 'You're quite a man, Jack Dalmuir,' Mercy said.

Her words, meant to make him smile, instead made him wince. He reached for her, then changed his mind. 'You think?'

She had no idea what to make of this, and so said nothing. They proceeded slowly, Jack managing his pace to hers. The town was bustling with shoppers and merchants, and they made their way towards the front, with women out together for a stroll, nursemaids with baby carriages and toddlers, and several clutches of young boys who had decided that the weather was far too good to be spent in school. The promenade was wide, lined with beach huts set high on the shingle, though none had been towed out to the water. The sea sparkled, flat calm, the same pale blue as the sky, and the air was heady with brine. Mercy lifted her face to the sun, closing her eyes for a moment to enjoy the heat on her face, and felt herself relaxing.

She opened her eyes to find Jack smiling at her. 'You

always do that,' he said. 'The first hint of sun and you do that, as if you are drinking it in.'

She smiled back. 'I love it, now I don't have to worry about ruining my complexion.'

His smile thinned at this inept reminder of her past, but he chose to ignore it. 'I'm lucky. I've skin like old leather, and never burned in the sun when we were on holiday, but some of the bairns went from milk-white to red-raw on the beach on the first day, poor souls.'

'Goodness, never tell me the sun shone on the west coast of Scotland, Jack. I swear there's a by-law there that requires it to rain at least once every day.'

He laughed. 'In my memory, the sun shone every day of those holidays, but I might be misremembering.'

'Is that a new pier they are building over there?' Mercy asked, pointing at the skeleton construction jutting out into the sea. 'Would you like to go and take a look? Silly question,' she added and, when he demurred, took his arm. 'Come on, Jack, I'm anxious to hear what improvements you would make to the design.'

He laughed at that. 'Very well, then. Be careful what you wish for.'

Work on what would become Brighton's West Pier had begun the year before, but Mercy could see little sign of the finished construction, only a series of tall iron columns like way-markers stretching from the promenade all the way out to sea. A temporary pier built of wood and scaffolding provided a platform for the men, stretching out beyond the furthest of the columns, where a steam engine powered what she assumed must be a drill. Though it wasn't actually being used, the clanging, shouting and hammering forced her to raise her voice.

'It doesn't look as if they have made much progress,' she said.

Jack gave a huff of laughter. 'Have you any idea of the amount of work it takes to fix just one of those columns into the seabed? They're threaded, like screws, you know, and they have to go deep down to get purchase, and to be strong enough to support the pier.'

'How foolish of me not to have thought of that.'

'Aye, very foolish.' He grinned. 'The pier is to be over a thousand feet long too, and it's about three hundred wide, so that's—let me think—how many columns?'

'A great many?'

'A great many. The architect wanted to have them installed by the end of this year, but Robert Laidlaw put him right. Robert is the man responsible for manufacturing those columns.'

'A Glasgow man, perchance?'

'If you want the best engineer, you go to Glasgow. You're learning! They'll put girders and ties on top, but you won't see any of that work when it's done. All that everyone will talk about is the fancy wooden platform and the pretty ironwork and whatever buildings they put up. History will remember the architect, needless to say—it's always the case—but for my money it's the engineer who should get the credit.'

'I suppose that's true. It is always the architect who is commemorated. Does it—how do you say it?—stick in your craw?'

'A wee bit, but I've always said my beam engines speak for themselves, and they will, long after I'm gone and they're still doing their job. And if anyone's in any doubt about their origins, they have only to look and they'll see "Dalmuir Engineering, Glasgow" on every beam.'

'You really are quite a man, Jack Dalmuir. To have started with nothing not so very long ago, and soon your name will be on every beam engine in the world.'

'No, even I'm not that ambitious, nor so daft. Quality, not quantity, is what we do.'

'But you are expanding, aren't you? And, if you win the German contract, you'll be taking your name to the Continent.'

'That's the plan.' His smile faded. 'Or it was.' At the end of the pier, the steam drill began work with a deafening roar. 'We can't talk here,' Jack said.

Chapter Fifteen

They headed for the Chain Pier. Under other circumstances, Jack would have admired the craft that had gone into the suspension design, even though it was old-fashioned now, with its oak supports. Today it was the water that drew him, not the structure supporting him, and Mercy too, her footsteps quickening as they passed through the toll booth onto the esplanade, heading for the farthest point and the view to sea.

At the end of the pier they sat down on one of the wooden benches. They were alone, save for a few seagulls perching on the iron rails. He was sick with nerves. 'Mercy…'

'Jack…'

'Go on.'

She shook her head. 'No. I owe it to you to listen. You go first.'

The words were ominous. It sounded as if she'd already made up her mind, and that threw him. He couldn't remember what it was he was going to say. All he wanted to do was to pull her into his arms, not to kiss her, just to hold her and breathe in the scent of her and lose himself in her and stop thinking.

He had one chance at this, he reminded himself. 'I've always made out that I was a happy lad, growing up just me and my ma. It's true, I was happy enough, but when you told me the other day that you were expecting it brought up all sorts of memories.'

He'd thought it would be difficult. Flaying himself, was what he'd thought it would feel like, but once he started he found himself tumbling over the words in his hurry to speak them, dredging up even more memories that he'd forgotten.

'And the holidays in Dunoon,' he finally concluded, 'when everyone else had a da sitting at their table. I missed him. You'll think it's daft, for I never knew him, but that's the only way I can put it. I missed my da's presence.'

There were tears in Mercy's eyes that she made no effort to hide. Her hand was curled into his, he noticed now. He made no attempt to remove it.

'And, now that your mother is gone, you'll never know the truth unless there is a neighbour or a friend...'

'I wouldn't do that. It's done and dusted now and, even if he's still alive, what would we have to say to each other? I'm well enough known, Mercy, for him to find me if he wants. He clearly doesn't want to.'

'Oh, Jack.'

'Like I said, it's done. I hadn't thought of it in years, until you told me about our—your child.'

'Ours,' she said, squeezing his hand. 'Whatever we decide today, the child is ours. You have a right to have a say in its upbringing, Jack, I won't deprive you or the baby of that. I had decided that, even before you told me this.'

His eyes were hot with tears. Mortified, he clenched them shut.

Mercy was looking away when he opened them, though her clasp had tightened. 'There is a packet steamer coming in to dock,' she said.

He had himself back under control, but he was no clearer on where he stood with her, and his elation and relief gave way to something that felt very like fear, a panic he couldn't understand now that he had her assurance about the child.

The child. Not *her*.

Mercy. From the first time he'd met her, there had been a connection. They got along. They understood each other. He felt it every time he saw her, something pulling them together. And when he was apart from her it was still there, a niggling thing reminding him of what he was missing. He didn't want to lose her, but he hadn't a clue how to put whatever he was feeling into words.

'I know it's difficult for you,' Mercy said while he was still struggling to find a way to articulate his feelings. 'You're a man who likes to be in control,' she said wryly, 'And I am a woman who is only just learning how to take control—a lesson you have been helping me learn. And this situation, it's not one either of us expected to have to deal with.'

'That's true, but it's hardly unique,' Jack said warily, for he had the distinct impression that she was reciting a speech.

'No, and the conventional solution would be for us to marry.'

'I didn't ask you to marry me because I felt it would be expected of me, I asked you to marry me because it was the best solution,' Jack said. He sounded defensive. Too defensive. 'What I mean is, best for the child, and for us too. And if you once more mention my looking for a helpmeet...'

'I won't, but you had a plan, and this...' She disengaged her hand from his to place it flat on her stomach. 'This wasn't part of it.'

'No, but it's happened and now I've had a chance to get used to the idea.'

He could have kicked himself. Stop sounding like a pragmatic engineer! They were talking about the rest of their lives together. Together? 'What I mean is—what I'm trying to say is that I want to marry you.'

Her stricken look gave him his answer. 'I'm so sorry, Jack. I think it would be a mistake.'

Though he'd half-expected it, her rejection still felt like a kick in the guts. 'Why...?' He cleared his throat. 'Can you explain why you think it would be a mistake? You can't still be comparing me with Harry Armstrong?'

'I never did compare you. *Never.*'

'So what is it, then? Are you afraid that, once you've taken my name, I'll expect you to be mine to command?'

She shook her head vehemently. 'That's what panicked me the other day but afterwards, when I had calmed down, I saw how wrong I was, how unfair I had been to you. I *know* you.'

'Then what is it that's stopping you?' He could hear the panic in his voice. He couldn't lose her. Not again. 'Is it the money? The pension you'd lose if you married again? I don't know how much it is, but I can have my man of business set something up for the same, so you've funds of your own and you don't feel as if you're relying on me. I can well afford it, if that's what's bothering you.'

'Oh, Jack.'

There were tears in her eyes. His stomach was churning. He was going to lose her, and he couldn't bear it. Never mind the bairn, it was Mercy who mattered most to him. Mercy he wanted for his wife. They were meant to be together. He'd felt it from the first. His instincts had prompted him into that half-hearted proposal in Dunoon. The child had given him the excuse to propose again, and he'd made a cack-handed job of it. Now he was trying to propose for the third time, and the way she was looking at him made him feel sick with dread. What was it he was missing?

'Look,' he said urgently. 'I know you had a terrible experience first time round, but it would be different with us.'

'I know that, Jack. I truly have put the past behind me. Harry has nothing to do with this.'

'He didn't want you to marry again.'

She smiled faintly. 'I hope you're not suggesting I marry to spite him.'

'I want you to marry me because you want to marry me.' Was it that simple? For the first time today, he felt as if the words were right. 'Mercy…'

'I don't want to marry you.' There was a finality

in her voice that turned his nausea into dread. 'I have tried to persuade myself...'

'*Persuade* yourself?'

She winced. 'I know everyone will say it is the right thing to do for the child...'

'I don't want you to marry me for the sake of the child!' Jack exclaimed. 'I want you to marry *me*.' He took her hand, his heart racing. 'I want us to be together. Did you ever ask yourself why it was so difficult for us to say goodbye?'

'We agreed...'

'I know what we agreed, but I think we were wrong. I *know* I was wrong. The baby set me on the right track, but I'd have come to my senses sooner or later. I missed you, Mercy, and it wasn't diminishing, it was getting stronger. Did you not feel the same?'

'Yes. No. I don't know. What has this got to do with the baby?'

'Nothing at all. I love you.'

The words struck them both like a thunderbolt. Mercy's mouth fell open. Jack felt as if something had clicked into place that had been out of true before. 'I love you,' he said again with more confidence. 'I love you and I don't want to lose you. That's why I want to marry you.'

'No.' She pulled her hand free. 'It's for the child.'

'I thought it was. That's why I proposed the other day.'

'And today—that's why you proposed today.'

'Yes. I mean, that's how it started out. I thought it was for the child, but then...'

'Then, when you thought I would refuse, you pretended to be in love with me, but you're saying that because you think it will stop me feeling guilty about ruining your life if I say I'll marry you.'

'You've got it the wrong way round! I love you. If you *don't* marry me, you'll be ruining my life.'

Mercy jumped to her feet. 'Don't say that, Jack. That's not fair. You were *perfectly* happy without me.'

'I was. I thought I was. I wasn't unhappy.' He got up and tried to take her hands again, but she backed away. 'Since I met you, I've been happier than I've ever been. And without you, I've been unhappy. I've missed you.'

'And I missed you, but...' But what? Her mind was frozen. Jack loved her. Jack loved her! If it were true... But it wasn't. 'If you loved me,' she said, 'Why didn't you say so before now?'

'I didn't know. I mean, I must have known, but I hadn't put it into words. I was so taken up with the news about the baby.'

'Exactly. This is about the baby. You don't love me but perhaps have persuaded yourself you do. To sweeten the pill.'

He stared at her incredulously. 'That's the most ludicrous thing I've ever heard.'

Was it? Did he really love her? Oh, but if he meant it, if he really did love her...

'I mean it, Mercy. I know it's sudden, and I can see that you might be thinking I'm only saying it because I'm so desperate to marry you, but it's not that. I'm desperate to marry you right enough, but it's because I want you. I just didn't see that until now, when I thought I was losing you.'

'But I told you, I had no intention of keeping your child from you. I have no notion at all of how we might manage it.'

'For the love of God! This is not about the child—I mean, it is, but not only that. It's about me and you. I love you. I want to spend the rest of my life with you.'

'But you never said.' She wanted to cry. She wanted to throw herself into his arms. She so desperately wanted to believe him, it hurt.

'I didn't know, until now,' he said again, and this time she let him take her hands. 'It's been there all along, the feeling that we—we— Ach, I don't know how to say it without sounding like a sap. Like I'm missing part of myself when you're not here. I've sprung this on you, and I've not even given you a chance to tell me how you really feel.'

As if her heart was doing flip-flops. Terrified. Panicked. Wanting to believe him. She so wanted to believe him, because she felt... No, she didn't feel the same. She couldn't feel the same, because he was deluded. Wasn't he?

'I don't know,' she said, which was wholly inadequate but at least had the merit of being the truth. 'I have no idea what I'm feeling. I didn't expect—you never said—I never thought...' Her voice was shaking. 'I simply don't know. I think I'd like to go home.'

'You need to think, mull things over. Of course, take all the time you need.'

The mixture of anguish and hope in his voice almost overset her. She longed to tell him what he wanted to hear, but if she did, and if they married, how would she ever know the truth? Jack would maintain the lie that he loved her because he was Jack, and if it was a lie then he'd surely grow slowly miserable? And she would be miserable because she had allowed herself to believe his lie, though it was well-intentioned. If it was a lie…

'I've thrown you, and I've kept you here far too long. You're looking quite wabbit,' Jack said, interrupting this convoluted chain of thought.

She forced a smile, because she knew it would make him feel better. 'A wan rabbit? You have thrown me. You've said the one thing that I didn't expect to hear.'

'It was a surprise to me too, but true nonetheless. Come on. We'll get a cab from the rank at the end of pier, and then you'll be home in no time.'

The journey passed mostly in silence, with each of them lost in their thoughts. When the cab arrived in Chelsea, Jack paid it off, saying he would walk the rest of the way.

'Will you come in for a cup of tea?' Mercy asked him, when Lucy opened the front door.

'I will,' he said, following her into the parlour. 'Don't worry, I'm not going to say any more. Not because I've nothing more to say, but because I've said more than enough for today. I just didn't want the day to end like that.'

'That's exactly what I was thinking.' Mercy sat down in her usual chair, and Jack took the sofa opposite her. His sofa. Their sofa. She longed to sit beside him, to rest her head on his shoulder, to have his arms around her. Did he love her?

'Stop thinking about it,' he said, getting up as Lucy

knocked on the door, and taking the tea tray from her with thanks. 'Here, I'll be Ma for once.'

He made the tea precisely as she liked it, putting a tiny splash of milk in first and pouring himself a cup which she knew he wouldn't drink, just to keep her company. They talked about Brighton, and he told her of a trip to Edinburgh when he'd been much younger, to see the Trinity Pier, a forerunner to the Chain Pier built by the same man.

'Not a Scot,' Jack said when she asked him, 'but the son of one. I should probably go,' he added, when she set her empty cup down beside his untouched one.

'In a minute.' She got up to sit beside him on the sofa. 'If I was not carrying our child, you would not be here with me today.'

'And you're thinking that you'll never know now whether I would have stayed away for ever, were it not for the child.'

'Yes.'

'I would have come looking for you, sooner or later. When I saw you on the bridge the other day, I knew I had to see you. I'd have come to my senses eventually.'

'How can you be so sure?'

'Because I came to my senses today. I had no idea I was going to tell you that I love you but, once I said it, it felt—it felt right,' he said, looking sheepish. 'I can't explain it more than that.'

'I've never been in love.'

'There you are—that's something else we have in common.'

'If I was in love with you, Jack, shouldn't I be throwing caution to the winds and myself into your arms?'

'And thinking that nothing else mattered, except being together? Don't be daft. Nothing else is so important, but that doesn't mean it doesn't matter.'

'My sister says that marriage is hard work. She says that it is doomed without love, because it's too much of an upheaval.'

'Then we're at least halfway on the road to success, because I know I love you.'

'I want to believe you, Jack.' She reached up to touch his cheek. His skin was warm, his neatly trimmed beard soft to the touch.

He caught her hand and kissed her palm, and she stopped trying to resist him, leaning towards him, whispering his name. He moaned softly, pulling her into his arms. Their lips met, clinging for a long moment, and she closed her eyes. She had missed this so much.

They kissed. A long, slow, deep kiss that drowned out everything save for the relief of being in Jack's arms again. She wrapped her arms around his neck and nestled closer, relief giving way to desire, to the fluttering in her belly, the heat in her blood, the scent of him and the taste of him. Their tongues touched. He pulled her tighter against him, their kisses becoming deeper, their breathing more shallow, her body alive and tingling, urgent for more. Frantic kisses, his mouth on her neck, her hands under his coat smoothing over the muscles of his back, frustrated by his clothing. His hand was on her breast, drawing a soft, pleasurable sigh from her. Then more kisses, and they were standing, wrapped in one another's arms.

He muttered her name. Then he groaned, swore softly and set her free. 'It's not right.'

Mercy, caught in the heat of passion, stared at him uncomprehendingly. 'Not right?'

'I don't mean it didn't feel right. I mean it wouldn't be right. Not when matters are unresolved between us.'

Unresolved? How could she have forgotten? Her body was throbbing, urging her to forget a little longer, as heedless as she had been of the circumstances and of her pregnancy. She wrapped her arms around her waist.

Jack winced. 'I forgot. I can't believe I forgot. Are you...?'

'I'm perfectly fine. It wouldn't harm the baby.' Mercy grimaced. 'That is one of the more embarrassing discussions which I listened to at the Lying-In Hospital.' Her smile faded. 'To be honest, I forgot too.'

Jack ran his fingers through his dishevelled hair and straightened his waistcoat. 'All the same, we can't. It won't prove anything, save what we already know— that we can take each other to the stars.'

'Would we be able to do that if we weren't in love?'

'Mercy, I want to say no, but I've always been as honest with you as you have with me. I've never felt like this with anyone else, that's all I can tell you.'

She lifted her hand to his cheek again, and he caught it again, but this time after kissing her knuckles he let her go. 'Take your time. There's a lot to think about.'

'You didn't take time to think on the pier. You simply blurted it out. If I have to think about whether I love you or not, isn't it likely that I don't? Oh, Jack, I'm so, so sorry,' she added hastily, for he had flinched.

He shook his head, tried to smile then gave up the attempt. It made her heart ache that she'd hurt him. She longed to tell him what he wanted to hear. Did that make it more or less likely that she loved him? 'What if I can't decide?' she asked wretchedly. 'What if you discover you're mistaken?'

'I won't. I can't explain it, but I'm certain of how I feel, and I want you to be certain. I don't want you to pretend to feelings just to make me feel better, do you hear me? Now, more than ever, we need to be honest with each other.'

'I know. I wish it wasn't so difficult.'

He laughed softly. 'Look, I don't have answers for you right now, Mercy, but I promise—whatever you decide, we'll find a way to sort it out. Together, do you hear me? It's our problem, not yours alone. I want you to be happy. Whatever that means, whatever it takes, that's my primary concern.' He kissed her forehead again, pressing her hand reassuringly. 'One step at a time. You know where I am when you're ready to talk.'

Chapter Sixteen

A week later, Mercy sat on the bench by the lake in Regent's Park in despair. Jack wanted her to be happy, he had said, even if it meant that she wouldn't marry him. It was this, above everything else he had said to her, that made her believe he loved her. Now she had accepted that, she could see it in everything he said and did. He saw a Mercy that no one else saw, saw strengths she had learnt about herself that even she hadn't known she possessed. Jack loved her, and she wanted to love him back, but the more she tried to examine her feelings the more tangled they became.

She was acutely conscious of how unfair it was of her to keep Jack waiting for an answer and also acutely conscious of the child growing inside her. She could not keep her condition a secret for much longer. If she was not going to marry Jack, they would have to find a way to protect their child and preserve a place in its life for its father. But when she tried to think in practical terms how that might be done, she felt as if her head would explode.

It's our problem, Jack had said, she reminded herself. *One step at a time.*

She frowned down at her hands. Jack wouldn't marry her if he thought it would make her unhappy. Wasn't that what she'd thought in reverse? The very same thing she'd thought, in fact, the night before they'd gone to Brighton—that she would not marry him because it would make him unhappy. Did that mean she was in love with Jack?

Her spirits lifted. For the first time in days, she felt as if she was making progress. But what on earth was the next step? When would she *know* that she was in love with him? With a mewl of frustration, Mercy got up and began to walk back through the park.

When Lucy informed her that she had a visitor, her heart leapt and then plummeted. Jack! Jack wanting an answer. She didn't have an answer. But the person taking tea and cake in her parlour was not Jack.

'Sarah! How lovely to see you. It's been an age.'

'Mercy!' Her friend jumped to her feet. 'Would you like some tea?'

'Thank you. Have you resolved the family crisis that kept you in the country?'

'In a manner of speaking.' To her astonishment, Sarah blushed. 'Clement and I are getting married.'

'What? Good heavens.' Mercy jumped up to hug her. 'Oh, Sarah, I am so pleased for you.'

'Are you? I wasn't at all sure, given your own experience of the institution, that you would be.'

'Oh, Sarah, I don't hate marriage. I hated being married to Harry.'

'I don't wish to contradict you, but I distinctly remember having a conversation, here in this very parlour, when you declared that you had no intention of ever marrying again.'

'I have long ceased letting Harry colour my views on any subject.' Mercy took a sip of her tea. 'If you are happy, Sarah, then I am happy for you. And Clement too, of course. My brother has said nothing to me, though, nor to Prue as far as I'm aware.'

'Perhaps he's forgotten.'

'Forgotten that he is betrothed?' Sarah's big blue eyes were sparkling. She gave a gurgle of laughter. 'You are teasing me!'

'A little. He wanted to come today, but I wanted to speak to you first.'

'You can't truly have imagined that I would be anything other that delighted?' Mercy said, puzzled. 'Prue and I were so certain that you would make a match of it, and so disappointed when things cooled between you.'

'That was my fault.' Sarah cut another slice of cake and began to make it into crumbs. 'Do you remember the conversation we had, when I told you I was in love with Clement?'

'Of course I do. I was so sure that you would resolve matters between you, and then your family crisis intervened, and I confess I've been rather preoccupied.'

'With little Verity and Prue. Prue told me that Clement was making a case study of Verity.'

'And of your sister, though she seems thankfully unaware of that fact.' Sarah grimaced. 'When I finally plucked up the courage to tell him of my—my reservations, shall we call it—about childbirth, he decided that the best thing would be to study the matter closely. Prue and Verity unwittingly provided him with the means.'

'And so you were persuaded by the results of his study that it was a risk worth taking?'

Sarah laughed. 'It eliminates one worry. You might recall also, during that conversation, that I was— that I— Oh goodness, it's not like me to be so mealy-mouthed. I was not convinced that I would enjoy love-making. Don't worry, I am remembering that my darling Clement is also your brother. Let me say only that you were right. I enjoyed it very much.'

'Enjoyed?'

'I told you that I was going to try him out as a lover.'

'Sarah! You never did! Oh, my goodness.'

'Yes.' Sarah's face fell. 'The problem was, even though we… Despite the success of that, I still couldn't persuade myself to marry him. It was such a huge step. I simply couldn't make up my mind to take it. And, though Clement was sure, he said he needed me to be sure too. That's why I retreated into the country and pretended to a family emergency.'

'I had no idea. Oh, Sarah, what a poor friend I have been.'

'No, you have been the best of friends, leaving me alone just as I asked you to. I needed to be clear in my own mind.'

'And you are clear now, then?' Mercy asked, fasci-nated. 'May I ask what—how?'

Sarah smiled, a soft, misty look in her eyes that Mercy had never seen before. 'I was coming back from the country. I took the train. I was going to tell Clement once and for all that I couldn't do it because I couldn't

keep shilly-shallying around any longer, it wasn't fair.
I didn't know he'd found out that I was arriving—I still
don't know how he found out, actually. Anyway, I got
off the train. You know what it's like at Euston. Everyone shouting and rushing, porters clattering, steam and
the screeching of brakes and noise. I was quite disori-
entated from having been in the country so long, and I
confess I was finding that I was already bracing myself
to face him. Dreading it, but determined, you know?'

'I do,' Mercy said fervently. 'Go on.'

'I got to the end of the platform. The smoke started
to clear and I saw a man standing there and—oh dear,
this is so embarrassing—my heart actually leapt. I
knew even before I saw him properly that it was Clement. And I said, what on earth are you doing here? And
he said, waiting for you. And I thought, *Sarah, you
have been an idiot. You're in love with this man. Stop
wasting time.*'

'Oh.' Mercy dabbed frantically at her eyes. 'Oh, that
is so…'

'I know, ridiculously romantic.' Sarah brushed a tear
away. 'Me! Like the heroine in a novel. But it's true.
He smiled at me, and he put his arms around me, and
I felt that this was where I belonged. I was home at
last. I didn't forget all about the other things—the tur-
moil and upheaval, the unanswered questions and the
compromises that doubtless lie ahead—but I'll have
Clement by my side, and I'd rather have that than not.
It's that simple.'

'I'm so sorry,' Jack said when Mercy opened the
door to him much later that night. 'I was down-river

all day and didn't get your telegram until I returned to my rooms.'

'There's no need to apologise.' Faced with him in the flesh, the butterflies that she'd been trying to tame ever since she'd sent the telegram began to flutter wildly. The next hour would determine the course of three lives. 'Come in,' Mercy said. 'Have you eaten?'

'No.' He followed her into the parlour. 'I'm not interested in food now.'

'Neither am I.' She had not eaten a thing since Sarah had left. She waved him to the sofa and after a moment's hesitation sat down beside him. 'I'm sorry to have kept you waiting so long for an answer.'

'I told you I'd wait. I want you to be sure.'

His voice, however, betrayed him. Meeting his anxious gaze, she felt her butterflies disappear. She loved this man and he loved her. 'I love you.' The words, that she had never spoken in her life, sounded strange, rusty. 'I love you, Jack,' she said, smiling.

His fingers curled tightly round hers, but he didn't return her smile. 'Are you sure? I need to know that you're sure, Mercy. I don't want...'

'To end up living a lie? To have me pretending to love you for the rest of our lives because I find I am mistaken and I don't want to hurt you?'

'Aye,' he said ruefully. 'All of that.'

Her heart lifted. He truly loved her. 'I don't want that either. 'I love you, Jack. I am absolutely sure, though I wasn't until today.'

'Can you tell me what changed?'

'I'll try.' She would tell him about Sarah and Clement later. It was the essence of her thinking that mattered now. 'You said that you wanted me to be happy, above all else, and I wanted you to be happy above all else, but I kept thinking of all the things we would be giving up if we married. Freedom, independence, making our own decisions—things that have been hard won in both our cases, in very different ways, you know?'

'It sounds familiar. Go on.'

'I was looking at it all the wrong way. What mattered is not what I'd be giving up, but what I'd gain if I married you. You. You make me happy. I know it's not that simple, that there will be all sorts of compromises and difficult decisions to make, but why would I choose to live without you when I can have you by my side? If I make you happy, and you make me happy, surely that's the best and only foundation for a life together? It must be love. It can only be love.'

'I couldn't have put it better myself,' Jack said, his voice cracking. 'I love you so much.'

'And I love you.'

'Mercy!' He pulled her into his arms and kissed her hungrily. 'You've no idea how much I've been wanting to hear you say that. How hard I've had to work not to let myself wonder what I'd do if you couldn't say it. I love you. I know we've not an easy road ahead of us, not least because we'll be a family before we know it. We'll need to decide where we want to live. I've already started making plans to delegate a great deal more, but there will be times that business takes me away.'

'I know that. You have men depending on you for their livelihood.'

'And you, Mercy. I'm not expecting you to simply fall in with my plans. I don't want a housekeeper.'

'I'm going to be a mother. I think that might take up quite a bit of my time.'

'And I'm going to be a father. But first, I'm going to be a husband.' He kissed her again. 'I'm looking forward to that. I love you so much. You'll get bored with hearing it.'

'Never.' She sighed blissfully, rubbing her cheek against his. 'I love you. Now that I've said it, it feels so right, I can't understand why it took me so long.'

'We're here now, and I promise you—whatever happens in the future, making you happy will be my first task of every day. I love you.'

'Oh, Jack.' She sighed, wrapping her arms around him. Their mouths met and they kissed again, a long, tender kiss that deepened and deepened and, when it finally ended, their breathing was ragged. 'I love you so much.'

'I love you too,' Jack said with a smile that made her pulses race. 'Let me show you how much.'

He got to his feet, pulling her with him. Sweeping her into his arms, he made for the stairs and her bed chamber. Their kisses grew frantic as they undressed each other, their hands and their mouths urgent after so many months apart. But once they were naked, lying together on the bed, he entered her slowly, watching her intently as he moved inside her, telling her he loved her and, as she reached her climax, kissing her deeply and calling her name before he too fell over the edge.

'I love you,' Jack said, his voice smoky and sated.

'I love you too.' Her head was resting on his shoulder. Their legs were tangled together. She snuggled in closer and his arm tightened on her waist.

'I love you, Jack. I have never in my life felt so completely happy, as if I am in exactly the right place at the right time.'

'I'm home,' he said, smiling tenderly at her. 'That's what I was thinking.' He kissed her, slowly and deeply. 'I'm home, and I'm planning to stay right here for the rest of my life.'

Glasgow Herald, 1st May 1866

New Holiday Home for Glasgow Children Opened!

On Saturday next Toward Castle, near the popular resort of Dunoon on the west coast, will open its doors to welcome the first lucky children from the Glasgow Gorbals for a holiday 'doon the watter'.

The new castle has been built on the site of the previous ruin for Mr and Mrs Dalmuir, who have until recently been inhabiting the gatekeeper's cottage with their young son, Alexander. The couple have also restored the surrounding estate and gardens, creating several play areas and a place to play football for the children who will holiday there. The stables have also been restore, and now house a number of small ponies upon which the children will learn to ride. A cart will transport those children too young to ride themselves, but the miniature steam train and carriages which have been laid out will doubtless prove much more of an attraction.

This innovative holiday home for children

from the city is the brainchild of the beautiful Mrs Dalmuir, inspired, we are told, by her husband's fond memories of going 'doon the water' as a child.

Her husband is, of course, Jack Dalmuir of Dalmuir Engineering, world-renowned manufacturers of beam engines. The company has recently expanded, following its success on the Continent, to take on another hundred employees, though Mr Dalmuir himself has, in his own words, been 'taking a bit of a back seat' since his marriage.

It is a union which appears to be flourishing as much as his business, for the happy couple were delighted to inform us that they are expecting their second child in the summer.

The first diminutive guests will arrive in Dunoon by a specially chartered steamer. We hope that our readers will join us in wishing this laudable endeavour every success.

* * * * *

Historical Note

I have once again been unable to resist returning to the Armstrong family, and unable to resist making the male line as repugnant in this next generation as they were in the first. Harry Armstrong is the third child of the patriarch Lord Henry Armstrong, who first walked on stage in the *Armstrong Sisters* series, but has since made cameo appearances in several other of my books.

If you want to know more, there's a family tree on my website. Am I finally done with this family? I suspect not!

The city of Glasgow was at the heart of the Industrial Revolution and is at the heart of this book. Since I have no idea how a Glaswegian from the Gorbals would speak back in the eighteen-sixties, I've let him use modern slang. I know it's not in the least bit historically accurate, but I love the words and phrases because they are so evocative, and I had such fun putting them in.

Jack is my own small tribute to an amazing city where I went to university and lived for many years, and to my paternal grandfather, who wasn't an engineer but a boilermaker in a shipyard. My maternal grandfather was a captain in the merchant navy. I couldn't resist paying a little tribute to one of his ships, the *SS Caledonia*, which was actually a rather posh passenger steamer from the Anchor Line, and not the cargo ship which transported Jack's beam engines to London.

Dalmuir Engineering is my own invention, but Jack's career is based loosely on some of the other world-famous Scottish engineers of the time, including John Frederick Bateman, who led the work to bring Glasgow's water supply from Loch Katrine to Milngavie in the eighteen-sixties. And, in case you haven't noticed, it's Grayson Maddox, another of my Glaswegian heroes, from *A Forbidden Liaison with Miss Grant*, who gives Jack his early break in life.

The steam engines which powered the pumping stations at the centre of Joseph Bazalgette's visionary project to clean up London were all built in Glasgow, and there are a few more historical snippets and connections for those of you who share my love of them.

In 1867, the lake where Mercy and Jack go skating in Regent's Park cracked. Tragically, forty people died under the ice, and as a result the lake was drained and the level reduced to four feet. The Magdalen Hospital for Penitent Prostitutes, the Asylum, or House of Refuge, and General Lying-In Hospital which Mercy visits were all positioned next to each other in Lambeth. Toward Castle near Dunoon really does exist. The original castle was the ancestral home of the Clan Lamont, but I've taken a few liberties with the dates of the rebuild, which was done in about 1820.

There's a lot more history in this book that I don't have the space to go into here. For more details of sources, and blogs connected with my research, check out my website. Any mistakes are all my own doing, and I hope they don't detract from your enjoyment of Mercy and Jack's story.

If you enjoyed this story be sure to read the first book in Marguerite Kaye's Revelations of the Carstairs Sisters duet

The Earl Who Sees Her Beauty

And why not check out her other miniseries Penniless Brides of Convenience?

**The Earl's Countess of Convenience
A Wife Worth Investing In
The Truth Behind Their Practical Marriage
The Inconvenient Elmswood Marriage**